Dude With a Cool Car

Concrete Angels MC series, Book 2

Siobhan Muir

ISBN: 1-947221-13-2
ISBN-13: 978-1-947221-13-0

DEDICATION

Dedicated to Maranda PA who read My Forever Cocky Biker
Encounter in one day and asked me when the next one is
coming. Here it is, Maranda. Thanks for loving my books.

ACKNOWLEDGMENTS

Writing a book is never really a one-person job, and writing a series is especially difficult alone. Keeping track of details is so much easier when you have help, especially when you're writing a series. Not only does it take a great deal of hard work, editing, and research on the part of the author to get things correct, but without my compatriots, there'd be a lot more mistakes. Any mistakes are my own.

Great thanks to Paige Prince for editing and making sure I knew what these handguns looks like and how they work. Thanks to Bianca Sommerland for creating the pre-made cover that just made the story pop into my head and the plot bunnies run wild. And thanks to Mary Decker who reminded me that those old cars have specific colors. I only changed the Corvette, Mary.

As always, great thanks to my readers for cheering me on. Seriously, y'all make my writing worth the detailed effort.

CHAPTER ONE

Cooper

"This has got to be my bad karma coming back to haunt me." I rubbed my eyes in frustration before putting the binocs back to them and squinting through the lenses. "And Backlog will be right behind it."

Or right behind me. I took a moment to glance over my shoulder at the wooded slopes around me. Ponderosa pine forests were far more open than those in temperate states, but they still offered a little cover. I relaxed when I heard birds chirping and caught sight of a chipmunk skittering to the top of a nearby rock.

No predators here but me.

I turned my attention to the compound below. I'd been up in the dry hills above Fort Collins for almost a week and I wasn't any closer to answers than when I first arrived. I was investigating the disappearance of Agents Dirk Hopkins and Arnold Eisenburg, and everything pointed to Backlog, the shadowy organization I'd been tracking for two years. Both Hopkins and Eisenburg had been members as far as I could tell, but the tracks were subtle.

"Hence why it's called a 'shadow organization,' jackass." Talking to myself made my isolation seem less

1

lonely.

My own investigation had to be shadowy because I suspected Backlog had infiltrated my agency, the Marshal Service. I didn't know who to trust. Even my partner, Anna Fitzsimmons, had said some things that made me wonder if she'd been inducted into the organization.

And that would really suck. I liked Anna. She was a damn good Marshal and, I'd thought, a pretty good friend.

Only my supervisor knew what I was doing and why, and I'd vetted the hell out of him before I confided in him. He'd squared it so it appeared I was on extended leave for anyone checking on my absence, but he'd been sending me messages about impending scrutiny.

I'd gone off the grid and purchased a burner phone to keep the technonuts from tracking me, but that would only last so long. I really needed some damn answers. Like why was Agent Eiseburg undercover in the Concrete Angels Motorcycle Club and what was his connection to Dirk Hopkins?

Especially because both of them are now dead.

I focused the binocs on the yard below me again. Had Backlog cut its losses and had the agents killed? Or did they pay the Concrete Angels to take them out? Either way, I needed to know if the motorcycle club was part of Backlog's arm or just an unwitting accomplice in the deaths of two federal officers.

Frankly, I couldn't care less about Hopkins' and Eisenburg's deaths. Both were less-than-stellar men. Hell, Hopkins had been indicted on rape, embezzlement, illegal wiretaps, and sexual harassment. Eisenburg's arrest had been on the horizon when he turned up dead in the wake of a wildfire. The news reported that he'd burned to death, but the autopsy proved the gunshot to his head had squelched his personal fire first. He'd been executed and left where the fire could obscure the evidence.

The question was, who ordered the execution? Backlog

or the Concrete Angels? Eisenburg was no prize and my investigation had found several accounts where money had been stored and then transferred away. Lots of money. So, had he been stealing from his undercover work or had he been paid by Backlog?

Too many fuckin' questions.

And here was another one: why the hell did the Concrete Angels' compound look like a cute, well-maintained mountain motel? While there was a big aluminum barn where they kept their vehicles and workshop, and another large building that appeared to be barracks, the higher-ranking members' residences and the clubhouse were downright quaint. Each window sported a flowerbox full of marigolds, petunias, and some sort of white daisies. They reminded me of my grandmother's garden back in western Washington, and I shook my head.

What kind of a motorcycle club gives a shit about flowers?

Apparently, the Concrete Angels had an honest-to-goddess grounds crew who lovingly took care of the landscaping. I had to admit I was pretty damn impressed.

I shifted on the rocky ground between two juniper shrubs and scanned the yard again. A bunch of younger men and women, prospects to joining the club, lounged around the various buildings, though they avoided the cabins in between the clubhouse and the vehicle barn. The latter stood open to allow for the breeze to cool the interior while several CA guys worked on their bikes. The pool behind the clubhouse had a nice assortment of half-naked people lounging around or swimming, but no one I recognized as the top leadership.

I was planning to swing back to the yard when a goddess of golden-brown skin, sleek lines, and an elegant Afro sauntered toward the diving board at the pool. She wore a two-piece suit I'd heard the ladies call a "tankini" in rust, rose, gold and black. The lines of the suit perfectly molded to her round ass and curved belly. The top had a V-neck and showed off her cleavage perfectly.

A large handful each. Nice.

My cock hardened at the sight and I had to squirm a bit to get my tightening shaft in a comfortable spot while lying on my belly. Not the easiest thing to do when I'm a "grower" rather than a "show-er." I liked my women with boobs, belly, butt, and thighs, and she fit my fantasy chick to a T.

I watched her strut onto the diving board, bounce a few times—and her tits bounced beautifully too—and cannonball into the pool with her knees against her chest. The other swimmers yelped and shouted at her when she came back up, but she grinned, unrepentant.

Damn. That's my kind of woman.

Except I was supposed to be investigating her motorcycle club and she probably was some other guy's old lady. The thought wilted my dick and I swore under my breath. It was stupid, but I didn't want her to be attached to anyone.

"You can't always get what you want."

No, and I'd learned that the hard way at the Marshal's Service. My boss's boss singled me out more often than not to take on the shit jobs, the ones no one wanted, just to push my buttons. The funny thing was I became one of the best at closing cases, especially the difficult shit investigations no one wanted. I guess I had to thank him for that.

Nah, he wouldn't appreciate it.

Not after I dragged his ass into custody after I exposed him and all his Backlog cronies. The jackass had tried to get me to quit. But instead, he created the very monster dogging his heels to bring him down. I never gave up or admitted defeat when it came to my investigations. And he was the first one I'd go after once I had enough evidence.

Yeah, that's the tricky part.

And I'd get it. Come hell or high water, I always got my man. Marshal Cooper DeVille definitely scored in that department. And I'd get the assholes in Backlog, too.

The goddess in the tankini finished her swim and toweled off in the shade of an ash tree. She laughed at a couple of the other women at the pool and flipped off one of the men making a snarky comment before sauntering her gorgeous ass into the clubhouse. I switched my view to the front doors to see if she'd come out and she didn't disappoint.

She'd put on a pair of small round sunglasses that reminded me of John Lennon, some flipflops, and wrapped the towel around her waist like a terrycloth skirt. It didn't matter what she wore. This surveillance operation just got a lot more enjoyable with her sauntering around.

She made her way down the line of cottages that served as the personal residences and stopped at one midway down the row. She dug out her keys then paused, as if listening to something. I adjusted the binocs to focus on her figure as she tilted her head, her brows creasing.

What? What does she hear?

She turned her head and lifted her gaze until it met mine through the binocs.

I froze and held my breath. The eerie feeling of having been discovered washed over me and I couldn't stop staring through the lenses.

Sweet glory, can she see me?

She dipped her chin in a quick nod and I gasped. *Holy shit, she* does *see me.* But I couldn't look away as she laughed, winked, and let herself into the cabin. The number on the door flashed across my view.

Cabin number thirteen.

Oh yeah, this job had bad karma written all over it.

CHAPTER TWO

Karma

Do you know how much I get blamed for everything? People would say, "Oh, that's bad Karma." Like I was some sort of unruly pet or spoiled food. Or they'd say, "I've done my good Karma today." Like I was a project they had to complete.

But people had rough things happen to them, particularly because of choices they'd made or actions they'd done, and wanted to blame me for them. "I guess it's my Karma."

Or they used me as a threat. "I so want to be there when Karma catches up to him."

Don't get me wrong. I was all about retribution and comeuppance, but I had standards and sometimes people did enough stupid shit that they naturally attracted consequences quickly. Like Roy, AKA Arnold Eisenburg, the undercover FBI agent who'd posed as a biker in the Concrete Angels Motorcycle Club. Turned out he was embezzling from both the FBI and the Concrete Angels, and Loki didn't take too kindly to the theft. The FBI didn't like it much either, but only Loki had the vagina to do anything about it.

Definitely not "balls." Balls were soft and squishy, and made a guy drop to his knees and vomit when barely brushed. Something that sensitive wasn't an example of courage and gumption, in my opinion. A vagina, on the other hand, could take a pounding, give pleasure, and still be tight the next time. Bold as brass and twice as beautiful.

Loki offered me an extra fifteen years of life in this world if I helped make Roy's consequences come that much sooner. It was a no-brainer for me. The guy was a pig, an asshole, a liar, and a thief. I'd never liked him so fucking him up for screwing over others was just icing on the cake of life for me.

No one messed with me, because I was Karma, and if anyone wanted shit done, they paid me in life years. Loki was immortal, so he had life years to spare. Humans had a lot less currency, but their passions burned brighter and they were greedy when it came to retribution. I was always happy to help if they could pay me.

Loki wasn't willing to pay me for Special Agent Dirk Hopkins, but I would've done him in for free. He raped my good friend Numbers when she was still at the FBI. He gave her more black moments than I'd seen in most horror flicks, and that wasn't something I could just let go. But Loki said he'd take care of it and if the news report was anything to go by, it sounded like it worked.

I caught the story on the TV behind the counter at the Gas 'N Snacks while I was grabbing some of my favorite treats after filling up my bike. Our inhouse chef, Grub, was fantastic, but I had a craving for Reese's Peanut Butter Cups and those couldn't be duplicated. Besides, I was still trying to get over the odd thing that had happened a few days before.

There'd been a guy in the hills above the compound watching us. *Correction: Watching me.* He'd used binoculars and wore drab clothing helping him blend in with the scrub, but I could see him. Supernatural beings had that going for them and I was nothing if not supernatural. Despite knowing he was there, I couldn't see the details of his face or body. I had to give him credit. He'd hidden himself pretty well behind the juniper bushes, but I suspected Loki knew the guy had been snooping around, too.

He'd jerked when I winked at him and that perversely made my day. Sometimes just the barest communication had a major effect and my good mood persisted. *Good Karma for everyone!* I laughed as I paid for my gas and goodies, and headed back out to my bike.

I opened up one of my panniers and slid the snacks in just as someone pulled up to the pump behind me. The engine of the vehicle purred like a tiger, deep and throaty, and I shivered with pleasure. In addition to Reece's Peanut Butter Cups, I had a soft spot for vintage cars, and this baby was totally vintage. A Pompeian Red 1962 Cadillac Coupe DeVille, its chrome mirror-clear, settled into the shade of the gas station and I drooled.

The guy driving the Caddy wasn't vintage at all. He slid from the driver's seat in acid-washed black jeans and a black t-shirt under a red and black plaid flannel shirt. He was tall with broad shoulders, but he had an athletic rather than robust build. Best of all, his energy zinged along mine with a sizzle of recognition, as if I'd met it before.

I raised my gaze to the guy's face and let my Karmic Vision™ take over. Most people looked like opalescent figures with their auras transposing their life energy over an opaque white matrix. But this guy appeared like a peacock with brilliant emerald green swirling with hunter and teal. Deep royal blue tendrils mixed with royal purple and gold. Oh, glory to the Goddess, I wanted to soak him up and blend him with my own kaleidoscope of colors.

But the flashes of dull oxblood red and sickly brown stopped me. *He's hiding something that really pisses him off.*

Disappointment soured my stomach and I pulled back into normal vision. I hadn't found many humans who had a matching set of colors for me to blend with. They were a rarity and to be treasured. I'd been around a long time, and they were few and far between. But those uneasy colors equated to a warning signal I'd learned the hard way not to ignore.

I gave him my best polite smile and zipped up my pannier.

"Nice bike. Harley Road King Special, isn't it?"

Damn, his voice sounded like smoky bourbon barbeque, sweet, tangy, and bursting with flavor. *Too bad he's not on my menu.*

"Yeah, a 2017." I nodded. "You know your bikes."

"Yeah, I've developed an eye for Harleys lately." He kept talking to me as he moved to the back of the car to fuel up. "I'm still a fan of the classics, but I've always liked the Road Kings. Just started riding?"

"Nope." I didn't want to talk to him more, but I couldn't get myself to start the engine. "Where'd you get a 1962 Coupe DeVille?"

What the hell am I doing? I didn't want to talk to the hot, sexy man who smelled like sandalwood and warm rich leather. *It's going to be fine. I can ride away anytime.*

"I found it in an old junkyard in Mobile, Alabama." He started the flow of fuel and moved to grab the squeegee. "The frame and the engine were in great condition, but the body needed a lot of work. It was my home project that kept me occupied after my divorce."

Maybe it's the divorce that's pissing him off. Why did my inner voice sound so hopeful?

"I'm sorry to hear about the divorce." And that was my cue to leave.

He waved it away as he cleaned the windshield. "It's been a few years now. The car came to me at the right time and I figured it was a sign."

"A sign?"

"Yeah, since we share the same name and all." He moved closer and held out his hand. "Cooper DeVille, at your service."

I laughed, I couldn't help it, but I took his hand.

Oh no, it's not going to be fine.

Explosive energy zinged between us through the grip of our hands. I wanted him with an intensity I hadn't felt in, well, ever. I raised my gaze to his and the energy switched on my Karmic Vision™ to show me his aura again. The streaks of anger remained, but they were threaded with lines of silver and brilliant ochre surprise.

Oh, shit-oh-dear.

In all my years of living on this plane of existence, I'd learned a thing or two about energy and the colors that when with it. The Goddess had Her plans for everyone and those of us in the plan rarely knew or understood it when it happened to us. But I'd studied enough to know that mates, long-term connections, showed up in metallic colors, particularly silver and gold, depending on the species.

This man, human despite the colors flowing through his aura like an oil slick, only flashed silver when I touched him. That meant he was my long-term connection. My mate.

Oh hell no!

I yanked my hand back and wiped it on my thigh.

"I gotta go." I rolled the kickstand up and cranked the starter on my bike. "See you."

Now why the hell had I said that? I shook my head and kicked backward to get around the Caddy.

"No, wait." He took a few steps after me. "I don't even know your name."

Yes, he does. But I wasn't sticking around to fill him in on that little chestnut. Panic flared in my gut as he tried to step in front of me, but I maneuvered around him and peeled out of the gas station. I heard him swear behind me but I floored the throttle and headed up the highway. It didn't matter that I was headed away from the Concrete Angels' compound. I just needed to get away from Cooper DeVille, my fated mate, and the only human who might really understand who I truly was.

And that couldn't happen.

****

Cooper

"Fuck!"

I roared the word as I yanked the gas nozzle out of Rosé, grateful I'd used my credit card so I could take off quickly. I hadn't expected to meet the Concrete Angel goddess I'd seen through my binocs so soon, but I wasn't about to let the opportunity go to waste. I thought things had been going better than well until panic flashed across her expression and she'd released my hand like it was on fire.

It kinda was.

I slid into the driver's seat and cranked the engine, encouraging the old girl to head out after my goddess. The woman had already disappeared out of sight, but I had this odd sense I could pretty much follow her anywhere if I kept focused long enough. Which was weird as hell, since I didn't even know her name, but at the moment I wasn't willing to question it too much.

I squealed out of the gas station, Rosé's fins fishtailing, and headed up the road. My goddess wasn't going to the Concrete Angels' compound, which I'd expected, but given the panic on her face, maybe she was just running.

"Sonuvaprick!"

The swearing didn't make me feel better. I just wanted to touch her again. Something extraordinary flooded through me when we shook hands and I'd been rocked back on my heels. It felt like a combination of orgasm, contentment, and that nice alcoholic buzz you get after drinking whiskey, and I wanted more of it. Hell, I just wanted to sit next to her, with her pussy on my face, or her mouth on my cock. I wasn't picky.

I stared up the winding mountain road and cursed again. Damn, the woman was fast on that bike. If it wasn't for the unnerving sense of where she'd gone, I probably would've lost her in the Rocky Mountain wilderness. But I slowed Rosé down when I hit County Road 162. *Where the hell is she going?*

This road went past the Manhattan Cemetery and wound its way toward the Red Feather Lakes. I half expected her to turn off toward the Bellaire Lake picnic site, but my inner sense told me she'd gone farther north and east. I eased Rosé onto a graded dirt road with signs to Molly Lake and drove through the trees until I reached a small parking area past the powerline easement. My mystery goddess rested in the shade of an aspen grove with a scowl on her face.

I parked the car beside a granite outcrop and turned it off. After the rumble of the road under my tires the silence around the lake was deafening. No one else had picked out this lake for camping or hiking today. It was just the goddess and me.

Her ferocious scowl didn't give me a lot of hope for positive interaction, but I was nothing if not dogged. I got out of the car and leaned against the side closest to her.

"Hi."

"What the fuck are you doing here?"

Not the best start, but better than icy silence.

"I followed you."

"No shit, Sherlock. Why the hell did you do that?"

I spread my hands and shrugged. "I never got your name."

She raised an eyebrow. "You followed me into

Bumfuck Nowhere Colorado to get my name after meeting me for all of two minutes? That's creepy."

I wanted to argue that it wasn't creepy, but it did seem like I'd stalked her. The very thought made my stomach cramp and bile work its way up my throat. I couldn't help but be drawn to her and ever since I'd taken her hand, I had this buzzing in my head attracting me to her like a compass needle.

I ran my hand over the back of my neck. "Yeah, I can see your point. But what's weird is I knew where you were going. Ever since we shook hands, I've had this feeling where I can kinda sense you no matter where you are. Well maybe not specifically where you are, but a general direction. Does that make sense?"

She groaned and dropped her head back, closing her eyes. "You unbelievable bitch!" She opened her eyes and pointed at the clouds in the sky. "You know I don't have time for this, right? He can't be my mate!"

I blinked. Mate? I knew humans were considered mammals, but not that we took mates. Unless she meant in terms of sex and reproduction, which I'd be happy to provide. At least the sex part.

"Uh, what?"

"I fucking don't have time for this. Do you hear me?"

A rumble of distant thunder flowed across the mountains around us from the building storm clouds and she scowled deeper.

"It's not funny."

"Who are you talking to?"

She hissed a breath through her bared teeth and shook her head. "No one. Look, Mr. DeVille—"

"Coop."

She shook her head again. "We can't do this. It won't work."

"What can't we do? I just wanted to talk more after you took off. And I wanted to learn your name." I opened

13

my hands to show my harmlessness. "Look, I didn't mean to scare you or freak you out. Hell, I'm kinda freaked out that I could sense where you were. We can just sit here and talk. I'll even stay right here."

She narrowed her eyes at me and I realized I'd dropped into the careful tone of voice cops used when trying to calm suspects. *Shit, don't blow it now.*

But she surprised me by turning to face me completely as she leaned on her bike. "Why do you want to talk?"

All the usual suave responses disappeared out of my thoughts before I could access them and I sat there scrambling for something to say.

Because you're beautiful and hearing your voice turns me on.

Because I can't get enough of being near you.

Because I'm desperate for company and you're the first person who's noticed me.

Oh yeah. All those things didn't sound stalkerish at all. I damn near choked on my sarcasm. No matter which way I looked at it, following her to get her name was creepy as hell and now I had no idea how to salvage the situation. *Way to go, DeVille.*

I honestly didn't know why I'd needed to follow her. It didn't make sense. Yes, talking to a member of the Concrete Angels would help my case against Backlog, but that hadn't been why I'd followed the goddess on a motorcycle. I'd simply needed to know more about her and to be close to her. And that was just fuckin' weird.

"You know what? You're right. This was a stupid idea." I nodded, self-recrimination and frustration zipping through me. "I'm gonna go. This has bad karma written all over it. Story of my life."

I lurched off Rosé and dug my keys out of my front pocket, but her voice stopped me.

"What did you say?"

"I said it's the story of my life."

"No." She shook her head as I paused in the front of Rosé's hood. "Before that."

"What, about karma?"

She nodded. "Do you believe in karma?"

"Hell yeah, I believe in karma. What goes around comes around, which is why I'm gonna head on outta here and leave you alone. I'm sorry I scared you." I resumed my trek to the car's door and had it opened before she appeared next to me.

She frowned and bit her bottom lip as if she debated what she wanted to do, but then she laid her hand on top of mine where it gripped the car door. That weird shock of recognition dialed my need to be near her up to about ten thousand and I gritted my teeth to keep from pulling her closer. *Just stay still, DeVille. Don't fuck this up.*

She gasped and swallowed hard but she never released my hand. She met my gaze and shrugged one shoulder. "My name's Karma."

To be honest, it sounded more like a title, but that didn't make any sense.

"Seriously? Your folks named you Karma?" So much for the smooth talker. "Sorry, that came out wrong. Hell, I've pretty much screwed up this whole conversation. I might as well finish it by telling you your ass looks fat on the bike, and that'll seal the deal."

"My ass looks fat on my bike?"

"No, it looks awesome, but with my track record so far, that seemed like my next illogical move." I ran my hand over my face, pretty sure I'd be leaving this place soon.

Karma threw her head back and laughed, a joyous sound that made my bones melt and my heart leap with delight like a kid on his birthday. Oh man, I thought I knew what I wanted in life, but at that moment, all I wanted to do was make her laugh. Forever. And ever, till death did we part.

"All right, Coop. I guess we can talk." She squeezed my hand one last time before releasing me. "Let's sit on the picnic table by the lake out of the sun."

She strode away from me in her ass-hugging jeans and my mouth watered at the curves under the denim. *Get your mind off of sex, jackass, or you really will get bad karma.* Another naughty voice suggested bad Karma would be hot as hell, but I shook my head and closed Rosé's door to follow her.

It gave me a good look at her leather vest, what bikers called their "cuts." The image in the center showed a gargoyle on a bike with flaming wheels, stone wings trailing behind it. Her name "KARMA" sat above it and the rocker below said "ENFORCER." Holy shit, this woman could've kicked my ass and buried my body without anyone knowing the difference. Maybe I was the lucky one today.

"I noticed your cut. It doesn't say "property of" anywhere." I settled on the picnic table bench across from her.

"Oh, good, you noticed." Her voice cracked with sarcasm, but a smile curled her lips.

I groaned. "Can we just agree that I'm gonna say stupid, sexist, and thoughtless things this whole conversation? That way you don't have to expect me to have my shit together at all."

She laughed again. "Don't worry about it. Most guys can't handle a woman being a full member of a biker club, much less the Enforcer. They just see tits and ass and start thinking with the wrong head." She shrugged. "I expect more."

"More?"

"Yeah, I expect you to see me as a person. I've definitely earned it."

I frowned. "How else would I see you?"

She tilted her head. "As something pretty to look at, as

something to fuck, the usual." She shrugged again. "I'm giving you a chance to be something other than typical."

Oh hell, this was a minefield. She was pretty, beautiful in fact. And yeah, I wanted to fuck her. Check that, I wanted to get intimate with her in hot and sweaty ways. But what I'd seen of her and just knowing she wore the title of Enforcer made me see her as more than just a pretty face.

Yeah, but how many guys see the tits first and dismiss her until she shoves a gun up their asses?

I nodded. "I can't guarantee I'll be anything other than typical, but I already see you as a person, even if I was crazy stupid about how I tracked you down." I rubbed the back of my neck. "Sorry about that. I don't have a clue how I knew where to find you. I just did."

Karma sighed and grimaced. "Don't worry about it. It's probably gonna be that way for a while. So what did you want talk to me about?"

"Uh…" My well-rehearsed cover story slid right out of my thoughts. *Where the hell is the cool and suave Marshal?* "You know, I totally lost my train of thought. Must've derailed in Denver."

"Alrighty then." She nodded and turned back to her bike. "I'll see you around."

"Wait!" Shit, was she leaving? *Get it together, Coop!* "How 'bout we head to the Shambala Center? They have a nice little coffee shop there that serves what they call magical teas." I spread my hands when she raised an eyebrow. "What do you say? Safe place, public venue. I promise to be a gentleman."

She snorted and shook her head. "If I wanted a gentleman, I wouldn't have stuck around here with you." She shrugged at my raised eyebrows. "I don't know how I know that, I just do."

"It's that thing about trusting your gut, right?"

She nodded and I nodded back.

"Yeah, me too. So Karma, can I treat you to a magical

tea and pastries that taste remarkably like they're made with twigs and sawdust? Or should we hang out here?"

"I think we should stay here. I mean, twigs and sawdust usually light my fire, but I'm trying to watch my figure." She winked and I laughed, real delight washing through me.

She wants to hang out and talk to me!

I hadn't heard that voice in a while. The inner nerdy teenaged boy who never got the pretty girls to notice him. I'd grown up since then, and matured. My body had filled out and I had a decent physique, but that teenaged boy still did the happy-dance when the ladies noticed.

Now don't blow it with her.

Easier said than done.

CHAPTER THREE

Karma

Cooper DeVille was my true mate. How the hell had that happened? I was Karma, the energy of 'what goes around comes around' in physical form. How the hell could I have a mate? I hadn't existed in physical form one hundred years ago. I had no idea how Loki pulled it off, but he harnessed my energy and gave me a body. We figured out together that staying in this form required life year payments. Fortunately, there were several beings who wanted retribution done quickly, and I'd gotten used to being here and "living."

But that didn't explain how I could have an actual fated mate.

I liked his laugh, though, and wanted to hear it a lot more often. Karma can be funny. Sometimes. And his laugh did funny things to my insides.

"Okay, so you followed me out here, derailed your train of thought, and you know about the magical teas at the Shambala Center. What brings you out here to the Rockies?"

He gave me a half-smile. "Camping, actually. I took some time off to get back to nature. I used to hike all the time in college, but once I started working for real, I stopped having time to do anything fun."

"What do you do for work?"

"I'm an investigator."

"Like a P.I.?" I raised my brows. "I thought that had a lot of downtime."

"Not when you want the pay the bills." He snorted. "Lately it's been full time, all the time. So I decided to take a break. Search for hidden trails and secret waterfalls rather than someone's cheating spouse or runaway siblings."

"Yeah, that would drive me insane." Though part of what he did was my doing. If he caught the adulterers or thieves, that belonged to my purview. "Are you based here in Colorado, or really getting away?"

"Denver, actually, but I didn't want to go anywhere close to the city. I wanted to go somewhere new." He nodded to my cut. "Are you really a member of a motorcycle club?"

"No, I just wear this leather cut because it looks cool."

For a moment, his expression froze in the "wha..." look, before he grinned and laughed again. "Yeah, okay, maybe that was a stupid question. What does "enforcer" mean?"

"It means I enforce the rules and bylaws of the club, and I do what needs to be done when it needs doing." I didn't tell him that included taking care of members who'd screwed the club or killing off enemies. Fortunately, those were rare occurrences, but when their karma came up, it was my job to follow through.

"So, that means you're part of the leadership, right?"

I raised an eyebrow. "Yeah, maybe. Why?"

"That's very cool. I've never met someone who rode in a real motorcycle club. Just those weekend warrior fools who think being badass is riding around on a cruiser with a little neon orange flag waving off the back."

The image was so incongruous to the Concrete Angels,

I couldn't hold back the laughter. "I can see why I'd be an anomaly."

"Now, don't go using those big words on me. I might not be able to follow the conversation."

I snorted. If he wasn't smarter than he pretended to be, then I was human. "I'll try to keep it simple." I straightened and gave him an amused smile. "It's been entertaining to meet and talk with you, Coop, but I gotta get a move on."

"Aw, and we were having such fun out here in the middle of nowhere." His smile lost some wattage, but he hid his disappointment well. "Well, if you gotta go, you gotta go. Can we trade cell numbers then? I'd like to have another one of these serendipitous meetings again."

"Now who's using the big words?" I grinned at his smug expression. "Sure, we can exchange numbers. Just don't call me. I rarely answer. I'm better at texting."

He nodded as he gave me his number. "You don't answer calls?"

I shrugged. "I don't like to be interrupted by sound, but I answer when it's important. It depends on who's calling."

"I hope I make it to your important-callers list." The smile he offered made me think of naughty things in more horizontal situations and I turned my face away before he saw me flush with excitement. I had a bad habit of showing when I wanted sex.

What the fuck is wrong with me? Sex didn't phase me at all. It felt good and scratched the itch of arousal when it came up. I didn't have the hangups that humans carried around with them. Granted, I required my partners to be old enough to know what they were doing—no teenagers, or virgins if I could help it—and I didn't keep them long-term. Too much drama with that.

Fantasies of getting busy with Coop already infiltrated my thoughts and I wanted to have some quiet space of my own to savor them. But I didn't want him to know I was having them.

"We'll see." I cleared my throat. "So, I'll see you around, Coop."

"Yeah, I hope so. I'll text you."

I grinned. "You do that. Maybe I'll text back." I winked and swung my leg over my ride.

To be brutally honest, I kinda hoped he'd text me before I made it back to the Concrete Angels' compound.

****

Cooper

Thank every deity out there that Karma hadn't written me off as a creepy stalker. Not that I wasn't stalking her, sort of. But at least she'd given me permission to contact her. I'd texted her a few times since I met her at the lake and she'd actually answered. Still, after three days I still hadn't figured out a way onto the Concrete Angels' compound. And I didn't see any casual way to have her invite me up to her place.

So, I'd been observing from my bush-and-rock nest above their little oasis, hoping to get more of a sense of who I should be following and who I needed to avoid. I had candidates for both lists.

The guy known as Loki scared the living shit out of me. He walked around with a perpetual half-smile and everyone got the hell out of his way. Sometimes he would mess with some of the members just to see how they reacted. The few times he glanced my way on the hill, I dropped to the ground and hid behind the rocks, my heart pounding in my chest. I didn't need his attention.

But the guy who seemed to be his right-hand man had a quality to him that made me want to pay attention. I'd never been interested in watching guys beyond surveillance, but this man had strength, power, and grace all rolled up in a warrior's body. He also had tats across his chest and shoulders, which only added to his badassery. He was the kind of guy I'd want as a best friend, 'cause he'd always have my back. Everyone around him treated him with deference and respect, and I never saw him get into fights. His presence seemed to sooth most people.

Another person I thought might be useful was a small woman. She, too, commanded respect and response from the other members of the club, and the few times one of the probationary members got handsy with her, she damn near broke his fingers off one by one. She seemed to be in the know, though, and it would be worth learning more about her when I got the chance.

But the one person I couldn't take my eyes off whenever she appeared in my field of view was Karma. She made my heart pound for a completely different reason than Loki. My palms sweated and my cock stiffened, and I wasn't anywhere near her. Just the way she moved had me thinking of hot, sweaty nights on cool cotton sheets, and I had to rub one out a couple of times to find my sanity. I'd never had a woman affect me so strongly before, and it made me doubly determined to get inside the compound.

Fortunately, the probationary members gave me the chance.

I'd been keeping track of all the members of the Concrete Angels, but when a small group of the junior members headed out, I scrambled to tag along. I kept my distance, driving like a tourist enjoying the winding mountain roads. When they pulled into a small hole-in-the-wall liquor store on the outskirts of Fort Collins, it gave me the chance to make my move.

"Fuck, man, how the fuck are we gonna get all the beer and shit back?" The lanky kid with peach fuzz on his face in mangey bits scowled at the cases and his bike as they set them on the ground. "It's not like I can carry it one-handed."

The other dimwitted punks seemed to be at a loss as

they stood around scratching their heads. I hid my grin as I came out the door behind them with a fifth of Captain Morgan.

"Everything okay, guys?" I asked as I headed to my Caddy.

The crew turned suspicious eyes on me until they got a look at my car. Those old Cadillacs might be heavy and bulky, but just about everyone likes to look at them.

"Is that your car?"

I ignored the stupidity in the question and nodded. "Yup. Every sexy inch of her."

"Wow, that's cool." Mangey grinned and sauntered closer. "How big's the trunk?"

"Fifty-one point three square feet." I put the rum in the aforementioned trunk. "Why?"

"You wanna come to a party? You could bring your girlfriend, too."

That went well. But I narrowed my eyes. "What do I gotta do?"

"Just let us borrow your trunk. You bring the beer and we're good to go."

Hook, line, and sinker. I pretended to consider, switching my gaze between the five punks who wore varying expressions of hopefulness. When I came back to Mangey, I let a smile curl my lips.

"Yeah, okay. Where are we goin'?" I left the trunk open and the guys brought the cases of beer to load them up.

Mangey gave me what he thought was a confident smirk. "All you gotta do is follow us. You got a girl to bring?" The way he licked his lips made my skin crawl, but I shook my head.

"Nah. Not currently. Don't you have girls where we're goin'?"

The guys shared looks and I bet dollars to doughnuts they were thinking of the woman who'd almost broken their fingers.

"Yeah, but it's just better if you bring your own. Most of the women there are the club's old ladies." Mangey shrugged, uncomfortable.

Maybe he's not as dumb as he looks.

I shrugged as I got into my Caddy. "Fine with me. Lead the way."

"All right." Mangey grinned and sat his bike as I closed the Caddy's door.

He waved to everyone and headed out. I let the others follow him before I drove after the group, pretending not to know where we were going. I also pretended that the only reason I wanted in to the compound was to find evidence that the Concrete Angels were working with the Backlog organization. But in reality, I just wanted to see Karma up close again.

My cock stiffened in my jeans when I thought of her, and I had to think about car maintenance to make it go down before I showed up with a woody.

It's all for the evidence.

Right, and I'd be nominated as the next President of the United States.

CHAPTER FOUR

Karma

Good glory, the world's a fuckin' mess right now.
I rolled my head on my neck to loosen the muscles,
trying to relax after all the work I'd done this week.
There'd been SCOTUS hearings and rape allegations and
on top of that, I had to set up some of the resulting
consequences for the November midterm elections. No
matter how people saw it, it would definitely be exciting.
But that meant more work for me. And none of it paid in
life years.

*Maybe I should take a shower to wash all that shit off
me.*

The Concrete Angels were planning a party and I
needed the break in routine. Of course, as the Enforcer I
had to keep people in line, but that's why I'd warned them
about InstaKarma™. Since I was watching, they'd get
consequences for their actions a helluva lot faster. Most of
the card-carrying members of the Concrete Angels had
learned. It was the scooters who still needed lessons.

Speaking of the scooters, Attila had sent them off on a
beer run to bring back enough for the club to enjoy for the
party. But he'd deliberately withheld the keys to the pickup

truck and van we had at the club's disposal. He said it would help the youngsters build character if they figured out a way to get it all back on their bikes. Scott and Schnoz had gased up the pickup for their less-than-triumphant return.

"Riders comin' in."

I swear Egyptian had been watching too many old westerns to say shit like that. They pulled open the gates to let the scooters in and one other vehicle.

A Pompeian Red 1962 Cadillac Coupe Deville.

Somehow, I wasn't surprised that Coop had figured out a way inside the compound. He might be on vacation, but he was a charmer and if he wanted to get into anywhere, he'd get the owners to invite him in. *Which is exactly what the scooters have done.*

Coop parked the Caddy in front of the Clubhouse and slid out of the front seats like a slick predator. I don't know why I thought of him that way, but he definitely wasn't the innocent he pretended to be. Something about this little surprise felt orchestrated.

His gaze immediately found mine and he winked before he sauntered to his trunk and popped it open. Several cases of beer sat in the back of his car along with a bottle of Captain Morgan.

Schnoz, Scott, Attila, and Dollhouse gathered around the back of the car, their expressions a mix of surprise and suspicion.

"Who the fuck are you?" Scott didn't screw around.

Coop gave his easy smile and held out his hand. "Coop DeVille. Your boys needed a way to get their beer home and invited me to come along."

Scott stared at Coop's hand then swung around to glare at Attila. "Way to go, jackass. Now you have to give Gopher Pyle there his cut and we have this yahoo comin' around." He shook his head. "This is all on you."

He turned and stalked away with a scowl. Aw well,

Scott wasn't the most trusting type. That's why he got along so well with his old lady, Numbers. Of course, it helped that she as a badass forensic accountant who used to work for the FBI before she got raped. She didn't easily trust either. It had been a pleasure setting her assailant's karma in motion.

Attila scowled, his gaze sliding up and down Coop's form. "Do ye jest volunteer to ferry around beer for any asshole who begs ye?"

Coop shrugged, dropping his hand. "No, but those boys couldn't figure out how to carry it on their bikes and they invited me along if I'd haul it up here. Seemed like a good deal."

"He's right. It is a pretty good deal." Michael grinned and reached out for Coop's hand. "Michael. Nice to meet you, Coop. That's a pretty sweet ride you got there."

Coop snorted with amusement as Michael released him. "Well, it's good for carryin' beer."

Michael laughed. "Yeah, I see that. Come on. Let the scooters unload the beer and we'll get this party started."

"All right." Coop nodded as he stood back. "What are we celebratin'?"

"Karma." Michael said it like meant consequences, but Coop's shoulders tightened and his gaze slid around the yard, looking for something.

When his gaze found me, heat leaked into his expression and he grinned. "I didn't know it was her birthday."

Michael laughed. "No, not Karma the woman, karma the results of actions and their consequences. We caught a guy embezzling from us and he met with some real world consequences."

"Shit. Embezzling? That's stupid. Did you get all the money back?" Coop shook his head as he retrieved his bottle of Captain Morgan.

"Not yet. But we got most of it and his silent partner,

so it's all good."

"You know, I'm a private investigator. If you want, I could do some legwork and find out more about him and where he could've stashed the missing funds. You know, if you're havin' trouble finding shit on him."

Michael paused and narrowed his eyes. I wondered what Coop was up to because it seemed like a weird offer for a guy who'd walked into a biker's compound five minutes earlier. But Coop was the picture of easy-going earnestness and I couldn't find a crack in his façade.

"Yeah, we have our own forensic accountant, I think we're doin' fine." Michael's voice held reserve.

Coop shrugged. "All righty. Well, if you run into any snags in your research, let me know. I've been doin' this a long time and have seen all the ways assholes try to hide shit. One time, I was trackin' a woman who stole money from one of the biggest banks on Wall Street. She used the money to purchase an antique necklace worth four million bucks. Then she cut it up into different pieces and gave them to her friends to sell using an auction house, laundering the money and making about twice that amount on the pieces."

"Damn." Attila nodded his head, impressed. "How did ye catch her?"

"I had a jeweler pose as a buyer and he found the serial numbers marked on each diamond." Coop grinned. "Traced the money back to her. The bank wanted interest, but that's not how it works. They got their money, I got paid, and she got thrown in jail."

"Nice work. Sounds like y'er as crafty as she was."

Coop nodded at Attila's compliment. "Glad you think so. Helps in my line of work."

"She sounds smart. Maybe we should see if she wants to work for us when she gets out." I stepped into the conversation and Coop's expression went from affability to smoldering heat as his gaze rested on me.

"I'm not sure she'd be trustworthy. More than likely she'd just steal from you, too."

"How do we know we could trust you?" Michael tilted his head, his gaze narrowed as it switched between Coop and me.

Coop shrugged. "It'd be a business transaction. You'd pay me to be trustworthy."

Attila grinned and Michael chuckled, though his gaze still held suspicion. I didn't blame him. Coop's interest in helping seemed a little too quick and easy. *And the worst part is he's your mate.* Yeah, that still threw me for a loop. It meant if he ever did anything wrong, it'd be my job to take care of it.

And doesn't that just make me want to throw up?

"We'll think about it. But in the meantime, there's a party to be had." Michael smiled as he clapped Coop on his back. "Park your car over by the workshop and we'll get it started."

Coop grinned and nodded, sweeping his gaze back to me. He gave me a seductive smile as he slid into the driver's seat and turned the engine over. Glory, he could rev me up like that damn car.

"Hey, Karma. Got a minute?" Michael pulled me aside as the tailfins of the Caddy disappeared behind the barn.

"Yeah,. What's up?"

"You know this guy?"

I shrugged. Michael wasn't any more human than I was, but it still surprised me when he picked up on things I hadn't said or shown. "I met him a couple of days ago. Why?"

"Think he's on the up-and-up?"

I tilted my head back and forth. "Maybe. I believe he's an investigator, but I also think he's a lot more interested in the Concrete Angels than just stumbling across us."

"Do you think he's already on an investigation?"

I frowned, trying to put my gut feelings into words.

"Kinda. He's looking for something, but I don't know what it is and I don't think he's made a decision about it yet."

Michael nodded as Coop reappeared in the yard. "Keep an eye on him. Find out what he knows and what he's looking for. I'm gonna talk to Loki about putting him on an investigation to find out where and to whom that money went."

"We still haven't found all of it?"

Michael shook his head. "Numbers is encountering roadblocks she's never seen before and something tells me we're dealing with an organization that's bigger than the FBI."

I bit my bottom lip. "What's bigger than the FBI?"

Michael clapped me on the shoulder. "I dunno, but I have a feeling we're gonna find out sooner rather than later. See you in a bit."

Coop ambled up with a grin, his hand wrapped around the bottle of Captain Morgan rum. "I knew I'd see you around. Let's get this party started."

"Why did you help the scooters?" I nodded my chin in the direction of the wannabe members congratulating the soon-to-be Gopher Pyle.

He followed my gaze then returned it to my face and shrugged. "I figured they belonged to your club. Not too many motorcycle clubs based up here and I wanted the opportunity to see you again. So, I took a chance." He nodded to me with a wink. "Definitely paid off."

His cheeky grin made me laugh even though my gut warned me he had other motivations in coming here. Oh, I believed he wanted to see me again, but I suspected it was secondary on his agenda. I didn't want to admit having him show up here was a welcome surprise for me.

"You could've just texted me." I tilted my head and raised my eyebrows

"Would you have invited me in for the party?"

I shrugged. "Definitely don't need to, now."

"Would you invite me to the next one?" His smile turned challenging.

"We'll have to see how well this one goes."

He laughed and I couldn't help but grin at his amusement. "Fair enough. I remember our conversation at the lake. I'll try to improve at each encounter. Then maybe you won't give me the suspicious look every time you see me."

"What suspicious look?"

"The one that says you're trying to figure out my motivation for wanting to be where you are."

I blinked as my smile melted off my face. Could he read me so well already? *He is my true mate.*

"I'll give you a hint. It has to do with how attracted I am to you and your snarky conversation." He'd leaned close and I could smell the scent of bubblegum on his breath.

"Do I smell bubblegum?" I raised my eyebrows as he pulled back with a grin.

"Yup."

"Why do you smell like bubblegum?"

"It's my toothpaste." He winked as he offered me his arm. "Shall I escort you to the clubhouse, Karma? I figure it's more gentlemanly than just cracking open this bottle of rum and chugging it." His gaze slid around the yard where men and women already had beers in their hands. "Of course, in this crowd I might actually fit in doing that."

"Not with rum." I gave him a mock scowl. "Unless you're a fuckin' pirate, you do not chug rum. The bartender in me would kick your ass."

"Not to mention the Enforcer, right?" His eyes sparkled with his amusement.

"That's right. But I still want to know why you smell like bubblegum." I needed to know this as if it would explain why I was so attracted to him, and why the Goddess had decided he was my true mate.

He paused long enough to open the doors of the clubhouse and usher me through. But instead of picking up the conversation again, his expression morphed into astonishment as he took in our clubhouse interior.

Loki had bought the place back in the '80s when it was an abandoned, run-down motel left over from the 1960s. The banks had foreclosed on the property and no one was willing to take over the maintenance and costs of repair. Loki got the whole thirty-five acre plot for a song and moved his motorcycle club there. We'd all pitched in to upgrade and remodel the place, which was why the main members resided in the individual cabins that had been the original motel rooms.

But the clubhouse was our crowning achievement. What used to be an old, dark, dingy motel lobby had become an open, airy space with pool tables, a brass and oak wood bar, and a comfortable sitting area with a 70-inch LED TV. The chairs and couches set out for folks to sit on were plush with bright and neutral colors mixing in a pleasing mosaic.

We'd also upgraded the pool out back and a full 5-star restaurant quality kitchen for Grub, our cook. Our laundry room boasted top-of-the-line laundry machines and members had petitioned Loki for a basketball court to be built beside the barracks.

"Wow." Coop gaped as I led him over to the bar, my usual haunt. "This place is amazing. And nice."

"What do you mean, 'nice?' Why wouldn't it be nice?"

He set the bottle of rum on the bar and turned to survey the rest of the clubhouse. "I dunno. I guess I was expecting the place to smell like sweat, cigarette smoke, rancid alcohol, and sex, and have dark faux wood paneling and no light." He pointed upwards. "The skylights in the ceiling are a nice touch. They really open the place up."

"That's what I said when we were renovating." I pointed at the gaps in the ceiling. "Loki's from a place

33

where it's dark and cold all the time and I'm like, oh hell no. We need light. Fortunately, Schnoz agreed with me and helped me cut holes in the ceiling to make it a reality."

Coop nodded. "I'm gonna have to revise my ideas about motorcycle clubs. This place is classy." He turned back around to face the bar as I slipped behind it.

I reached under the counter to hand him a whiskey glass. "Want me to pour? Or you gonna do that?"

He shoved the bottle toward me. "I'll leave it to the professional."

I gave him a half-smile. "Tell you what. I'll pour the rum if you tell me what's up with the bubblegum toothpaste."

He laughed. "Deal." He watched me expertly open the rum and pour two fingers into both glasses. "Cheers." He lifted the glass and clinked it to mine.

We both sipped and I raised an eyebrow. "Now spill."

He shrugged. "Ever since I was a little kid I've hated the taste of mint. My mom couldn't figure out a way to get me to brush my teeth because all the toothpaste on the market was made with spearmint, peppermint, or straight mint. And it would make me gag. One time she made me brush my teeth after we'd eaten a huge Thanksgiving dinner. You can imagine what happened."

"Oh glory." I gaped at him in horror.

"Oh glory is right. There was vomit and dinner remnants all over the bathroom. We both ended up having to take a shower to wash ourselves off. And Dad had to hose down the bathroom before anyone could go in there." He grimaced and shook his head. "As a result, my mom went to the library and looked up recipes for toothpaste that she could flavor on her own. In the end, we decided that while apple was my favorite flavor, vanilla made my breath more tolerable. When they started coming out with other flavors, I tried a bunch of the kids' pastes, and settled on bubblegum being the best."

He grinned, showing off his clean pearly whites and I laughed.

"Note to self: No mint juleps for Coop."

"Hell no." He made a disgusted face. "That shit's awful. No peppermint patties or mint ice cream either."

I grinned as I sipped the rum. "I'll remember that." I tilted my head and narrowed my eyes. "So, now that you're here, you sure you want to hang out?"

He raised his eyebrows and set down his glass. "Why would you ask that?"

I shrugged. "I know how motorcycle clubs are portrayed, especially in the media and on TV. A lot of people have this skewed view of them and don't know what it's like. Hell, even Scott's old lady was pretty sure we were a cult."

"Are you?"

I glanced at him, trying to decipher the expression on his face. "No."

"No? Don't you all live on a compound and share resources and you have to pass some sort of esoteric test to become a full member?"

When he put it like that, it did sound kinda hinky. "But if you want to leave at any time, you can. And pooling resources for living expenses makes sense. Everyone looks after each other, more or less. It's economics."

"True. But don't you demand absolute loyalty?"

I narrowed my eyes. He wasn't hostile, but the questions put me on the defensive. I liked my life and I liked the Concrete Angels. *And I want him to like us, too.* Which was weird, even for my true mate. I'd just met him and I didn't know him well enough to trust him completely. But I wanted him to think well of my life and my adopted family.

"No, not absolute, just the usual amount."

He raised his eyebrows. "What does that mean?"

"It means that the members consider the club and its

members before they consider money or 'power' when making deals with any outside entity." I leaned against the bar counter. "It means they value the people of the club above any personal benefit. Don't believe everything you hear about motorcycle clubs not caring who they hurt. We protect our members because no one else will and many law enforcement agencies want to destroy us just because we operate outside their understanding."

He flinched and glanced away with a grimace. "Yeah, well, they've had a lot of experience with the clubs who aren't on the up-and-up and engage in illegal activity."

Now it was my turn to twitch. The Concrete Angels tended to be a gray club. We conducted business that was lucrative, but not strictly legal, and we had our limits and codes. But the law enforcement agencies and groups didn't agree with our methods. I eyed him, wondering if he belonged to such an agency and was only here to get evidence on us.

"Is that why you're really here, Coop?" No point in pussyfooting around. If he was only trying to bring us down, I wanted him gone, true mate or not. "Are you some undercover agent trying to get dirt on the Concrete Angels?"

Before he could answer, the new member Scott had designated Gopher Pyle stumbled up and wrapped an arm around Coop's shoulders.

"Hey man, there you are! I gotta thank you. You got me my cut and my road name." He grinned. "Lemme get you a beer."

Coop's face relaxed from surprise to an amused smile and he nodded. "No problem. Hey, you did me a favor. Got me in to see Karma, so we're square."

"Well, hell, what're friends for?" Gopher straightened his shoulders and his grin turned smug as if he'd orchestrated the whole thing. "Come on. The party's moving out to the pool and Grub's cooking a mean barbeque."

"Damn, that does sound good." Coop peeled himself off the stool and nodded to me. "How about we go outside and enjoy the pool and food? And if, you know, you wanna put on a bikini or something, I won't say no."

I raised an eyebrow. How did he know I had a bikini? "You got swim trunks hiding on you somewhere?"

"Yup. In the bag in my car."

"Don't you come prepared?"

"Well, I wasn't a boy scout, but they weren't the only ones who learned having supplies made life easier." He winked before Gopher dragged him away toward the pool.

I watched them go, tapping my finger on my glass of rum. It didn't escape my notice that he hadn't answered my question about being an undercover agent. I sensed he kept secrets from me, which wasn't surprising considering we'd known each other all of five days, and most of those we'd spent apart. But I had a feeling his secrets were bigger than just he didn't like mint or he'd been previously married.

And what about your secrets? Yeah, I wasn't ready to tell him I wasn't human, at least not in the way he expected. How would I share that the monsters he feared — drug dealers, human traffickers, corporate executive officers — didn't hold a candle to the angels, shifters, and minor gods he hung out with here?

CHAPTER FIVE

Cooper

Saved by the bell.

Or by a soon-to-be drunk biker who dragged me out to the pool before I had to answer Karma's question. I didn't want to answer it. I suspected even my superior lying skills would stand up to her observation. Being undercover had been pretty easy for me in the past, but even the most creepy and observant drug dealers and sex traffickers hadn't caught on to my deception. Something told me Karma would see through it a lot faster. And that scared me.

I had to find out how the Concrete Angels were connected to the deaths of Agents Hopkins and Eisenburg, and if they killed the men on the orders of the Backlog. Or if they'd simply done it themselves.

But tonight, no one was talking about anything but celebrating. It'd been a long time since I'd celebrated anything, but kicking back beside the pool with a cold beer, sweet barbecued ribs, and the fantastic view of Karma in her bikini did me a world of good. This time the suit consisted of brightly colored flowers and leaves on a black background, but the print highlighted her generous breasts and ass, and my cock loved it.

I'd already changed out of my jeans into my swim trunks to give my cock more range of motion. But even those grew tight in the crotch as Karma's sexy ass swayed past me on her way to the pool. Somehow we'd managed to find matching swim suits. My trunks weren't as brightly colored, but they had the same pattern of leaves and flowers in more neutral colors. The Scottish guy with shoulder-length hair and a beard ribbed me about it. I learned his road name was Attila and the women they'd brought in, called honeys, would sigh when his brogue hit their ears.

My choice in suit hadn't been intentional, but I kinda liked that Karma and I matched.

"Tryin' to get Karma to be your old lady, are ye?" Attila had sauntered over in an honest-to-glory kilt and nothing else.

I shook my head. "What exactly does that term mean? I admit I'm trying to get a date with her, but that's about it. Doesn't old lady mean a long term gig?"

"Aye. It means she's yours to do with as ye please." He bit his bottom lip and rocked his hips. "If ye catch my meanin'. It means she's taken and woe betide any man who tries anything with her without yer permission."

I snorted as I watched her jump into the pool. "Woe betide anyone who tries anything with her without *her* permission. She's the Enforcer, isn't she? You'd be stupid to take advantage of her. She'd kick your ass six ways from breakfast."

Attila followed my gaze as Karma swam across the pool with smooth strokes. "Aye, that's the right of it. Even if she wasn't the Enforcer, she's a force to be reckoned with. A few have tried and they werena seen again." He shrugged as I turned my wide eyes to his. "She's fiery, that one. And you'd best be 'ware of it. But if you can gain her regard, the shag would be amazing, I'll wager."

I couldn't argue with him there. Hell, I'd just like to kiss her. My cock saluted the idea and I shifted a little to relieve the pressure. *Damn, think about something else.*

My gaze slid over the assembled crowd and I found the snarly guy Karma had called Scott standing beside a blonde woman wearing glasses and a reserved smile. Something about her seemed familiar, as if I'd seen her face before, but I couldn't quite place where.

"Hey, Attila, who's the woman next to Scott? She one of the honeys?"

Attila tore his gaze away from another giggly woman whose boobs seemed as big as her head, and looked in the direction I'd pointed.

"Nah, that's Scott's old lady, Numbers."

"Where'd she get the road name of Numbers?"

"She's a wiz with 'em. Magic in accounting. Used to be FBI."

"Holy fuck. Why the hell is she here then?"

"Loki hired her to check our books and her former boss dinna like it so much. Wee wanker." Attila scowled as he shook his head. "He brought the FBI here trying to pin shite on us and terrorize her. But she was the one who sniffed out who embezzled from us, and we took care o' that."

Things started to become clear. "What was the guy's name who came after her?"

Attila eyed me with surprise and I realized I'd jumped into cop-interrogation mode. "Why do ye want to know?"

I forced myself to shrug. "I'm a PI and puzzles like that intrigue me. Michael mentioned that you hadn't found all the money and I offered to do some research to see if I could find other avenues where the money went. You just added another piece of the puzzle."

Attila kept looking at me and I did my best to play it cool. He had a right to be suspicious and I'd overplayed my hand. But if my own suspicions were right, Numbers was the woman who'd accused Agent Hopkins of rape. I just needed Attila or someone in the Concrete Angels to confirm it.

"I doona remember his name, but I know he was her boss and she was afraid of him."

I nodded and shrugged again, stuffing my disappointment down. "If he raped her, I can understand her fear."

"Why? You been raped?" Attila wore disbelief like a hat.

I shook my head. "No, but I understand what it's like not to trust anyone around you to have your back."

Oh boy, did I understand. When my agency had been infected with Backlog members, I couldn't trust anyone except my boss, and I worried he'd get compromised while I was out here investigating. But Marshal Gary Battlebourne had been painfully honest throughout his career and I had to trust someone. I just hoped he stayed that way.

"Aye, it's a crazy world."

Attila nodded, his eyes still narrowed in thought. He sat back with his hands behind his head. A tattoo of a wicked skull wearing a beret with a sword through the bones, the blade passing through the left eye socket, flashed on the inside of his arm. I recognized the Special Forces tattoo before I realized his expression had turned mischievous.

Aw hell.

"So what about you, Coop? Are ye here for an investigation or somethin' else?"

That was too close for comfort and I let a lazy smile curl my lips. "Your boys over there couldn't bring back the beer without help, so I volunteered to do a civic duty. But since I've met Karma before, I took the opportunity to see her again."

"Have ye? Where at?"

"A local Gas 'N Snacks. I ran into her while filling up my car and we talked." More or less after I chased her through the winding mountain roads.

"Talked, did ye?" He raised an eyebrow as a smirk curled his lips. "Looks like it was some talk to get ye to walk in here voluntarily. Ye must have it bad for our Enforcer." He paused. "Ye do know what the Enforcer does, aye?"

I nodded slowly. "She takes care of what needs to be done."

"Aye, she does." He lost his smile and a shiver ran down my back. "That means if yer investigatin' what ye shouldna, she'll kill ye quick. Hear me?"

I met his gaze while I chose which way to respond. I could show fear and he'd think the message got across. I could blow him off and he'd probably believe me to be overconfident and stupid. Or I could become belligerent and he'd really think me stupid.

Well, with those choices...

"I know what she does and I know what it means." I kept my voice level. "I'm not here to cause trouble. I just wanted to see Karma and brought the beer."

He nodded slowly, his gaze still searching mine for secrets. *Nope, not gonna tell you those, buddy.* Evidently, he satisfied himself with whatever he found and nodded.

"Right, then. Ye'll do." He rolled to his feet as Karma pulled herself, dripping, out of the pool. "Oy, Karma! Ye'd best be seein' to this man, here, before he does somethin' stupid like get too pissed to talk to ye."

Talking to Karma wasn't the problem. But getting just the right information out of the Concrete Angels? Yeah, that was a trick and a half. Maybe I could get her talking about their connection to Agent Dirk Hopkins without tipping her off.

"He wouldn't do that. He'd miss out on too much."

Her voice washed over me like sultry velvet and my

42

heart rate went up. Not from fear, but from arousal. The woman could make me hard as a pipe with just a few words. Hell, she could probably read the dictionary to me and I'd be holding back my orgasm.

"No, ma'am, I wouldn't do that." I held her gaze as she sauntered over to me, her hips swinging with erotic enticement in each step.

Damn, she's sexy and I need her.

The thought came out of nowhere and I'd never experienced the emotion stitched to it. It wasn't simply desire. It wasn't a delicious treat picked up on a run to a quickie mart. This was something deeper and more necessary, a staple in my diet like eggs or butter, and I *needed* it.

Before I could say anything more, she'd straddled my hips and settled onto my lap, her wet pussy soaking my trunks with pool water.

"But I don't want to talk at the moment."

"No?" Did my voice squeak? I cleared my throat.

"No."

She bent as she grasped my face and tilted my head enough to press her lips against mine. I moaned as the softness of them cinched my attention. But when she pushed her tongue into my mouth, I lost coherence and control. I groaned as I wrapped my arms around her body and pulled her close to my chest, desperate for more contact. My cock hardened against the front of my trunks and I ached to rub it against her hot core.

Oh, my glory, I need her.

I couldn't breathe. I couldn't think. I could only feel, and that drove the need to be naked and inside her. I forgot the reason I was in the Concrete Angels compound. I forgot the investigation and Backlog. I just needed her like I needed air to breathe and water to drink.

"Would it be possible to stop eating his face long enough for me to talk to him, Karma?"

A new voice filtered into my awareness, but the primal side of me wanted to ignore it. Karma, on the other hand, had other ideas. She pulled back to meet my gaze, her lips swollen with our pleasure, before she glanced away.

"Sure, Loki. Talk away." She helped me turn my head to face the really scary guy I'd seen through my binocs.

He wasn't as tall as Michael, or as broad as Attila, but he carried presence and power with him like he'd been born to it. I swallowed hard, his attention on me uncomfortable. He had piercing blue eyes, a neatly trimmed beard, and long, wavy reddish-blond hair. I didn't notice details about other guys usually, but this guy had beauty and power all rolled up in a slightly amused smile curling his elegant lips. Made me nervous as hell.

"So, you're the dude with a cool car, *ja*?" He tilted his head. "Michael says you can investigate where our money has gone."

"Yeah." I nodded, afraid to say more.

"What makes you think you can do better than a forensic accountant?"

"I got friends in low places. And lots of experience." It was hard to hold a serious conversation with a hot woman sitting on my semi-erect cock, but I didn't think I could move her off my lap unless she wanted to go

Loki nodded slowly. "*Ja*, I can see you do. Okay, Coop "Dude with a Cool Car" DeVille, you can look for our money. You can get started on that as soon as Karma's done with you." Again, an enigmatic smile wreathed his lips. "Tomorrow is soon enough, *ja*?"

"Wait." He turned with a raised eyebrow. "Who stole the money from you in the first place?"

"Why do you need to know that?"

I shrugged. "I gotta have a starting place somewhere."

He nodded again. "Roy." He grimaced and shook his head. "Also known as Agent Arnold Eisenburg of the FBI."

Bingo.

I raised my eyebrows. "The FBI stole money from you?" I whistled my surprise. "That takes a lot of gall. How do you know it didn't go back to the Feds?"

He shrugged. "If it did, our forensic accountant would've been able to track it there. And she found some of it. But not all of it. He and his partner weren't sending it to the FBI."

"He had a partner? Here or in the FBI?"

"In the FBI. Neither of them are problems now, but the money is still missing. You find it, and there'll be rewards, *ja*?"

"Yeah, okay. Sounds good. I'll get on it first thing tomorrow."

Loki eyed us with speculation and the ultra-scary smile curled his lips again. "*Ja. Det er bra.*"

"What?"

Karma snorted. "He said that's fine."

"What language was that?" I watched Loki saunter away to join Michael and the snarly guy I'd met earlier.

"Norwegian, I believe. He throws out words every now and again to keep us on our toes." She wriggled her ass on my lap again. "But I'm not worried about your toes. Unless that's a fetish of yours."

I grimaced. "No way in hell. I'd rather focus on something softer and far more sexy. Like you."

She grinned before she kissed me again and my cock rose to the occasion. Damn, I wanted to be somewhere private, where I could strip her out of her bikini and marvel at all that glowing golden skin. And if I had to investigate her pussy while there, I'd take one for the team.

"I think that can be arranged." She backed off my lap and I groaned as my cock stretched the wet cloth. "Follow me."

She sauntered away toward the clubhouse and I didn't waste any time rolling to my feet. I'd gotten the go ahead to investigate the Concrete Angels, had been given the name of the agent who'd screwed them, and now the sexiest woman I'd ever seen wanted to spend some quality alone-time with me. Fuck yeah, life was lookin' up.

CHAPTER SIX

Karma

I must be out of my mind.

I felt more than saw Coop follow me away from the pool and the zing of pleasurable anticipation sped up my heart rate. *He's a human.* Yeah, it didn't matter. The Goddess had seen fit to make him my true mate and that meant I was completely attuned to his every move when close to me.

The scooters noticed my progress with hungry eyes, which had everything to do with the bikini I wore, but they'd learned long ago not to touch. It was satisfying giving them immediate consequences to their less-than stellar ideas of how to treat women, but ultimately disappointing that they only learned to fear the women members rather than decide we were people.

Not that I'm a person in the traditional sense.

Traditional or otherwise, I definitely felt emotions. At the moment, I wanted to get down and dirty with my true mate. I waved to Dollhouse and Calhoun as I sauntered through the clubhouse, and both ladies smirked as they waved back. I suspected their grins came from Coop trailing behind me like a puppy on a leash.

I stepped out into the yard and continued my way to my cabin, enjoying the quiet. Most of the members were in the clubhouse or around the pool, and it was always loud when they got together. A few of the guys like The Friar and Torch were fooling around in the barn workshop, but the rest of the yard sat deserted. I took a deep breath of the silence and let it seep into me.

A spike of lust and desire shot through my awareness as I neared my cabin, lucky number thirteen. Humans made a big deal out of that number, but in reality, it wasn't any less lucky than any other number. That didn't mean I didn't play up the consequences on days with the number thirteen, or four, but it was just a day.

And today, I'm gettin' lucky.

"Come on in, Coop." I stood aside and allowed him to enter in front of me. *All the better to ogle his ass in those trunks.* "And when you're ready, feel free to strip naked."

"What?" He spun back toward me and his eyebrows reached his hairline.

"Strip. Naked." I let a lazy smile curl my lips as I pulled the towel off my hips and draped it over one of my two tall bar stools. "I want to see what all those clothes have been hiding from me."

He snorted and shot a look toward the open window. "Here? Now? What about in the bedroom?"

Oh ho, my lovely mate is modest.

I tilted my head as I sauntered over to the front window and lowered the blinds, the slats allowing the light through. "There. Now strip."

He laughed and yanked his t-shirt over his head, exposing chiseled pecs and abs with a line of hair arrowing straight down into his colorful trunks. My mouth watered as my gaze followed that line to the large bulge pushing against the front, stretching the fabric tight. Oh yeah, I'd get to sample the goods hidden there.

I raised my gaze to take in the muscles across his back

and shoulders as he turned to pull off low-heeled cowboy boots. A few scars marked the skin of his back, a testament to his experience and life. I didn't know what he'd done to earn them, but they were a wicked reminder he hadn't always been safe.

My inner guardian rose up at the thought, swearing to protect him against all enemies from then on. He straightened with his back to me and shoved his swim trunks over his hips, exposing his tight ass. *Was he walking around commando in his jeans, too?* Oh that was a lovely thought. I licked my lips and swallowed hard. I'd have to pay closer attention.

At last, he turned around and ran his hands through his hair in a nervous motion as if he worried about my opinion of his body.

Two thumbs way, way up.

"Damn, you're sexy." Not the most elegant of phrases, but definitely conveyed what I was thinking. *The drool might give me away, too.*

His grin warmed my heart in ways I'd rarely experienced. "You think so?"

"Oh yeah." I sauntered around him, trailing my fingers over his shoulders and down his other arm. "I know so." I stopped beside him and slid my hand down the crease in his back to his butt. "I love how tight your ass is."

He chuckled but said nothing, allowing me to explore his body as I chose. I focused on his chest and torso, taking my time to learn the shape of his muscles. He had perfectly round nipples just above the curve of his pecs and a dusting of dark hair that helped build the line down to his groin. I followed the line down to the thickening cock rising from a matching thatch of hair around his balls.

Sweet glory to the Goddess. He missed his calling as a porn star because the length and girth of him definitely had my attention. Rising in a delicious curve, his cock damn near reached his navel. And I wanted to lick the whole length. I also wanted him to wear some cock jewelry to mark him as mine.

One step at a time, Karma dear.

I slid around in front of him, still trailing my fingers over his skin until I stopped with my hand over his heart. I met his gaze and found him completely focused on me. His heart beat a quick tattoo under my palm, but he stood still and attentive, his deep brown eyes nearly black as the pupil grew almost to the edges of his irises.

"Do you want me, Coop?"

He licked his lips but never looked away from my gaze. "Yes, ma'am."

"How much do you want me?" I stepped to his right, stroking his chest with my fingers.

"I want you more than I've wanted anything in a long time, ma'am." His gaze followed mine.

"What would you do to get what you want?"

He swallowed hard. "Anything."

"Anything?" I raised an eyebrow. "Anything I ask?"

"Yes, ma'am."

A delicious curl of pleasure mixed with power slid through me. "So, if I asked you to eat my pussy, would you?"

"Yes, ma'am." He licked his lips again and his cock flexed between his thighs.

"If I asked you stand here naked while I ran my hands over you, would you let me?"

"Yes, ma'am."

"What if I asked you to let me suck your cock but forbid you to come. Would you do it?"

His breath caught as his cock jerked, and his thighs trembled, but he nodded. "Glory, yes, ma'am."

I moved back until I stood facing him, his body quivering in anticipation. "Would you still be willing to do as I ask if I told you to eat my pussy and bring me pleasure without being able to come yourself?"

Coop swallowed hard and shivered, his eyes growing bright with desire. "Y-yes, ma'am."

Sweet glory, Coop is a submissive. I'd lived long enough among humans to know about the BDSM lifestyle, and while I had Dominant tendencies in my sex life, it hadn't been my focus to pursue or practice regularly. Especially with humans. But with Coop practically quivering for me to take the lead, my Domme nature rose to the fore.

"Hmm, you seem very sure of yourself, Coop. But I think we need some ground rules." I grasped his chin and made sure he met my gaze. "I need to be clear on what this is. Are you willingly giving me permission to use you as I see fit?"

He swallowed again, and gave a jerky nod. "Yes, ma'am."

"Are you sure this is what you want, Coop? Because if I find out you're lying to me, I will walk away without a backward glance." I wasn't sure I could actually walk away, but I needed him to know honesty was everything here.

"I'm not lying. Not with this. Not with something this important." His voice came out with the strength of truth and an undertone of pleading.

I nodded slowly. "Is this truly what you want? Because we can enjoy each other in vanilla ways."

He shook his head and his hands clenched into fists. "I don't know what that means, exactly, but I know I want to be with you and please you. I *need* to please you."

"Have you heard the term BDSM?"

He shrugged. "It's a kind of fetish, right?"

"It can be. It depends on the players." I stepped behind him and gathered his arms until I held his wrists at the small of his back, my knuckles resting against his ass. "For example. Some folks like to be bound while their Mistress takes Her pleasure from them. Would you like to be bound?" I tugged on his wrists and brushed my lips over his shoulder, enjoying the scent of his sun-warmed skin.

He hissed and groaned, dropped his head back to brush my cheek. "Yes, ma'am."

"Hmm." I licked his shoulder before a nipped it, making him jump. "What about pain?" I bit him a little harder and he yelped.

"No, ma'am."

Yeah, he wasn't going to be a pain slut.

"What about spanking and impact play?" I slapped his ass, enjoying the tensing of his muscles, before smoothing my hand over the skin. "Do you like such sensations?"

He shook his head. "I don't think so, ma'am."

I nodded again as I released his hands and returned to face him. "All right. One last question before we start playing." I made sure I had his complete attention without the haze of lust and desire clouding his eyes. "When we play, I will be in control. In control of your needs and your pleasure. You will bow to my will and tend to my needs in order to fulfill yours, but that might not include your own release." I raised my chin. "Is that something you can handle, Coop? Are you willing to put all rights of pleasure in my hands?"

He blinked and took a deep breath, leaving his hands behind his back as if they remained bound. "I've never been with anyone who has these kinds of requirements, but they don't scare me. Or they don't scare me more than my interest in trying. I want to be with you, Karma, and if this is how I have to do it, I won't hesitate. Ma'am."

His response had my pussy creaming and my heart expanding like the Grinch after Cindy-Lou Who took his hand at Yule. It was the perfect answer and I admired his courage. I would still take it slow, learning him while he learned me, but he made me want to play for the first time in years.

"That's very good to hear, Coop." I settled my mind

into Domme-mode and straightened my shoulders, pushing my breasts out toward him. His gaze latched onto the bikini cups holding them and he licked his lips. "Hey, eyes up here."

He jerked his gaze up to mine and blinked slowly, still lucid enough to get my last instruction.

"There's just one thing left we have to establish. Your safeword."

"Safeword?"

"Yes." I gripped his jaw again and met his gaze. "It's the word, something out of context, that stops all play. Stops it cold and allows you equal footing with me again. Most people new to the lifestyle chose stop light colors to get the understanding across. Green for good-to-go, yellow for slow down or readjust things, red for hard limits and stop play."

"Those really make the play stop?" He frowned.

"It does if you trust your Domme to do as She promises." I slid my hand to his shoulder and down his muscular arm. "BDSM only works if the partners trust each other to be honest and to uphold their roles. I must trust you to tell me when you need something and you must trust me to uphold the rules of play."

"Even if it means you stop?"

"Particularly if it means I stop." I squeezed his elbow with my fingers. "Giving me control over your pleasure is a big gift and must be treated with respect. But you're the one in control. I can only give you as much or as little as you want. If I overstep and lose your trust, I will lose everything. In reality, I serve you, give you what you need. I need to be needed. That gives me peace and well-being."

His gaze softened and his head tilted. "I *need* you, Ma'am."

Again, my heart grew another three sizes and I wanted to throw my arms around him in jubilation. *But Dommes don't do that.* I had to show my approval in other ways. I gave him my warmest smile.

"Very good. I'll be everything you need today, Coop. But I need to hear your safeword so there's no confusion."

He blinked. "I thought we were going to use the stop light analogy."

"We can if that's easiest. But if we continue our relationship"—*oh please, please, please*—"I'll want you to select a safeword specific to you. Clear?"

He nodded. "Yes, Ma'am."

"I like that. Ma'am. Effective, yet subtle, even in public." I nodded with satisfaction. "Okay, Coop, here's how we'll start. I want you to go into the bedroom and lie down on your back on the bed. You will grasp the headboard and remain there until I come to you. Is that clear?"

He swallowed and his cock flexed at my orders, but he nodded.

"No, I need verbal confirmation that you understand me."

"Yes, Ma'am."

"Very good. Go on now. I'll be there in a minute."

He turned and strode to the room without looking back, his ass and back flexing deliciously with his movement. *Holy fuck, he's sexy.* I wanted to chase him into my room and tackle him, but I'd take my time to do this right. The Goddess had made it clear he was my true mate, but that didn't guarantee I wouldn't fuck it up if I got careless. Especially if Coop hadn't known he was a submissive before.

Oh my glory. Oh my glory. The realization that I had to be extra careful hit me like a ton of bricks and a cold sweat slithered down my back despite the warmth of the day. Taking a deep breath, I forced myself to head into my kitchenette. I didn't use it much because Grubb was the best damn chef in Colorado, but I still had snacks and tea for when I needed a quick pick-me-up.

I leaned against the counter and breathed deeply, trying to calm my racing heart. I'd found a submissive to play with, and he was my perfect partner according to the Goddess, but he was so new to the lifestyle. He represented the clay before the artist made pottery. Or the marble before the sculptor used a chisel. I'd never had a dedicated sub before, but Coop made me want to whip out a collar and bind him to me without trying his paces.

Calm down, Karma. Don't give yourself bad karma you'll have to repay later.

I closed my eyes and thought back to times when I'd been in my Domme role. Unfortunately, they were few and far between, and it had been a long time since I'd indulged that part of myself. I needed control to give Coop what he needed, and right now I was like a kid with a new puppy. The puppy wanted to please, but the kid didn't know enough to treat it right.

You do know enough, you just have to calm down enough to remember. That was the Goddess's voice, and She was right. *And he's new to this, so you both can build your relationship the way it should be, based on what you need rather than what others 'recommend'.*

Right. The rules of BDSM changed based on the partners. Whatever they decided between them, those were the correct rules to use.

I shivered with excitement and anticipation before I stood up and straightened my shoulders. Coop needed a Domme with confidence and calm, not an overexcited teenager with bossy tendencies. I took a few more moments to settle myself before I took a deep breath and headed for the bedroom.

An image of sucking him off while he sat tied to the chair made my pussy clench with need and I shivered again. *That day will come, but it's not today. One step at a time.* Yeah, I just hoped I had enough control over myself to make that a reality.

CHAPTER SEVEN

Cooper

I lay on the bed and tried to still my breathing. I hadn't been this excited for sex in a long time. I still couldn't understand why the idea of Karma having control made my cock hard enough to pound nails, but I knew I wanted it this way. Maybe that was the reason my marriage had fallen apart. Andrea hadn't been a bad woman when we married, and I'd been a pretty good husband considering my profession as a Marshal.

But sexually, she'd been the kind of woman who wanted to be babied and pampered, not doing much beyond opening her legs in hopes it would get me hard. But though we'd been trying for a baby, it was harder and harder to get the urge to have sex with her, even for that reason. Pampering her became a chore.

I'm ashamed to say I spent more and more time away from home, working on cases to take my mind of my frustration. I didn't know what was wrong, only that something was and our sexual relations dwindled. Andrea had gotten more and more hostile and I'd bristled right back at her. She accused me of having an affair, but the only thing I did right in our marriage was remain faithful.

I soon learned her accusation was more projection than belief when I caught her fucking the smarmy househusband of a military woman down the street. I don't know if he actually gave Andrea what she wanted or if he'd simply been more available than me, but his presence in our bed was the nail in the coffin of our relationship. I'd threatened to arrest his ass for adultery as I chased him out of our house with his pants still around his ankles. Finding him pumping in to my wife on the counter of our kitchen had infuriated me.

Gave me a whole new meaning for Home Economics.

A rueful laugh pushed its way out of my chest. The divorce had gotten ugly, though we both agreed she'd get the house and I wouldn't pay alimony. I'd felt betrayed, but in retrospect, she probably had as well. I couldn't give her the kind of sex she wanted so I avoided her, and we'd hurt each other.

But after Karma laid out the rules of how she liked sex, it made me wonder if I'd avoided Andrea because she didn't make all the sexual choices and wanted me to treat her like a damsel. The thing was, I worked in law enforcement. I made all the decisions all the time. I dimly recalled the few times I'd fantasized about the faceless woman of my dreams having me pamper her based on her choices, giving me clear directions and taking the decisions out of my hands.

"Holy shit."

The insight stole my breath and released some of my frustration at my ex. Maybe she'd needed me to do to her what I'd needed her to do to me. She'd once screamed at me that if I'd been more of a man, our marriage wouldn't have fallen apart. It had infuriated me because I was the man all the time on the job and needed someone else to take the heat for a while.

"Oh my, someone's been alone in his mind too long."

Karma's voice jerked me back to the present, and I

realized my cock had wilted like dead flowers left in a vase without water. I grimaced as my heart sank. I didn't want to disappoint her right off the bat. At least it had taken years with Andrea. I'd only known Karma few days.

"I'm sorry, Ma'am." I tried to will my erection back into place, but my dark thoughts had pretty much killed it. I moved my hand to reach for my cock.

"Hey. What did I say about your hands?"

I froze and swallowed hard, trepidation and excitement pounding through me in equal measures. "You said to grasp the headboard, Ma'am."

"That's right. I said grasp the headboard." She nodded as she crossed her arms over her chest. "Are you changing your mind about this arrangement?"

A curious tightness filled her voice and it matched the tightness in my throat at the idea of ending our play. "No, Ma'am."

"All right, then. Back they go." She pointed at the back of the bed and I resecured my hands around the rustic spindles. "Very good, Coop. Now, I want you to spread your legs so I can suck your cock."

I blinked, trying to understand her words. "Suck my cock? I thought I was supposed to give you pleasure." She raised an eyebrow and I hastily added, "Ma'am."

She stopped at the foot of the bed. "Oh, you are going to give me pleasure, Coop. It's my pleasure to suck on your hard shaft and lick the head, savoring the taste of your pre-cum. All I need is you to get hard for your Domme. Can you do that for me, Coop?"

My cock had already started to swell with her sultry words and the smile curling her lips lit my fire. Holy moly, she was sexy and I desperately wanted to please her. If letting her suck on my cock was what it took, I'd stay hard until the end of time.

"Ah, there it is, your lovely cock." She settled between my legs with her shoulders brushing my calves. "I think I want to sniff your balls first." She dipped her head and pressed her lips on the inside of my thigh just where my scrotum hung between them.

I moaned as she inhaled, my hands tightening on the spindles above my head. Her lips and nose tickled the crease between my thigh and my balls, and exquisite pleasure slid through my body. She dragged her nose over the skin of my testicles and I saw stars.

"Oh, those are lovely. How do they taste?"

Before I could respond, slick heat engulfed my scrotum and I hit a high note I hadn't heard in my voice since I was twelve. I rocked my hips, wanting more heat, or less ticklishness, I wasn't sure which. She reached between my legs and grasped my shaft as she licked and laved my balls. I wanted her to stroke my dick, but she only held it out of her way as she enjoyed her ministrations.

Karma pulled back with lust and arousal filling her face and I desperately wanted to give her more. If all I had to do was lay there and take what she was giving, I'd do it for a long as possible.

"Oh yeah, your balls are delicious. I'll have to revisit them later." She looked up my body at me. "But I think I want to taste your cock instead." Her fingers massage the hair of my groin in little circles, not touching my dick or balls, but stimulating them nonetheless. "I'm going to enjoy your cock, but I don't want you to come until I say. And you can't let go of the headboard. If you do either of those, I'll have to punish you. Do you understand?"

Glory, her words made my cock jerk as arousal surged through me. "Yes, Ma'am."

"Very good, Coop. Don't let me down now."

She pulled the head of my dick to her lips and ran her tongue over the glans. I groaned and tried to shove it deeper into her hot, wet mouth, but she held my hips down and sipped the pre-cum sliding from my slit. Glory, the feel of her tongue on my most sensitive skin made squirm.

She chuckled as I tried to get closer to her mouth, but took her time, licking and kissing my hard shaft. I tightened my hands around the spindles, hoping that I'd be able to find calm as she ignited my arousal. But her lips and her tongue fractured my usual focus. I tried to think of cleaning out my car after a long stakeout or spending time looking over the divorce papers. But her caresses splintered my thoughts.

Her tongue swiped over the edge of the head and I whimpered as she pulled her mouth away. To my relief, she slowed down and changed the rhythm, helping my building orgasm to slide to the back of my mind again.

She tickled and suckled the underside of my cock and I was able to turn my mind away to float on gentle pleasure.

"Oh no, you don't. You will not ignore me."

Karma slid her mouth all the way over my cock and down until I hit the back of her throat. Her tongue massaged my hard shaft and her tight heat brought my attention back to what she was doing. But when her hands massaged my balls, my release renewed its threat on my sanity.

Then she swallowed.

"Oh, my sweet glory, Karma."

Abruptly, the sweet, hot, wet pleasure ended as she pulled off. "What did you call me?"

"Uh…" I gasped for a few moments, trying to grasp what I'd missed. Her voice told me I'd said something wrong. "Ma'am. Ma'am, thank you, Ma'am."

"Good man, Coop. You mustn't forget, now, or you won't get what you want. Understand?"

"Y-yes, Ma'am."

"Good."

She dipped her head again, licking my dick until the arousal built again. She kept her attention shallow, just massaging the edge of the head and the crown, as if she licked and sucked because she was enjoying the flavor and texture of my cock. I'd never had a woman take such joy in sucking my dick. All my previous partners had given the impression they wanted to get it over with, like it was the price they paid for something they wanted more.

But not Karma. She fondled and massaged my penis like it was the best treat she'd had in years and she wanted to savor it for as long as possible. She even hummed while she did it as if she'd just remembered why she loved sucking cock. And maybe it was true, but damn if it didn't make me want more.

"Fuck yeah."

A deep chuckle welled up from her chest and flowed over my groin, increasing the friction and pleasure. I moaned and rocked my hips again, but she continued to hold me still. She dipped her head and swallowed my cock whole, deep-throating me until I couldn't tell where her hot mouth ended and I began.

She did something with her throat and tongue to make the pressure increase again, and the hot, slick delight worked its way from my balls to my brain. I tightened my hands on the spindles of the headboard as she worked her mouth faster and tighter. Moans and whimpers flew from my throat without my say-so and my hips rocked despite her hold on them.

When she deep-throated me again, I was fine until she rolled my balls in her fingers.

"Oh, glory, Ma'am. If you keep doing that, I'm gonna come."

"Uh-uh." She gave me the negative as she kept up her rhythm and I whimpered a high note.

"Please, Ma'am. Let me come." I held on to my release by a thread, her tongue's caresses making it damn near impossible.

She pulled back long enough to consider my face as I gritted my teeth against the orgasm clawing at my balls.

"No."

She returned to my cock and sucked on it like it would disappear without her attention. I groaned and squeezed the spindles harder, holding onto my release with every fiber of my being. I could let go and let her down. Despite the pleasure she administered, some part of me needed to hold out as long as she required it. I needed it like I needed air to breathe and failure to hold out wasn't an option.

But when her fingers trailed down below my balls to my taint, I wailed against my release.

"Please, Ma'am. I can't hold back. Please let me come, Ma'am."

"You may come, sweet man."

She swallowed my dick again and squeezed my balls, and I was lost. My orgasm roared through me, sweeping away my fears, my worries, hell, even my insecurities about trusting this woman. I'd worried about withholding my true profession when she said we needed to trust each other, but her attention to my body washed it away. She gave me the most unbelievable pleasure and I couldn't imagine being without it.

I need this. I need her, my Ma'am.

The thought came through clearly as I settled back into the bed from my lofty flight. She licked and sucked my dick, taking all the cum I pumped into her mouth as she hummed with approval. She swallowed it all down and cleaned my skin with her tongue, sending erotic aftershocks through me.

"Oh, you're my sweet man, Coop. Well done." She smiled as she backed off the bed. "I think you deserve a reward for being so good. Would you like a reward?"

"Yes, Ma'am." I nodded vigorously, though my body rested in a languorous drape on the bed.

"Keep your eyes on me. Do you understand?"

"Yes, Ma'am."

She slid off and stood with a satisfied smile on her lips where I could easily see her without turning my head, or sucking in my gut. Fortunately, I'd spent enough time working out at a local gym and going for runs in the mornings that I didn't have much of the beer gut left as a result of my divorce. I'd heard the best revenge against an ex was to make my body better than when they had it, and I'd put the advice into practice.

Now I was glad I had, even if it hadn't been for Andrea's appreciation.

"Keep your attention on me, Coop. Don't drift, please."

How the hell she knew I'd been thinking of the past, I had no idea, but I jerked my attention and gaze back to her beautiful body. She reached behind herself and pulled on the strings of her bikini top until it loosened and she lifted it off her breasts.

Hot damn and fuckin' A.

Her golden-brown skin grew lighter around her more coffee-colored areolas and pert, large nipples. My mouth watered as I took in her full breasts. I wanted to suck on them until she orgasmed from the pleasure of my tongue on her soft skin. Or maybe she'd press those full mounds against my cheeks so I could smell her delicious scent surrounding me.

"Do you like my breasts?" She slid her hands under their full weight and pushed them up, making the large nipples point straight at me.

"Oh glory, yes, Ma'am."

"Very good." She grinned. "You may look but not touch. I have something else in mind as your reward."

"You do, Ma'am?"

"Oh yeah."

She grinned as she dropped her hands to her hips and pushed the tiny bikini bottom off her perfect, rounded ass. My gaze zeroed in on the neatly trimmed wedge of curls covering her mound and I moaned, licking my lips. If I could get my mouth on her pussy, I'd be in heaven.

"Don't let go of the headboard." She sauntered over to the bed and smiled down at me. I swallowed hard at the scent of her arousal wafting up from between her legs.

"No, Ma'am. I won't let go."

"Good. Now, are you ready for your reward?"

"Yes, Ma'am."

"Excellent. Push yourself down the bed a bit until your arms are almost straight."

I moved a little, wriggling my ass and my shoulders lower on the bed. She moved the pillows away from my head until I lay completely flat. My dick, so recently flaccid, started to fill again as she ran her hands over my body, adjusting and positioning it with attention to my comfort.

"Keep your hands where I can see them."

The statement reminded me of every cop I'd worked with and I twitched in surprise. Had she figured out what I was? She gave me a sharp look and I licked my lips, trying to reassure her that my attention hadn't wandered.

"How are you feeling, Coop? Are your arms okay?"

"I'm fine, Ma'am. My arms are fine."

"What color?"

She fixed me with a stern look and it took my endorphin-addled brain a few moments to understand the importance of the question.

"Oh, uh, green. My arms are green."

The sweet smile curling her lips as she straddled my waist made the momentary efforts at thought worth it. But even better was the placement of her sweet-smelling pussy not more than eighteen inches from my mouth.

"Very good. Now, here's your reward. You're gonna eat my pussy and make me come." She chuckled at my wide grin. "But you can't let go of the headboard until I allow you to do so. And you can't use your hands. You can only make me come with your nose, lips, and tongue. Is that clear?"

"Ma'am, yes, Ma'am."

I wanted that pussy more than I wanted my next breath, but it was so damn hard to wait for her to get her body into position without using my hands. My knuckles strained as I gripped the spindles of the headboard when she maneuvered closer to me.

The scent of her pussy made my mouth water and I whimpered a little as she knelt above my face. If I extended my tongue, I'd be able to lick her lips and get the first taste of the honey coating them. But something held me back. I understood if I tasted her without permission, I'd be in a heap of trouble and might not get the reward she was offering.

It was weird to hold back. All the previous times I'd had sex with a woman, I'd never restrained my efforts or waited for my partner's explicit order. But with Karma, my gut said I needed to wait for her to give me the go-ahead. If I did, I'd get more than I'd hoped.

"Are you waiting to kiss my pussy, Coop?" She tilted her head and met my gaze as she positioned herself over me.

"Yes, Ma'am."

"Good man. Now, move your hands to my ass."

I widened my eyes with my grin but did as she ordered, letting my palms fill with her glorious ass. The skin of her butt cheeks felt silky smooth in my hands and I wanted to squeeze and caress them.

"You're allowed to caress my ass as you eat my pussy, Coop, but you better leave those hands there because if they leave my cheeks, you'll be punished. Do you understand?"

"How will I be punished, Ma'am?" I wasn't planning on moving my hands from her ass, but I wanted to know what the stakes were.

Karma reached down between her legs to stroke my face with one hand. "You won't be allowed to come again tonight. I'll give myself pleasure with a toy or my own fingers and I'll make you watch, but you won't be able to touch me or yourself. Your body and orgasms belong to me now."

"And if I still disobey you, Ma'am?" I wanted to know what might be worse, although watching her come without participating might just kill me.

"Are you planning to be a brat, Coop?"

"No, Ma'am. I just need to know all the stakes."

She nodded, her expression growing thoughtful. "You won't be allowed to sleep with me tonight. I'll either banish you to the floor or send you on your way back to your campsite with your cool car." She lost some of her amusement as she met my gaze. "Do you understand, Coop?"

Part of me wanted to test her to see if she'd uphold her statements, but another, stronger part of me handcuffed and gagged the first part. There was no fucking way I'd to go back to my campsite in the hills above the compound. Not only had I packed it up before I met with the junior members of the Concrete Angels, but I wanted to stay close to and serve Karma.

"I understand, Ma'am."

"Very good, sweet man. Now, hold onto my ass and lick my pussy."

"Yes, Ma'am."

I wrapped each hand around a perfect, taut globe and pulled my Ma'am's cunt to my face. She probably expected me to just chow down like a dog going after soft food, but I used my tongue to outline her perfect lips, tickling the hairs along their fleshy edges. Her sweet and tangy flavor burst over my tongue as she sighed, the sound full of pleasure. Satisfaction bloomed in my chest and I kept sipping at her lips.

I separated her inner labia and ran the tip of my tongue between her folds, stroking the sensitive skin there. Her hands gripped the headboard above me and her breasts bounded as she twitched when I hit a particularly ticklish spot. I kept my eyes on her as I stroked, trying to learn what she loved based on her reactions to my tongue.

Her wet cream slipped into my mouth and filled my senses. I loved eating women out, but this felt like more to me. More pleasing, more satisfying, more flavorful. I couldn't get enough of her personal taste - like Rainier cherries, sweet and tart together. I took my time enjoying her lips before I'd even touched her clit because I might have been the one pleasuring her, but that didn't mean I couldn't tease. I'd figured out the best sex wasn't the wham-bam-thank-you-ma'am variety. A little extra effort went a long way toward satisfaction, even during one-night-stands.

"Oh, Coop, yes. Rub your tongue on my clit."

Your wish is my command.

I realized how true that was as I pushed my tongue into the hood of her clit and massaged it slowly, listening to her throaty moans over my head. I laved the stiff little nub before I sucked it into my mouth and increased the pressure on it like she had on my cock. I'd learned years ago that the clit was a mini-penis and had just as many nerves there to elicit pleasure when rubbed just right.

I rubbed and sucked on her nub until it started to relax then I dropped my mouth to her slit and thrust my tongue into her hot vagina as my nose rubbed her clit. Hot tangy cream dripped into my mouth as she whimpered and rocked on my face.

Aw yeah, making my woman happy.

It became my ultimate goal to give her pleasure, even if I never got more of my own. I'd always taken care of my lovers during sex, but the need to do so for Karma took on a whole new level. She was my queen and my goddess. I'd make sure her pleasure outstripped mine because mine derived from hers. If she was satisfied, I was satisfied.

I rubbed my nose harder against her clit as I thrust my tongue into her wet pussy, and moaned along with her as her sweet cream filled my mouth. She rocked her hips on my face and I enjoyed the play of her ass muscles under my hands. I couldn't contain either my delight at her erotic motions or her pussy juices as they spilled over my chin.

I desperately wanted to use my fingers and thrust into her cunt while I sucked on her clit, but she'd required me to do this with my tongue and failure wasn't an option. I glanced up her body to gauge where she was in her pleasure and damn near lost my focus in her beauty.

Karma rode my face with determined intensity, her hands white-knuckled on the headboard in pleasure. Her full breasts bounced as she rocked and I wished I could hold them, tweaking their velvety nipples as my tongue drove her to ecstasy. She whimpered and moaned with each thrust of her hips and I couldn't help but moan with her. She embodied the most beautiful woman I'd ever seen and I wanted to just stare.

You have a job to do, jackass. Oh, yeah, right. I gently squeezed her ass cheeks as I sped up my tongue on her soft folds and clit. Her sweet tangy cream filled my mouth and covered my chin, but my scruff would hold her scent for hours and I was all for that.

"Oh glory, Coop. Make me come. Lick your Mistress hard and make her come."

Yes, Ma'am.

I couldn't disobey an order any more than I could sprout feathers - *but if she ordered it, I'd try* - and I rubbed the flat of my tongue against her nether lips before I grasped her clit and sucked hard. I pulled her butt cheeks apart as I squeezed their taut fullness and Karma exploded in my mouth. She wailed her release over my head and my own cock hardened to stone with both satisfaction and arousal. I'd made my Ma'am come hard and I reaped the joys of drinking down the flood of her release.

Karma's moves became jerky over my head as I tenderly cleaned every inch of her clenching pussy. I wanted to feel those spasms on my fingers or cock, but deep satisfaction settled into my heart with the knowledge that I'd made her come. I kept up my ministrations on her pussy lips and clit until she moved off of me, but that small action had opened up a deep well of "rightness" inside.

I'd been satisfied and pleased when my orgasm rippled through me and I filled her mouth with my cum. But it was a thin puddle when compared to the vast lake of pleasure I felt when I'd done what my Ma'am required of me. Seeing her pleasure and contentment fed my system like a drug and I needed more. This was the man I was meant to be and I'd strive every day, every hour, to be that man for her.

****

Karma

Coop was perfect. He'd come on command and he'd eaten my pussy with the skills of a pro, never moving his hands off my ass. He might have been new to the official rules of the lifestyle, but he learned quickly and seemed ready for the next step.

I want to collar him.

Whoa. That thought came out too soon. Yes, he was my true mate according to the Goddess, which meant I'd never be able to truly outrun him, but he knew too little about me. And honestly, I didn't know enough about him. Oh, I knew he'd be the best sexual partner I could ever have, but there was more to the man than what he did with his tongue and cock.

Although, right now, I want to try the cock.

"Good man, Coop." I sighed as I pulled away from his mouth and settled on the bed beside him. "That was perfect." I glanced down at his groin to find his cock straining with desperation and need, pre-cum leaking from the tip. But his hands and body relaxed at my words and a satisfied smile curled his lips. "Give your Mistress a few moments to recover and I shall take care of that cock."

He frowned a bit. "If it pleases you, Ma'am. I'm okay lying beside you."

"What's the frown for, Coop? Did I hurt you?" I hoped I hadn't. Sometimes the human men I fucked just couldn't handle what physical power I carried. I didn't mean to be stronger than them, I simply was.

"No, Ma'am. It's just you called yourself 'Mistress' and I think of you as Ma'am. I hadn't heard you say you wanted to be called that."

"Oh." I nodded. "Well, I am your Mistress, but if you want to call me your Ma'am, I don't mind." I bit my lip. "Or to make things easier, I can be your Madam, since Ma'am is derived from that."

He snorted softly, humor curling his lips. "Most people think of Madam as a reference to a brothel owner."

"Ah, but we aren't most people and when it comes to this relationship, we make the rules. You may call me "Ma'am" in public and I'll be your Madam in private, and the rest of those people can make their own ass-making assumptions. Okay?"

His smile warmed and his gaze filled with hopeful yearning. "Yes, Ma'am."

I liked being his Madam, and at least with regards to him, I was running a kind of brothel. A pleasure brothel where the rules were clear and he got what he needed at my say-so. I served his needs to be dominated so he could be the finest version of the man he already was. I provided release and relaxation, as well as pleasure. And giving that to him gave me the greatest satisfaction as his woman and his Madam.

"Hmm, I think your cock need some attention, Coop." I reached down his body and took his long, curved shaft in my hand. "Are you sure you were never a porn star? This big, bad boy could've had a good career."

He snorted and shook his head. "No, Ma'am. Never got into producing flicks. Watched enough of them, but never thought to participate in them."

I stroked his dick and enjoyed the velvety skin over organic steel. "Then the world missed out because I only want this cock on display for me and me alone. Are you into exhibitionism, Coop?"

He pursed his lips in thought. "You know, before today I would've said no. But if you asked me to do it because you liked it, I might consider it."

His response made my stomach flutter with pleasure and approval. He'd do it because I wanted it and I might require him to do so in the future. But at the moment, his honest response was enough.

"Not today. For now, I want this cock all to myself and I don't want Dollhouse, Calhoun, Viper or Numbers getting a good look at it. Hell, even Attila and Michael would love to see it."

He swallowed a bit nervously. "Attila and Michael are gay?"

I shook my head. "They're both bisexual. Does that make you uncomfortable?" I kept squeezing his cock in my hand, stroking slowly, but the shaft wilted a little.

"No." I squeezed harder and he grimaced. "Well, yeah, maybe a little. I'm straight."

"Oh, I know you are, and they know it, too. But there's a good chance they're not attracted to you or they realized you were already taken." I tilted my head and narrowed my eyes. "You know they're just as normal as you, right? They have "types" in all genders and they don't hit on someone they know is taken. They just have a wider variety of people too choose from. You get that, right?"

He frowned and shrugged, but I didn't accept non-answers.

"Answer me, Coop."

"I don't know."

I sighed. "You don't hit on everyone woman you see because she has tits and a pussy, do you?"

"No. I'm attracted to only certain women. Age, shape, and personality make a difference to me."

"Yeah, it's the same with bisexual people. They don't see all men or all women as a target-rich environment. They have their types based on age, shape, and personality just like you, but instead of just one gender, they're looking at both men and women. The challenge they face is finding those men and women who are partial to their own gender."

"Why's that a challenge?"

I raised my eyebrows. "What if Attila falls for someone who wears a male body? He has to make sure that guy is into guys or it's a no-go. And worse, gay guys are just as biphobic as straight guys, sometimes worse. Because like you, they believe the myth that bisexual people are always looking for something better, even while they're with someone. It's bullshit, but it persists."

I could see he didn't quite believe me so I tried one more tack. "Would you hit on Scott's old lady, Numbers?"

He frowned. "No. No way in hell. Not only am I yours, Ma'am, but she's taken."

"But aren't you attracted to her?"

He shook his head. "She's attractive, but she's not who I want. And I don't poach."

I rolled my eyes. "Women aren't big game and men don't own them. In fact, if you're going to be my lover, I technically own you. And last I checked, I'm the woman in this relationship."

"You know what I mean. She's taken and it's disrespectful to her and to Scott to hit on her with the intention of hooking up."

"I'm glad to hear you think that way. I'm pretty sure Michael feels the same when he sees an attractive man or woman. He might think they're sexy, but he refuses to be a disrespectful dick and try to hook up with someone who's taken." I narrowed my eyes again. "Here's another question. Would you go looking to hook up with someone single, like Dollhouse, if you're with me?"

"Fuck no!" He rose out of the bed and took my hands, meeting my gaze with earnestness. "I want you and only you, Ma'am. You have my focus and my faithfulness. I'd never cheat. Hell, I didn't cheat on my ex, even when she cheated on me."

Anger kindled at his ex-wife's infidelity, but I didn't allow it to derail this discussion. "Easy, Coop. I'm not suggesting you would, I'm trying to make a point. Neither Michael nor Attila for all their rough looks would do that either. They're just as faithful as you with whomever they've chosen. Just because they're attracted to all genders doesn't make them less faithful. Or less respectful. They won't hit on you because they know you're both straight and taken. Do you understand now?"

He met my gaze, searching my face for something. I wasn't concerned about the likelihood of his straying—I knew he wouldn't—but I wanted him to treat the other members of the Concrete Angels as people, even if Michael was no more human than I was.

He nodded slowly. "Why are you making sure I know this?"

"Because I won't tolerate you treating the bisexual members of the Concrete Angels with any less respect. I expect you to treat them as normal while you're with me. Because they are normal. Do you understand, Coop?"

"Yes, Ma'am." But he frowned as if I'd given him a lot more to think about than he'd expected.

I decided not to push him on it, but the mood had shifted away from sex and I didn't feel like recapturing it. But I was in the mood for his hands on my body again.

"Come on. Let's go take a shower and I'll let you wash

my body."

Some of the arousal returned to his eyes and his lips curled into a smile. "Yes, Ma'am."

I rolled off the bed and he followed me, all sexy masculine grace. A little spike of lust shot through me as his muscles flexed with his movement, but I kept the flare off my expression. Maybe I'd give him another orgasm in the shower with my hands because I definitely wanted to get my hands on him again.

I want to collar him.

No question about it. But all things had their time, and now wasn't it. But it gave me something to strive for.

CHAPTER EIGHT

Cooper

After one of the sexiest showers I'd ever taken, and another orgasm for me, Karma watched me dress in my jeans and t-shirt with the intensity of someone viewing a dance performance. It made me conscious of my movements enough that I slowed them down to show her the best versions of my chest, arms, shoulders, and ass. The unspoken request settled over me and I took pains to make it enjoyable for her.

This is so fuckin' weird.

It was. I'd never changed how I did things for anyone, not even Andrea. But I wanted to impress and please Karma with every fiber of my being. I needed her good regard and I'd do damn near anything to keep it. It was weird, but it felt weirdly right.

Karma put on a tight leather halter-top with beaded fringe on the bottom and no back. It hugged her breasts so they became enticing mounds and my cock hardened in my jeans despite the two orgasms I'd had in the last two hours. Damn, the woman could keep me in sexual need just from walking past me.

She also slipped into denim capris and some ankle

boots with matching beaded fringe like her shirt. The boots had heels that pushed up her butt and made the already round globes even more sexy. I resigned myself to being a walking hard-on, though I definitely wouldn't have blue balls.

By the time we stepped out of her cabin, the sun had dropped behind the mountains and long shadows painted the ground in blue. I hadn't realized how late it was, but I hoped I'd be able to stay the night with Karma. *If not, I'll find a cheap hotel in Fort Collins.*

Before we reached the clubhouse, Karma stepped in front of me, making me meet her gaze.

"I want to get a few things clear before we face the rest of the clubmembers." She licked her lips and it occurred to me she might be nervous. "I, uh, I've never brought one of my...partners in the lifestyle here to the compound. I've always kept my play confined to the club scene."

"Club scene?"

"Yeah, you know, the BDSM clubs. I used to play a little more often, but I did it at Club Willow in Fort Collins. I've never brought a playmate here." She bit her bottom lip with an unusual show of unease. "Not everyone knows my sexual lifestyle and I've never had a long-term boyfriend here. I don't want you to stop being you or stop serving me, but I don't want..."

"You don't want anyone to make fun of me or think me pussywhipped because I serve you."

"Yeah. Not everyone understands that the submissive has all the power in the relationship, and you choose to have me dominate you." She ran her hands over my chest before she met my gaze. "I want you to call me Ma'am among them, but I don't want to embarrass you in any way."

"Ma'am, I'm not embarrassed by being solicitous to your needs. And the only person I'm submissive to is you. And maybe Loki so he won't kick my ass." I grinned as she snorted with amusement. "But if you want to keep the nature of our relationship private, I can keep it subtle and not infringe on your authority. You're the Enforcer and I respect that. Just remember that I can hold my own, too."

She gave me a confident smile. "I know you can and don't let anyone treat you as less because they think women are supposed to be weaker than men. We both know that's not true."

Hell yeah, I knew that. Women put up with and survived more shit than men ever did and they managed to succeed. Men would've given up and run away with their tails between their legs under the same conditions.

"I know I'm not less than other men just because I serve you as my Madam." I leaned forward but stopped short of her lips. "May I kiss you, Ma'am?"

"You may."

I pressed my lips to hers as a new burst of satisfaction slid over me. Glory, I wanted this woman and loved touching her. And having her permission made the kiss even more electric. I loved so much about her, but I didn't want to voice the feeling yet. It was too new and fragile to be spoken aloud.

I stood back and smiled at her. She nodded and took my hand before we continued into the clubhouse. Something had shifted between us and a new confidence grew in the place of the newness. It had happened faster than I thought possible, but I refused to question it. I wanted this with Karma and I wasn't about to give up on it just because it was quick and different.

The clubhouse had grown rowdy in our absence and more people crowded around the two pool tables in the back while the booze and food flowed. Someone had set up a huge buffet table with a shit-ton of food on it and all of it looked like they'd hired a caterer.

"Are you hungry, Ma'am?" My heart rate jumped up at the idea of serving her. She'd told me to tone it down while in public, so I wouldn't do anything to betray her trust, but I could still get her a plate of food.

"Yeah. You get the food and I'll get the drinks. What'll you have?"

"Ice water."

She raised her eyebrows. "Seriously?"

"Yes, Ma'am. I want to be ready for anything and I can't do that if I'm six sheets to the wind." Plus I didn't want to be drunk off my ass and say something to break my cover in front of this notorious biker club. That would be bad.

She nodded and we split paths. I shoved the guilt to the side as I headed over to the buffet, grabbing two plates. I needed to be honest with Karma about my real reason for being here, but I didn't want to lose the fragile connection we'd started. Not only that, but she was my way in to get more information about the Concrete Angels.

Loki's statements about where Hopkins and Eisenburg had been sending the money made me think the biker club wasn't working for or with Backlog, but I wouldn't be sure until I investigated thoroughly. I walked down the buffet, filling the plates as I thought over what I'd found out so far.

As I picked the choicest items for Karma I found myself relieved that the Concrete Angels weren't actually working for Backlog. I liked what I'd seen so far and didn't want to be involved with a woman who had such low morals. Of course, I didn't know her well enough to know all her values or what she was willing to do for cash, but she definitely had a code she followed and I hoped it coincided with mine.

Sweet glory, let it coincide with mine.

Cheers broke up my thoughts and I shot a look toward the pool tables in the back where cash was exchanging hands based on who'd won the latest game. I took the full plates toward a table with a good view of the pool tables and set them down, waiting for Karma to join me there before holding out her chair. She winked and smiled as she slid into the proffered seat and I settled across the table from her.

"What's going on over there?" I nodded to the crowd.

Karma grinned and snorted. "Oh, it looks like Numbers is schooling someone at pool."

I craned my head to look as she set down a large tumbler of ice water beside my plate.

"Numbers? The former FBI forensic accountant?"

"Yeah. How did you know that?"

I shrugged. "I heard it from Attila." The crowd parted enough for me to see the woman I'd seen with Scott moving around the pool table with confidence and amusement as people slapped twenty dollar bills down on the table edge. She wore a leather cut with the words "Property of Scott Free" on it. "How'd she become Scott's old lady?"

Karma nodded as she ate something off her plate. "Yeah, she used to, but her boss, Agent Dirk Hopkins, raped her and got away with it. She left the FBI to start her own forensic accounting business, but he kept her under surveillance. She didn't know that until we found bugs all over her apartment. Scott was furious. Numbers too."

"So how'd she end up here as his old lady?" I'd gotten the connection between former agents Oriana Hunter and Dirk Hopkins, but it didn't explain how she'd ended up with the Concrete Angels. *Is she a Backlog plant?*

"Well, that's a kinda weird story." Karma nodded to the woman commanding the pool table. "It turns out her "good friend" Melrose was the girlfriend of Roy, but Roy was an undercover FBI agent trying to get dirt on our club. Melrose had befriended Numbers and lured her up here to the compound when Loki needed someone to look into our embezzlement problems."

"That seems like a dumb move on the part of an undercover FBI agent. Especially the one actually embezzling from you." In fact, that was downright stupid and undercover agents were generally the smartest of the bunch, me included.

"I don't think Roy actually knew Loki had asked Mel to bring her friend up here, and I'm pretty sure Mel didn't know Roy was undercover FBI." Karma shook her head as she enjoyed her chicken parmesan. "But once Numbers got here, Roy made himself scarce. Numbers didn't actually see him until after they found the bugs in her apartment. But she knew he was FBI right off. It was a huge mess."

"I'll bet." *And it'll be the same when they realize I'm with the Marshal's Service.*

"She tracked the money and figured out Roy was skimming to send to the FBI. But when she realized the FBI had her under surveillance two years after she'd quit, she no longer had any reason trust them. So she turned over all the information she could find on their scheme to Loki and accepted Scott's suit. It was very sweet."

I could've sworn I heard wistfulness in Karma's voice, but she glanced down at her food before I could read her expression.

"Loki said you hadn't recovered all the money. Seems weird since Numbers is a forensic accountant."

"She is, and she found our money. At least, she found most of it." Karma grimaced. "That's why Loki's taking a chance on you. Some of the money was shuffled back to the FBI's coffers as if repaying them for their undercover agent's expenses. More of it went into some "secret" off-shore accounts in the names of Arnold Eisenburg and Dirk Hopkins. They were making nest eggs off our income." She rolled her eyes. "But some of the money disappeared. They sent it to some accounts that looked real only digitally. But when the banks were contacted, they claimed they didn't exist, or our inquiry would be handed to the bank's auditor, but they had a backlog of files to go through."

And there it is. The good old Backlog, hiding in plain

sight. That's where the money went.

I nodded as I sipped my water. "How much money was sent into these fictitious accounts?"

"Almost three million dollars."

I choked on my water, damn near spitting it across the table. "Three million? That's huge."

Holy fuck. No wonder Backlog could infiltrate any law enforcement agency in the US and yet hide its presence. If they had agents in groups like the Concrete Angels, or worse, had the groups already in their pockets, they could finance their illegal activities for centuries and no one would be able to stop them.

"Yeah, it is. Not exactly pocket change. But that's why he's taking a chance on you and offering a reward if you track our money down."

I nodded. "Yeah, I can see why he wants someone to find the rest. He had Numbers track the rest of it, though?"

Karma nodded. "Why?"

"Tomorrow I'll talk to her about where she looked so I don't duplicate her work and have an idea of where to go from there."

Karma sipped her drink but dropped her hand on his arm. "Just make sure you meet her at her office here in the clubhouse. She doesn't trust men much after her rape and neither does her old man. Scott won't think twice about kicking the shit out of you if you scare her."

I lost my smile and nodded. "I hear you." I couldn't imagine the kind of struggle Numbers had to face each time a strange man came near her and I didn't blame Scott for being protective. "I'll talk to her tomorrow." I tilted my head toward the tables. "Right now, it's kinda fun watching her kick ass at pool."

It also gave me time to evaluate the woman. If she had a road name and an old man, more than likely her loyalties and priorities had shifted to the Concrete Angels. But given what I'd heard through the grapevine about her treatment after the alleged rape from the FBI, I wouldn't blame her one bit. They'd hung her out to dry and allowed her rapist to stalk and watch her. My loyalty would've evaporated, too.

Before Karma could respond, the mangey junior biker staggered up to our table and caught himself on an unoccupied chair, wobbling precariously. I rose half-way to my feet as he teetered toward the floor.

"Whoa, man, are you all right?"

The guy grinned and reached out to grasp my arm as the stench of beer and cigarettes washed over me. "Yeah, man, I'm great." He listed dangerously the other way, but managed to get one leg straightened under his body. "I just wanted to thank you, man. Without you, I wouldn't have gotten my cut *forever* and I'd still be just a scooter." He scowled and shook his head. "Losers."

"Yeah, I know. You're welcome." I nodded, waiting to see if he'd fall or stagger off. "Happy to help."

"I got my new road name now, too. Did I thank you for that? It's Gopher. Gopher Pyle." He grinned and swayed. "Has a nice ring to it."

"It does." I bit my laugh back, wondering if he was too young to remember the comic strip about another Pyle.

"I just wanted to say thanks if I didn't before and let you know if you ever need anything, like drinks or rubbers or whatever, I'm your guy." He leered at Karma, though I'm sure he thought he was being sexy. "And since you're fucking our Enforcer, I know you're a good guy." He reached out to thump me ineffectually on the shoulder. "I love you, man."

I snorted. "I love you, too."

"You're awesome, you know that?" He turned to Karma. "You know he's awesome, right?"

Karma smiled. "Yup, I know, Gopher. Why don't you find a friend to crash with tonight?"

"Yeah, okay. Cool. Love you, man."

Gopher wandered off, his path making him look like a sailor on Cinderella Liberty after being stuck on a ship far too long. He knocked over a couple more chairs and bounced off a couch on his way back to the pool tables, and I winced in sympathy.

"Did you tell him we were fucking?" Karma raised an eyebrow.

"No, Ma'am. He got to that conclusion all on his own."

"Great. That should be around the entire club by tomorrow morning."

I nodded toward the tables. "I don't think it'll take that long." Gopher leaned against a short man with a balding head and crazy eyes, waving vaguely back in our direction.

"Yeah, I think you're right. Might as well not fight it." Her gaze heated and my cock saluted her hint of sex. "I have to work tonight. Parties are my gig and I have to keep the rowdy down to a minimum. You wanna help me make my rounds as Enforcer tonight?"

I snorted. "As much as I'd like to watch you keep the rowdy assholes in line, I think I really should get started on finding your money. Mind if I stay in your cabin while you work? I promise to not go through your drawers."

She gave me a silken smile that set my heart pounding in my chest. "You better not, or I might have to reprimand you. Plus you might not like what you find."

"Oh yeah?" I grinned as we gathered up our dishes and took them over to the bins for collection. "Now you've totally piqued my interest."

"Hmm, will I have to chain you to the bed?"

As much as the thought fired my blood in some weird way, I shook my head. I needed to get my laptop and check a few things, and I couldn't do that if she bound me to the bed. Plus, I needed to check on my car. While I didn't think the members of the Concrete Angels would do anything stupid to a fine piece of machinery, I didn't trust they wouldn't put a tracker or a bug on it.

"No, Ma'am. I'll behave and just do my research until you come home."

We both paused and looked at each other as the word "home" hovered between us like a snowflake, both beautiful and fragile at the same time. The world of the clubhouse faded away as I met her gaze and it held, the silence pregnant with hope and possibilities.

"And will you be waiting for me to come home, Coop?"

Her question made me swallow against the powerful yearning rising in my chest. Home. I didn't have one and I desperately wanted one. I'd wanted one for years, but didn't really understand the meaning of the word. I had to clear my throat twice to get my answer out.

"Yes, Ma'am."

Her expression softened and the same yearning I felt in my chest sat reflected in her eyes. She pushed up onto her toes to brush her lips across mine and I moaned as I closed my eyes. She felt like home, even more so than the space she lived in. And I wanted more of that. I wanted her to be the place to which I returned.

"Come on, Coop. Let me take you to my place. I have to get changed anyway. The drunks forget who I am when I'm dressed like this." She took my hand and pulled me toward the front doors.

Despite our little interlude, my shoulder blades itched with the feeling of being watched. I let my gaze slide through the room and caught Loki, Michael, the crazy-eyed bald guy, and Attila watching us before we disappeared through the front doors. *So, they don't quite believe I'm as innocent as I say.*

I didn't blame them. I wouldn't trust a guy who'd miraculously shown up with beer and a promise to help investigate just because he'd met a woman in the crew. And they shouldn't trust me. My goal was to determine what had happened to the FBI agents and how deeply involved they were with Backlog.

The silence outside in the yard was damn near deafening after the noise in the clubhouse, but the feeling of being watched disappeared. I let out a little sigh of relief but kept my eyes open for anyone around us. I wouldn't put it past the leadership of the Concrete Angels to keep an eye on me. I'd have to be careful when I went to my car later tonight.

"What are you thinking about?" Karma's voice brought me back to where I was.

I shrugged. "I was thinking of where I'd start in my search tonight since I haven't talked to Numbers yet."

She nodded as we stopped at her cabin door. "I don't have any suggestions because I'm not in charge of that part of our organization. I guess you could start with Eisenburg and go from there. He'll lead you to his partner and maybe give you a hint of where else he sent the money."

"Dirk Hopkins."

"Yeah. At least, we think so. But the money went somewhere and they didn't seem to have it. So, Loki thinks there's a third party, someone we haven't identified yet, who pulled Hopkins' and Eisenburg's strings."

She let us into the cabin and headed toward the bedroom to change. I stopped in the main room and let my mind wander over the information Karma and the others had given me. Not much that was new except for their belief in a third party. *Backlog.* It had to be them, and it reinforced my suspicion that the Concrete Angels weren't working with them directly.

Unless Karma and Loki are lying and testing me to see how much I know.

It wouldn't surprise me. Karma might like the sex I offered, but that didn't mean she trusted me. I ignored the stab of guilt. At some point I'd have to reconcile the emotions I felt about her with the reality that my investigation had started with her motorcycle club, and they were my main suspects. I hadn't ruled them out, but my gut said they were pawns rather than perpetrators.

My gut or my dick?

Before I could come up with an answer, Karma returned to the main room dressed in jeans, her leather cut over a long-sleeved black t-shirt, and a pair of sleek, soft-soled boots that looked like light-hikers for space. She'd gathered her amazing mane of hair up into a headband that allowed it to cascade in a plume of curls down her back. It was sexy as hell.

"Damn, Ma'am. You're one sexy woman."

The smile curling her lips took on a hint of flattered delight. I wondered if anyone had told her that without wanting something from her. But I meant it. She was my fantasy come to life and I'd do my damnedest to find a way to make sure I could stay with her for as long as possible.

"Thanks." She nodded as she handed me the key to her cabin. It was actually an old-fashioned skeleton key. When I raised my eyebrows, she tilted her head toward the door. "If you have to go out to your car for something. Your bag, for instance."

I grinned. "Oh, yeah, I might need that."

"I expect to see you here when I get back tonight. Don't worry about waiting up. It'll be late, but I'd like you to be here." She turned her beautiful eyes on me and an odd shadow of vulnerability hid in their depths.

It warmed my heart and sparked an answering need to protect her. I almost snorted. *Karma doesn't need protection*. But it didn't stop me from wanting to. I smiled.

"I'll be here."

She grinned and nodded before heading out. I followed her to the door then stood there as she sauntered back toward the clubhouse. *Damn, she's so sexy.* And powerful. As she closed in on the larger building, her body language changed from relaxed and carefree to bold and intimidating. I'd just seen her assume her Enforcer role, and the transformation was impressive.

I just hoped my investigation proved she and the
Concrete Angels were innocent of Backlog's bullshit. Oh,
my gut and my initial findings suggested that was the case,
but I wanted proof to backup suspicions. I squeezed the key
she'd given me and thought about my plan of attack.

First, I needed my bag and my laptop, but there was no
way I'd use their Wi-Fi. I'd hotspot my phone to keep my
lines of communication free from listeners. I'd also check
my car and Karma's cabin for bugs with my handy-dandy
Bug and GPS detector. The special White Noise App on
my phone would ensure other listening devices didn't catch
my conversations in places I didn't trust.

I scanned the yard outside the cabins as I headed
toward the barn to my car. Most of the Concrete Angels
had retreated to the clubhouse to party, but there were a few
working in the barn. One guy stood in the shadows of the
workshop, damn near invisible as the sun ducked behind
the mountains. I wouldn't have seen him except the bright
blue plaid of his armless shirt stood out against his tanned
skin. He stood still, like he'd been carved from a statue, and
his gaze never wavered from mine. It was eerie as hell, but
since he didn't make a move toward me, I shoved him to
the back of my mind.

*You can look as long as you like. Just don't touch,
buddy.*

I made it the car and unlocked it before popping the
trunk and pulling out my bag. I gave a visual inspection to
make sure my camping gear remained where I'd left it
before I closed the trunk and set the bag on top. I dug
around to make sure all my toys remained where they
should. No one had disturbed my things that I could tell,
but that was another reason why I had the detector.

I turned off my cell and laptop before powered on the
little hand-held unit. It chirped to let me know it was ready
and I swung it around the car, looking for little toys left for

me by my current hosts. *Or Backlog agents.* I wouldn't put it past them to have gotten to my car when I wasn't looking.

The little scanner picked up three bugs. One under my front bench seat, one in my bag, and a GPS tracker inside the trunk. *Damn, those boys have been busy.* I made sure to go through my clothing to ensure their freedom from electronic vermin and locked up the car.

I glanced at the barn when I headed back toward Karma's cabin, but the silent man had disappeared. *Yeah, that's not creepy at all.* I sped my steps just a bit to reach the cabin and ducked inside, locking the door. I set Karma's key down on the kitchenette counter and went through my listening-device routine. I found two bugs and a camera, which I ripped out. No one should be keeping tabs on Karma.

My gut turned over at the thought of someone listening to what we'd done in her bedroom, but we couldn't put that genie back in the bottle. I'd just make sure we didn't have any other uninvited guests to our play time.

I sat at the little dinette table and set up my laptop and a little white noise generator, just in case I'd missed any electronic bugs. Then I took a deep breath and dialed my boss's cell.

"Battlebourne."

"Yeah, it's DeVille."

"Holy shit, DeVille. Where the hell have you been? I thought maybe the guys from the...organization had caught up with you." Neither of us said Backlog aloud over the phone.

"No, just been laying low while I check out the Concrete Angels."

"Yeah, smart. How's that going?"

"I'm in."

There was a short pause. "What?"

"I'm in. I got into the Concrete Angels' compound." I

could see the narrowed eyes through the phone.

"How the hell did you do that?"

"I met someone, made a contact, and got invited to one of their parties." Close enough. He didn't really need the details.

"Uh-huh. So what have you found out?"

I shrugged even if he couldn't see it. "Not much yet, but I got permission to start looking into their dealings with Agent Arnold Eisenburg and we know he was with the organization. But I gotta say, from what the CA members have been saying, I don't think they were in on what he was doing. I'm getting the feeling they were either pawns or patsies."

I could hear his brows come down. "You met a woman, didn't you?"

"What?"

"Come on, DeVille. I know you. You wouldn't be this lenient on a suspected group unless you met someone you liked. Just make sure you're thinking with your big head rather than your little one."

"Yeah, you do know me, and you know I don't think with my little head." At least not when it mattered. I could enjoy my time with Karma and still keep track of my investigation. But my gut kept saying the Concrete Angels weren't in on Backlog's gig. "My gut says they're not in the know."

"Let's hope it really is your gut and not your dick talking."

I didn't get snarky because I'd had the same thought. "Yes, sir. I'll get started tonight and see what I can dig up. What do you know about Agents Eisenburg and Hopkins?"

"They were both highly decorated FBI agents, but Hopkins got that rape accusation that kinda put him under the lens of Internal Affairs." Battlebourne paused and I heard other voices in the background. After a few moments, he resumed. "Someone high up made the rape charge slide under the rug and the accuser left the FBI. Guess she couldn't hack the pressure."

I scowled. Gary Battlebourne was a good guy overall, but his blasé view of rape pissed me off. I didn't have a sister or a mother or a cousin who'd been raped, but the idea that a man would use his size and strength to sexually hurt someone infuriated me. My ire trebled when I thought it could happen to Karma.

"Are you thinking the organization made sure it wasn't thoroughly investigated?"

"That would be my guess given his position within their ranks. They couldn't afford their favorite little FBI stooge to get his career derailed just because he dipped his wick where he wasn't supposed to." I heard the growl in Battlebourne's voice.

"Yeah, right. I'm going to talk to the woman who accused him tomorrow and see what she knows. Apparently, the Concrete Angels hired her to look into their financials when they realized someone was skimming. They've found most of it, but apparently there's about three million outstanding."

"Holy fuck!" Battlebourne barked and then whispered an apology to someone on his end. "That's not the "most" of it?"

"Yeah, apparently Eisenburg siphoned off a decent amount to destinations unknown. I've promised to look into it because I suspect the organization is behind it." I took a deep breath, hoping I'd allayed his concerns about me thinking with my dick. "That's why I don't think the Concrete Angels are in league with them. If the motorcycle club is looking for their money, I think they're just being used."

Battlebourne hummed. "Yeah, you might be right. See what you can dig up and let me know. I'll talk to you in a few days unless something comes up."

"Yes, sir. Later."

"Later."

The line went dead and I rubbed my chin. Every time I thought about the Concrete Angels working with Backlog, my gut said I was off base. They might have had a connection to Backlog when Eisenburg was undercover as Roy, but that ended with his exposure. And the bikers wanted their money back. I had a feeling they might not succeed, but they damn sure would try and might give Backlog a hell of an adversary. I wouldn't want Loki and his crew coming after me.

I sighed and used my phone as a hot-spot before I cracked open my laptop. Tonight I'd poke around and see what I could find out about Hopkins' and Eisenburg's deaths that the authorities hadn't divulged to the public and tomorrow I'd talk to Numbers and find out what she knew. Hopefully she'd be willing to talk to me. *And she won't figure out I'm actually a member of law enforcement.*

If she was half as smart as I guessed she was, I'd have to be really careful.

CHAPTER NINE

Karma

I kept a wary eye on Gopher and his buddies as the party got really rockin'. I could tell he was super pleased he'd secured his membership into the Concrete Angels if the drunk love fest he'd handed to Coop was any indication. But I wouldn't put it past him to do something super stupid that would put his cut in jeopardy. *Or at least make some sort of mess to clean up.* We'd lost members just as fast as we gained them for shit like that.

For the most part, the party was staying within acceptable levels of chaos and I could enjoy most of my time. And I was. Mostly. But my mind kept slipping back to the handsome PI staying in my cabin, waiting for me to get off work. *Too bad he's not working to get me off.* Yeah, I might wake his ass up and make him eat my pussy when I came in around 2:30 am after we closed the bar and set out the Alka-Seltzer, tea, fresh water, and bread. The hangover remedies would be needed tomorrow.

"Hey, Karma, you doing okay?" Viper stepped up beside me with her personal tumbler of fine Irish whisky.

"Yeah. Why?"

"Because I thought you'd like to know that your boy

toy found the listening and tracking devices in his car and in your cabin before he settled down for the evening."

Viper was in charge of our physical security around the compound. We didn't need much. Most people were smart enough to leave us the hell alone, but every now and again some stupid human kids would try to get through the fence. Fortunately, we had a couple of guys who didn't need much sleep and they patrolled the grounds when needed. Viper helped with the more digital eyes and ears.

I raised my eyebrows. "You put devices in my cabin?" That wouldn't work. I didn't want to share Coop's screams of pleasure with anyone.

"Yeah, just two listeners and a camera. Not very much. But he found them. He's pretty smart." Viper grinned and nodded. "He also never tapped into our Wi-Fi so we won't know what he's doing on the net. He's got a revolving encryption on his phone."

I nodded, suitably impressed. Coop said he was a PI. More than likely he was sneakier than the regular sneaks and hackers. For some reason, that made me feel more secure rather than less.

"And he got the ones I stashed in his car. The man's thorough."

She didn't know the half of it. But Viper was talking about finding electronic visitors, not sex, and I wasn't about to enlighten her.

"Flint and Torch are hanging out at the barn and are kinda keeping an eye on what he does when he comes out of your door."

I barked a laugh at that. Flint was a gargoyle, the original Concrete Angel, and Torch was a dragon. Yeah, that kind of dragon. He wore a human disguise pretty well and most people didn't know he could bench-press a Peterbilt with a full trailer. But when I looked carefully, I could see the head, neck, horns, and tail of his draconian self against the night sky.

Though Viper was as human as Coop, she had some talents that made me question her heritage, and she knew about all us "other" members of the club. Only a small cadre of the human inner circle knew about those of us who weren't human. But besides Michael, Luke, and me, no one else knew Loki was the real Loki, Norse God of Mischief and Trickery. Not even Torch and Flint, though it was hard to tell what the gargoyle did or didn't know. He rarely spoke, and never aloud.

"Thanks for putting them on watch. We'll all be safer for it, including Coop."

Viper nodded. "He's the one, isn't he?"

"What?" I blinked.

"The One. The center of your soul, your heart of hearts, the happily-ever-after. You know, all the clichés. Coop's your one-and-only, isn't he?"

One of the things I shared with Viper was a love for romance novels. Humans might be a pain in the ass and so damn greedy, but they also loved fiercely and with great creativity. And those who could write it down and weave a world just a little happier than ours? Pure magic. Viper was a big fan of cowboy and hockey romances, while I preferred the BDSM and paranormal romances, natch.

"Yeah, I think so."

Viper nodded with a smirk. "I figured. Otherwise it was too damn fast for you to bring him to your cabin. The few other guys you've fucked haven't ever gotten close to your home."

I hadn't thought of that, but she was right. I didn't bring people into my sanctuary because I wanted a place where no one could disturb me, especially if I had to work some big retribution magic.

For example, the scooters were getting a little too rowdy around Numbers at the pool tables and Scott was liable to do some serious damage to the room with them. Time to bring some swift and enduring results before they trashed our clubhouse.

"Let's take out the trash and we can keep talking." I'd already started moving toward the tables and Viper followed.

"Sounds good."

One thing I liked about Viper was her can-do attitude when it came to manhandling. She might have been human, but she could kick-ass better than most of the men. And she didn't take anyone's shit. She'd just as soon cut someone as smile and too many guys had underestimated her. *Including the guy who'd hurt her.* His karma had come back around for him and he was long gone—I'd made sure—but the damage to Viper had been done and now she had skin thick enough to give a rhino a run for its money.

And yet, she's still romantic. But only I knew that. And maybe Loki.

It didn't take us long to clear out the scooters and put them to work cleaning up the yard and the pool area with Attila watching over them. The Scot could hold his liquor better than most of the other club members and could keep everyone in line, even when schnockered. Gopher was too drunk to do anything beyond drooling so we hauled his ass to the barracks and let him sleep it off. Scott hovered around Numbers like a snarly junkyard dog, but things calmed enough for Viper and I to resume our post near the bar to keep an eye on things.

"I'm happy for you, you know." Viper sipped a lemonade to keep herself sharp. She could drink with the best of them, but she only allowed herself one most nights. Another byproduct of the asshole who'd hurt her. "You deserve to have love and a sexy man to fuck all the time."

"So do you."

Viper grimaced and waved the idea away. "Eh, I had my chance and I picked the wrong one."

"It ain't over until the robust woman sings, and I'm not hearing the aria."

Viper raised an eyebrow. "I thought it was 'fat lady'?"

"Hey, there's no body shaming here. It takes a lot of skill and strength to sing opera, and she doesn't have to be a wiry stick of a woman. You know, like you."

Viper laughed and punched my shoulder. "Shut up. There's no need to be jealous just because I'm hot in my leather pants and bustier." She tilted her head with a coy look out of the corner of her eyes and her black hair swung to shield half her face, tickling the tops of her breasts. "Everyone wants to be me. I've got it, so I'm gonna flaunt it."

I laughed, but my heart squeezed for her. She used her looks to hide the wounded heart underneath, and I wanted to tell her the beauty she possessed wasn't in her tight abs and ass. But we'd come to a mutual truce and understanding years ago. I didn't poke at her wounds or the pretty bandages she'd layered over them, and she didn't tell anyone she'd paid me fifteen life years to watch the man who'd hurt her get his karma.

Usually the payment of life years didn't come with any residuals from the person who gave them to me and I could do my job with detachment. But it had been different with Viper. I'd experienced the burning need to see retribution done and satisfaction filled me when the results came due. It made me understand the human condition a lot more than I had before, and it also educated me on how much I should charge for those kinds of consequences.

Yeah, a helluva lot more than I did.

Viper had become my first and closest friend, and she taught me a lot about being human that even Loki couldn't. And for that I owed her more than she'd paid me.

"You better flaunt it. I like watching a sexy woman walk around, and the honeys aren't cutting it."

Viper scowled. "Girlfriend, please. Those girls are too young to flaunt anything yet. Give them a few years and they might come close to my skills. And I stress *might*."

I laughed again. "True that. I think most of them hope to be you."

Viper abruptly sobered. "No, they really don't." She looked away and I cursed under my breath. But before I could say anything, she straightened her shoulders and gave me a smile as fake as a three-dollar bill. "But we can let them dream. Hey, I'm gonna go check on the barn to see how things are going out there. Be back later."

I nodded and watched her saunter out of the clubhouse, her head held high and her back straight. I knew she was hurting, but I couldn't think of what had set her off. Hopefully she'd tell me later, but Viper was a private person with lots of secrets. If I could wish one thing for her, it was that she'd find someone to offer her the steadfast romance she read about in her books. She'd become hard because she had to and she was the strongest human I knew. She'd taught me a lot about resilience, but I wanted her to have some ease, too.

Eventually, the party wound down and most people drifted off to bed. Neo, Dollhouse, and I cleaned up the remnants and set out the hangover remedies for the morning slog before we turned out the lights. I stepped out of the clubhouse doors into the clear night and took a deep breath. I had a hot guy waiting for me in bed, but I wanted to shake off the residuals of the party before I crawled in beside him.

He wasn't pure by any stretch of the imagination, and he still held secrets I needed to understand before I committed to him. But what we had between us represented all my hopes. It was pure and fragile and precious, and I didn't want to tarnish it with the sloppy desperation I'd sensed in the revelers. We were all searching for love and a sense of belonging, and some tried to find it in the parties.

Damn, I'm maudlin tonight.

I shook my head and strode to my cabin, hoping to leave my sappy thoughts behind. But the moment I opened my door, Coop's scent hit me and my heart turned all gooey again. I found him lying on the couch, his body curled up in the fetal position so he could fit. His laptop and phone sat neatly stacked on the table and his bag rested beside the chair, out of the walkway.

I smiled. He already understood my need for order and kept his clutter to a minimum. *And maybe he's the same.* As a man who spent his life running around investigating people and places on the go, he didn't have space for messes or clutter.

I pulled off my boots and set them near the door before I crouched next to him and studied his face in the dim glow of the kitchenette light over the stove. He wore exhaustion around his eyes and mouth, but sleep relieved some of the stress lines on his forehead. He was handsome when awake, but his beauty increased as he slept.

I pushed some of his hair back from his forehead and he opened his eyes, immediately awake. He hadn't moved, but all the relaxed beauty left his face as he focused his attention on me.

"Hey." I gave him a smile.

"Hi."

"That doesn't look very comfortable. How 'bout you come to bed with me?"

He sat up and rolled his head on his neck, trying to loosen up the kinks he'd surely gotten from sleeping in that position. "Yeah, okay, Ma'am. What time is it?"

"Oh dark thirty." I grinned at his snort. "Come on. Let's get you stripped down and into bed. I'll be right behind you."

He nodded and rolled to his feet, but he stopped and wrapped his arms around me before I could move away. I glanced up at him with surprised and he tilted his head.

"Do you want me to eat your pussy, Ma'am?"

His offer mirrored my earlier thoughts, but I smiled and shook my head. "Not tonight, Coop. I'd rather fall asleep wrapped up in your sexy body and soak up your warmth."

He raised his eyebrows. "Are you cold?"

"No, I just like having a handsome teddy bear man to keep me warm at night." I stepped out of his arms and pointed at the bedroom. "Now, go get naked and I'll be right behind you."

He gave me a sultry smile as he pulled his shirt over his head. I couldn't help the gasp of delight. I loved the line of hair between his abs, but his back was nothing to scoff at. Those muscles covering his bones and shoulders made me want to fondle and lick. But tonight, I wanted to snuggle.

"Tease. Get in bed."

He laughed and I waved him into the room while I locked the door and turned off the light over the stove. He used the bathroom while I undressed, and I took my time, folding and putting away my clothes carefully. If I expected my sub to do it, I needed to set a good example. Coop returned to the room and slid under the covers as I'd ordered. But instead of lying there, he lifted up the sheets and blankets when I came to the bed, offering me the space beneath.

"Come to bed, Ma'am, and let me warm you up."

Yearning and delight shot through me as I settled beneath the sheets. He dropped them over me and pulled my back against his chest, my ass settling at his groin. I wiggled a little to fit his cock and balls into the cleft of my ass, and he rumbled a chuckle at my back.

"Trying to get me hard, Ma'am?"

"No, just trying to get comfortable. Why, are you getting hard?"

"No, Ma'am. Just wondered if you wanted me to."

"Not tonight, Coop. I'm really tired and want to rest."

"Yes, Ma'am."

He settled down behind me, wrapping his arm around

my waist. I closed my eyes and listened to his breathing, so grateful to have him there. I normally didn't like to sleep with anyone. Most of the people I'd had sex with weren't the ones I wanted to sleep beside. They were good enough to scratch the itch of my arousal, but not trustworthy enough to share my bed.

But Coop was both trustworthy and sexy, and I wanted him to stay around me more often. For some reason, he made me feel safe and relaxed enough to sleep. Karma never sleeps, but while the energy of consequences carried on forever, living in a physical body required me to rest. And with Coop I could do it without fear.

I want him to stay forever.

It was a lovely thought, but a bit early to hope for. I'd take tonight and enjoy the hell out of it.

CHAPTER TEN

Cooper

I'd never slept so well in my life. Even as a kid I'd be up every few hours, my mind refusing to calm down for long. As an adult, it had gotten worse with the stresses of the job and the few undercover stints.

But lying wrapped around Karma shut my mind down and sent me into a deep, dreamless sleep. I'd never experienced it before, but I knew I needed more. She made me feel safe, content, and protected even though I was wrapped around her. I woke feeling refreshed and sharper than usual, and I realized I was already addicted to her.

"Good morning, Coop. Did you sleep well?"

I opened my eyes to find her standing beside the bed with a large mug of steaming coffee, wearing nothing but a short, peach-colored silk robe. I wasn't sure which image was more delicious—the hot coffee or woman in a robe barely clinging to her curves.

Both. Both is good.

"I did sleep well. How 'bout you?" I frowned, dismayed that she'd both gotten up before me and I never noticed her leave the bed. "Aren't you still tired?"

She shook her head as she handed me the coffee. "I

don't need much sleep."

I sipped the coffee and groaned. "Oh, glory, that's good. Thank you, Ma'am."

She grinned. "You're welcome. I'd bet dollars to doughnuts you're having a better wake up than most of the Concrete Angels. We made sure to set out all the hangover remedies last night, and I'm sure Grub added the raw eggs and small shots of hair-of-the-dog this morning."

I grimaced. "Oh, yeah, I remember those mornings. Thank Goddess I'm done with that part of my life. Those kinds of morning suck."

She tilted her head and gave me a perplexed smile. "You invoke the Goddess a lot for a…man. Why is that?"

I shrugged. "It made more sense to me. If the divine is supposed to be loving, protective, nurturing, and life-giving, it makes sense it has a female energy. Most of the men I've met are angry, threatening, destructive, and violent, even with their kids. I'd rather have a warrior goddess watching my back than an angry, vengeful god any day." I shrugged and sipped more coffee. My views on such things weren't met with a lot of enthusiasm so I usually kept them to myself.

But Karma smiled and I felt like I'd passed some sort of test.

"So, what are you going to do today?"

I shrugged. "I'm gonna talk to Numbers to see what places she dug up to trace the money. Once I know what she's done, I'll be able to start making inroads to the places she can't get to. I have a hunch about where your money has gone, but I won't know until I see what Numbers found."

Karma nodded as she rose and headed for the bathroom. "Smart. No point in re-inventing the wheel."

"Exactly." I set the mug down on the side table and swung my feet to the floor. "Are you gonna take a shower, Ma'am?" I hurried after her, hoping for the chance to see her naked under the hot water.

"Yes, that was my plan."

"Would you like me to wash your back?" I waggled my eyebrows and grinned as she laughed.

"That would be great. As long as you let me wash yours."

"Yes, Ma'am."

I ducked around her and turned on the water in the shower, adjusting the temperature to be comfortable for both of us. Then I dried my hands and turned to her.

"Let me take you out of that robe, Ma'am."

She turned her back and shrugged out of the soft, orange silk. I loved the way it slid over her skin with a soft hiss and my cock saluted both the sound and the sight. Damn, I wanted to brush up against her back and rock my hips with my cock between her butt cheeks. I loved how she'd wiggled her ass last night, making sure my dick fit in her crack as we slept. It had turned me on and comforted at the same time.

I hung the robe on a hook and handed her into the shower. She sighed as she stepped under the spray and my dick flexed in appreciation. I stepped in behind her, grateful she had a large upright shower. Nothing worse than trying to be sexy in a coffin box with nozzles.

Karma dropped her head under the water to wet her hair down and I took the time to grab the puff and fill it with bodywash.

"Let me wash you, Ma'am."

"You may."

It might seem weird to enjoy taking orders, but her commands filled me with a sense of purpose and belonging that I hadn't felt since I was a kid. My mom had been frail with a rare bone pathology that made her body brittle. She wasn't weak by any stretch of the imagination, but one little bump against a kitchen drawer could shatter her arm. I'd learned to always make sure she was stable and free of obstacles so she could enjoy life. I served her and it brought me joy and satisfaction to do it right. When she died, I'd felt adrift.

I needed to serve Karma to feel content and complete again. I needed to ensure her pleasure and comfort to secure my own, and it brought back the good memories of serving my mother with my superior strength. My mom was long gone, but I could offer the same strength to Karma.

I lathered up the puff and scrubbed it over her back and butt, following with my hands to smooth the suds on her skin. I loved the sensation of her soft skin slick with soap and my cock echoed my sentiments with more flexing. I dropped to my knees to wash her feet and legs, taking my time over her heels.

She giggled a little and turned, rinsing the soap off her back. I kept scrubbing her legs, taking my time as I rose up to her groin. I glanced up at her and found her gaze on mine, her attention anticipatory.

"May I clean your pussy, Ma'am?"

"You may."

Her voice came out in a purr as I soaped my hand and slid it between her legs, curling my fingers to fit between her folds. She tossed her head back and closed her eyes, rocking on my hand. I looked up her body, enjoying her clenching muscles and her hard little nipples. They stood out from her body, begging to be sucked, but I kept my attention on her pussy lips and her ass. I wanted her to be clean as well as pleasured.

I stroked her with more patience than I felt, but watching her writhe on my hand as she grew wetter and wetter, turned me on more than I thought possible. When I slid two fingers into her hot slit, she gasped and rocked her hips against them.

"That's it, Ma'am. Fuck my fingers. Let me give you pleasure."

To be honest, I wanted to eat that pussy so much my balls ached. But I contented myself with rubbing and stroking her up to a fever pitch before I strummed her clit with my thumb.

Karma came with a scream of joy and my name on her lips. I stroked and strummed and wished I could put my mouth on her pussy to lap up her cum. But I kept my ministrations constant until she came back down from her glorious flight of ecstasy. Then I soaped up my hand and cleaned her before rising to my feet to finish her torso and arms.

"You are insanely good at that, Coop."

I smirked. "Thank you, Ma'am. Let me know any time you need help in the shower and I'll be here."

She laughed and rinsed her body, taking the puff from me. Bone-deep satisfaction tumbled through me at the contentment I could hear in her laugh despite my hard, aching cock. Her pleasure and release gave me more satisfaction than any of my own orgasms. The idea surprised me, but I couldn't doubt its veracity.

"Okay, now you." She turned and stepped to the side, offering me the water.

"Me, Ma'am?"

"Yup. Not only do I want to wash your fuckin' sexy body, but I want to suck cock." She winked as she shoved me into the water. "Breakfast of champions."

I laughed as I filled the puff with bodywash and handed it to her while I soaked my body. My dick pointed at her with an imperative, but if she never touched it, I'd still be satisfied. She gave me a smile as she lathered her hands then motioned me to turn my back to her. I obeyed, closing my eyes as the water sluiced down my face and chest.

Karma started at my shoulders and neck, massaging as well as scrubbing my skin. Her fingers worked at some of the hard knots left over from sleeping on the ground for a few weeks while I observed the Concrete Angels' compound. I groaned as she rubbed the muscles down either side of my spine to the small of my back, digging her knuckles into them.

When she moved on to my ass, she kept her touches light, using the puff to clean the skin before she slid one hand between my butt cheeks and fingered my tiny hole. She didn't penetrate the ring of muscles, but her questing fingers made a thorough inspection. I widened my stance as I leaned forward on my arms, letting my head hang.

She pushed her hand between my legs and massaged my balls. I jerked and whimpered a little as she rolled the scrotum in her slick hand. Each touch set off a spark of arousal, making my cock jerk with need. Pre-cum dripped from the tip and I wished she would run her hands over my aching flesh.

"Turn around, Coop."

Her hand disappeared from my balls and its absence jerked me into motion. I needed her hands on me more than I needed my next breath. I stood in front of her, letting the water rinse my back as she rose to her feet, her breasts and arms covered in soap suds.

"Do you need the water, Ma'am?"

"No, I'm fine. Now, I need you to stand there with your feet hip-width apart and keep your eyes down on your cock. Do you understand?"

I swallowed hard and dropped my gaze. "Yes, Ma'am."

"Good man."

With my gaze down, I could see her hands and the puff sliding over my chest and belly, taking her time to clean each ridge and valley of muscle. It was sexy as hell to watch her detailed efforts on my skin, and my balls tightened up to the base of my cock as arousal surged through my system. Glory, I wanted her to touch my dick. With her hands. With her mouth. With her pussy. I didn't care as long as she wrapped something around my aching length.

"Good job, Coop." Karma dropped to my feet to clean the fronts of my legs. When her hands circled my cock, I moaned and thrust my hips before I could stop myself.

"Oh ho, someone's turned on." The humor in her voice kept me from letting my snark out from behind my teeth. "Turn and rinse off, then I'll do something about it."

I rinsed off my body as quickly as I could before I turned back to her, ready for whatever she'd give me.

"Let's switch places. I want to be sure you're all clean."

I whimpered as my cock made movement an exercise in desperation, but I slid out of the water and stood with my back to the wall. She rinsed her body and the puff before she turned her back to the spray and scanned me with narrowed eyes.

"Did I say you could take your eyes off your dick?"

"No, Ma'am. Sorry, Ma'am." I dropped my gaze to my straining shaft and waited, a thrill zipping through me at her tone of warning. I loved when she brought the sharpness back.

"Now, Coop, I want you to listen very carefully. I'm going to suck your cock until you can't hold back anymore. But you must not come until I tap your hip. Like this." She dropped her right hand to my left hip and patted it with her fingers. "Do you understand?"

"Yes, Ma'am."

"Good. Because I'm not going to take my mouth off your dick and I want you to keep your gaze on me while I suck you off. You can't close your eyes, you can't throw your head back. You have to watch me make you come. Do you understand?"

I shivered and nodded. "Yes, Ma'am."

"Very good."

She dropped to her knees in front of me with her back

in the spray of water, and it had to be one of the sexiest things I'd ever seen. I had to fight the urge to pull her back up, uneasy with her kneeling before me because the Madam never kneels, but she'd said this was her pleasure and she wanted to do this, so I left her alone.

"I had no-slip bars installed just for this instance." She grinned up at me as she moved my hips closer to her face and nuzzled my balls. "You hold on tight now, and don't come until I tap your hip. Of course, you're welcome to beg, but not until I tap your hip. Ready?"

The sensation of her nose on my sac had damn near short-circuited my brain, but I managed to nod and grasp the bathroom "oh-shit" bars. *And yeah, it'll be oh-shit if I come before she says I can.* Maybe they'd keep me from falling.

"Now, I'm gonna enjoy this cock. Keep your eyes on me."

When her mouth enveloped my dick, I almost closed my eyes, but I groaned and tightened my hands on the bars until my knuckles hurt. Watching my cock disappear into her hot mouth as the water slid down over her naked body was the most erotic thing I'd experienced in a long time. Normally, I'd close my eyes and just feel, but she'd forbidden it. So I watched and it turned me on more than I expected.

She met my gaze a few times as she swirled her tongue over my shaft and the intimacy of that connection settled deeper and deeper into my soul. I wanted to look away, afraid of what she'd see in my eyes, but her order was stronger than my fear.

She dragged her tongue down the shaft and back up before engulfing the head and shoving the tip into my slit. At the same time, she massaged my balls, rolling the soft skin between her fingers like the Singing Balls used in Chinese medicine. The combination of touches launched my orgasm before I was ready and I had to bite my lip hard to keep it at bay.

Oh, please, Goddess, let me hold back. Please.

But Karma tortured me, building the pleasure up so high I had to try to think of maintaining my focus away from my impending release. I tried to think of changing Rosé's oil, but Karma's tongue splintered my thoughts when she held my cock and licked my balls, sucking one into her mouth.

"Oh, glory, Ma'am, I think I'm gonna come. May I come, please?"

"Uh-uh."

I moaned as she went back to work on my dick, her hot mouth sliding up and down the sensitive flesh. When I hit the back of her throat, she swallowed and I saw fuckin' stars. I tightened my hands on the oh-shit bars and held on for dear life.

Then she tilted her head and took me deep, using the muscles of her throat to tighten and undulate against my shaft. I whimpered as I watched her swallow me down to the root. I wasn't small. I'd never been small so most women hadn't been able to do more the get two-thirds of me into their mouths. But Karma took me to the base and the eroticism of that action pushed me over the edge.

"Oh, fuck, Ma'am. I'm gonna come. I'm sorry. I'm gonna come! Karma!"

She rolled her eyes up to meet mine as my release boiled through me. I couldn't hold back and roared out her name, my cum shooting down her throat as she kept my gaze locked on hers. She swallowed and swallowed and I floated in the perfect place where time and the world no longer mattered. My Madam was everything and I'd serve her for as long as she let me.

I love her.

Despite the sexy lassitude, the thought shocked me and I stared at her in wonder and not a little panic as she licked my cock to clean it of cum. I kept my gaze on her and what she did to my dick, both enjoying it and whimpering from over-stimulation. She rose, allowing the still warm spray to wash the rest of my body. My breath sawed in my chest as I took in the implications of the emotion flowing through me.

I love her.

It was clear I'd lost my mind. Sure, Karma was gorgeous and she brought me more pleasure than I'd ever experienced with another woman. But love? I'd only been here two weeks and I'd only known Karma a handful of days. How could I know it was love? Hell, it had taken me two years to fall for Andrea, and that hadn't turned out well.

That's because Andrea couldn't give me what I needed.

Okay, true, but I hadn't known that until I met Karma. The question was could I trust my instincts on this when I'd failed so spectacularly in the past?

Is it real love when you haven't told her why you're really here?

There was a question I didn't want to think about so I shoved it to the back of my mind as Karma turned off the shower and stepped out to grab two big fluffy towels. Each one had a hood, like a kid's towel, but it was adult sized. She brought one and wrapped it around me, pulling the hood onto my head. Then she ran her hands all over my body, drying the water off every inch, including my deflating cock. I just stood there, breathing and thinking, as she dried my body with loving and careful efforts.

"There, you should be all dry."

She offered her hand to me and I stepped out of the shower, charmed and delighted despite my dark thoughts. She gave me a proud smile as she patted my ass under the towel.

"Go get dressed and we'll get started for the day." She made shooing motions toward the bedroom. "Oh, and Coop?"

I stopped. "Yes, Ma'am?"

"There will be consequences for coming without permission."

I swallowed hard despite the uptick in my heart rate. "Yes, Ma'am."

"Good." She nodded. "Get dressed now."

I wondered what I was in for later. *That, and I have to figure out what the fuck I'm really doing here.*

I pulled my clothes on, wondering if I'd FUBAR'd this investigation. Hell, I was sleeping with a member of the organization I was investigating. *And I love her.* Which was all sorts of wrong. But my gut said the Concrete Angels weren't directly involved with Backlog and the day's research would confirm that.

I shook my head and tried to focus. "Do you think Numbers will be up? I want to get a jump on where she left off. Do you think she'll be awake after the party last night?"

"Yeah, probably. She doesn't go as hard as the others when it comes to partying. It has something to do with her past at the FBI. Not that I blame her."

Yeah, I don't blame her, either.

"Coop?"

"Yeah?"

"You need to be careful. With Numbers."

I looked up and met Karma's gaze. "Careful with her?"

"Yeah. She doesn't trust men in general, and you're someone new. And Scott doesn't take kindly to anyone who scares her. He kinda thrashes someone first, asks questions later."

Yeah, I'd seen how Scott hovered around Numbers. Out of the way but watchful.

"I'll be careful and keep my distance from her. I'm just going to talk to her to find out what she knows so I can continue." And find out if the Concrete Angels were pawns or conspirators.

And wouldn't that just suck if I had to walk way from Karma? It would damn near break my heart and I wasn't sure I'd recover. It had been hard when Andrea fucked me over, but this would be me fucking me over, and that sucked big-ass donkey balls.

"Earth to Coop, come in please."

I blinked and realized I'd been in my head too long.

"Uh, yeah, sorry. Did you ask something?"

"I said, do you wanna meet up for lunch? It might be good to take a break."

"Oh." The idea of having pussy for lunch jerked my mind back to the beautiful woman who'd given me a BJ this morning. "Yeah, that would be great. How 'bout I text you when I'm at a good stopping point?"

"Sounds good." She offered me a sultry smile that made my cock rise despite my recent orgasm. "Maybe we could bring lunch back here for a little cookie & nookie."

I laughed as my cock saluted the idea. "Yes, Ma'am."

"Good. Let's go get some coffee and breakfast, in that order. I'm starving."

I finished dressing and followed her swaying denim ass out into the yard. I automatically checked our surroundings and found the same guy I'd seen the night before leaning against the barn wall, his beefy arms crossed over his chest. *So, they don't completely trust me.* I had to admit a combination of hurt and approval. I wasn't totally trustworthy for them yet, but hopefully I'd get answers that would satisfy my gut instincts.

And just maybe, I'd figure out what I'd do if I got answers I didn't like.

****

Karma

Coop remained pretty quiet after our early morning

fuck snack and I wondered what had put him in such a pensive mood. I'd seen Flint standing out in the yard and nodded to him. He'd acknowledged with a slow blink which I'd learned meant things were okay. Coop hadn't tried to slip out while I slept.

He held the door open for me to enter the clubhouse in front of him and followed behind, but I sensed when he came to an abrupt stop.

"Whoa."

I turned and raised my eyebrows. "What?"

"It's not a nasty, SOLO-cup strewn, vomit-streaked mess."

I chuckled. "Did you expect it to be?"

"Well, yeah. After a party like last night, I figured there'd be garbage and bodies all over the place, some of them half dressed." He narrowed his eyes and pointed at me. "You all are messing with my pre-conceived notions of how a biker club parties."

I laughed aloud as I led him over to the counter with the coffee and hot water machines. "Oh, I'm pretty sure we party just as hard as other clubs, we just make an effort to clean up before we crap out." It also helped that half of our club wasn't human and could remain upright when the humans had gone tits-up with alcohol. But he didn't need to know that secret yet.

Not until I know him better.

Yeah, the Goddess had asserted he was my true mate, but there was something he was holding back. Something that might make our connection a lot harder to maintain. I wanted to ignore my gut and tell her to fuck off, but I hadn't lived as long as I had by ignoring it. Coop had secrets—hell we all did—and until I knew most of them, I had to remain careful, true mate or not.

"I'm impressed. You even have hangover remedies. You come prepared."

"Yup. No point in feeling like shit the whole next

day." I poured us both two large mugs of coffee and handed him one. "Go pick a table and I'll bring you some grub."

He raised his eyebrows. "Aren't I supposed to serve you?"

I leaned close with a secret smile. "Actually, you got that backwards, sweet stud. The Domme serves the sub in all ways." His eyes widened as I straightened. "Besides, you had an eventful morning. Go sit down. I got this."

I turned back to the food Grub had cooked up this morning and thanked my lucky stars there was plenty. I hadn't eating anything except snacks the night before and my stomach reminded me the physical body needed fuel. I loaded two plates up with eggs, sausage, European bacon, English muffins, a blueberry and a banana-nut muffin, and a cup of yogurt.

"Good glory, do you need help with that?" Coop rose to his feet to take a plate, his eyes wide.

"Thanks. I'm really hungry this morning."

"Yeah, I can see that." He set the plates down and pulled out my chair for me, an action that warmed my heart despite being out of place in a biker club hangout. "Ma'am."

Pleasure filled my heart as I sat down and he settled into the chair to my left, his attention briefly swinging around the room, cataloging where people and exits stood. I'd seen him do that before and I wondered where he'd gotten the training. It seemed like a military or law enforcement thing, and reminded me that he had secrets I needed to learn.

I wanted to know him, but I didn't want to interrupt the ease of breakfast. We'd had a good evening and a fantastic morning. I wanted to stay in that happy, sexually-satisfied glow for a while longer. So we ate and chatted about little things that didn't matter until he'd finished his meal and cleared our empty plates.

"I guess I better get started. Where do you think I'll

find Numbers?"

Coop brought me another cup of coffee and set it down before grabbing my empty mug.

"She has an office here in the back." I pointed to the doors along the back wall. "Hers is labeled with 'Financial Advisor' next to the Black Room."

He raised his eyebrows. "Black Room?"

"Yeah. That's Neo's realm. It's completely black inside and no windows. Don't go in there unless you're invited."

He nodded slowly. "Okay, then. What does Neo do in his Black Room?"

"He watches everyone else and keeps track of our computer access." I watched Coop pale and sympathized. I didn't like Neo watching my every move online either, but it kept the Concrete Angels safe from law enforcement and entrapment issues. "Don't worry. He's discreet."

Coop grimaced. "Yeah, well, I'm still gonna use my own private access. My contacts wouldn't like me letting someone else into their networks and correspondence." He leaned down and kissed my forehead. "I'm gonna get started for the day, Ma'am. I'll see you for lunch."

I watched him saunter away and enjoyed his ass in his jeans, but his reaction to Neo's job unsettled me. *Come on, no one likes Big Brother watching.* That must have been it. Coop didn't know us very well and he wouldn't like someone watching him all the time. I dismissed my unease and finished the muffins before I rose to clear my plate.

"Hey, Karma. How are you this morning?"

Michael stepped up to the buffet and made himself some tea as he gave me a smile. I narrowed my eyes. Michael only smiled when he either wanted something or had something unpleasant to tell people.

"I'm good. Why?"

"So suspicious." He selected two of Grub's poppyseed muffins and grinned. "That's a good quality to have. Loki,

Luke, and I have something we need to discuss with you if you have a moment."

Oh boy. If the Big Three wanted to talk to me, something definitely had come up. And as one of the Enforcers in the club, taking care of something was my job description. *Please, Goddess, don't let it be Coop.*

"Yeah. I got some time." Not that I'd say no, but there was nothing pressing on my schedule for the day. I poured out the last of my coffee. A waste, really, but I didn't want to dump it on anything important if someone pissed me off. "Lead the way."

I shot a look at Numbers' office as Michael led me to Loki's and wondered if I'd find out something I didn't like about Coop. I knew from the bitter experience of others that the Goddess often made relationships hard, their paths full of pitfalls and obstacles that required the participants to really work for them. My gut sank. It was my turn to endure her machinations in matters of the heart, and I suspected it would be my hardest set of tests ever.

"How's it going with your man, there?" Michael nodded toward the Financial Advisor office with a smile. "He treating you well?"

"Yeah. Why? What have you heard?"

He wore innocence like a mask. "Nothing. I just wanted to be sure he wasn't causing you distress."

I stopped and grasped his arm. "Michael, don't dissemble. What is it?"

His smile dissolved until he became grave. "Come into Loki's office and we'll talk about it."

My gut sank as I followed him and I'm glad I poured out the coffee. We found Loki seated behind his desk with his feet up and his fingers steepled, his customary smirk in place. That never boded well, for friend or foe. Michael closed the door behind us and I stepped to one side, crossing my arms over my chest.

"Okay, what's up, Loki?"

"What? No pleasantries or morning news, Karma?" That damned smirk never shifted.

"No. What's going on?"

"That is a good question." He finally dropped his feet to the floor and sat forward, leaning his elbows on the desk. "It seems your man Cooper DeVille really is a private investigator."

I shot a look at Michael's unusually solemn face before I returned to Loki and narrowed my eyes. "Yeah, so? What's your point?"

"The point is, before three years ago, Cooper DeVille, P.I. never existed. Anywhere." Loki tilted his head. "Who do you think this man is, Karma?"

I raised my eyebrows and spread my hands. "I dunno. I thought he was a P.I. What am I missing?"

"The timing doesn't seem hinky to you?"

I opened my mouth to respond with the negative when my mind caught up with the implications. "That's right around the time Roy joined us and our money started to disappear."

Loki nodded. "*Ja.*"

I frowned. "You don't think Coop's FBI, do you? It would make sense that they'd want to get another agent in here."

Michael shook his head. "No. We checked the local FBI offices and some of the national, and Neo couldn't find anything. Numbers didn't recognize him, either."

"He might not be FBI. Maybe he's working for someone else. Maybe he's part of whoever's getting our money." Loki scowled.

I frowned, thinking before I spouted off and talked out my ass. "You know I can sense energy. I didn't get that vibe off him. He's got honor, Loki."

"Even criminals have honor to their crews, Karma." Michael sighed and shook his head. "He's hiding something, I just don't know what it is."

I didn't want to agree with Michael, but I'd felt the same thing. Coop was telling most of the truth, but he'd held back a few things. *And as they say, the demons get your soul by telling half-truths.* The problem was, I suspected Coop already had my soul, and my heart.

"Keep an eye on him, *ja*? Find out what he's really looking at, and use that famous Karmic Vision™ to make sure he isn't incurring a debt he'll need to repay. Know what I mean?"

My mouth dried out and my gut sank. Yeah, I knew exactly what Loki meant. People who lied, cheated, and snuck around always incurred a fairly obvious karmic debt and it showed up when I took a good Karmic look. And I hadn't looked at him with my Karmic Vision™ since the time he met me at the Gas 'N Snacks. What would I find when I looked at him with it now?

"Yeah, I know what you mean. He's planning to look through our records to find out where the rest of the money has gone. Do we tell him to stop?"

Loki shook his head. "No, we'll let it ride for now. It might prove useful in finding out who he really works for." He stopped as his phone rang. "*Ja*, Neo?"

"Luke on Skype for you, boss."

"*Det er bra.* Put it up on the big screen, Neo. *Tusen takk.*"

The large video screen behind the desk lit up with the face of Luke Everfall, our nomadic member. He had brown eyes and a red bandana wrapped around his bald head do-rag style, and perfectly arched blond eyebrows. He lounged on a luxurious couch with palm trees and bright blue skies filling the windows behind him. He had the rugged, don't-give-a-fuck biker look down, though under the blond goatee, his features were just as angelic as Michael's.

That might be because he's Michael's older brother.

"*Ja*, Luke. Thanks for calling. What do you know?" Loki waved at the man on the screen. "Michael and Karma are here with me."

"Good, 'cause I got some news about the dickhead who died in the mine."

"What kind of news, Luke?" Michael moved to stand beside me so we were all in the view frame.

"Someone's been looking into his death. A couple different someones, actually. All law enforcement."

Loki shrugged. "It's as we expected. Why is this a big deal?"

"Because there are people from a lot of different jurisdictions lookin' into it. Not just the LVMPD and Searchlight PD, but also the FBI from San Diego and Seattle, an ATF agent from D.C., and U.S. Marshal from Chicago. Even the NSA has been snooping around more obviously than usual. What the fuck was this guy Hopkins into?"

Loki shook his head. "I don't know, but our reasons for taking him out had to do with Scott's old lady."

"Yeah, well, something else is going on. Hopkins must have been into something bigger than just the FBI because there's a lot of people looking for what really happened to him."

"Or they're looking into what he was hiding." I tapped my chin with a finger. "Did Numbers ever find a connection between him and Eisenburg other than they worked for the FBI?"

"No, not in terms of money at least. Why?" Michael shook his head.

"I think we should have Neo look into what other things they had in common. You know, like a bowling league or a passion for flower arranging or making ice sculptures with chainsaws. See where they made charitable donations, stuff like that." I grinned as Michael and Luke both laughed. "Seriously, there are people out there who do that kind of shit."

"Not in Las Vegas, they don't. Too damn hot." Luke's

dry remark made Loki smile.

"See what you can dig up while you're there, Luke, but don't get too close to the cops. I don't want our club to be on their radar, *ja*?"

Luke nodded. "Yeah, I get you."

"*Det er bra.* We'll see what we can find out on this end. We have a private investigator taking a look, too." Loki's gaze shot to me but his expression didn't change. "We'll let you know if anything turns up. Keep your head down and don't do anything I wouldn't do, *ja*?"

Luke grinned. "Loki, is there anything you wouldn't do?"

"Not that I can think of at the moment."

Luke laughed. "That's what I thought. Talk at you later." His screen went blank as he disconnected the call.

Loki turned back around to face me. "It was a good idea about the other connections, Karma. I'll have Neo look for that."

"What about Coop, Loki?" Michael's face held sadness and wariness.

"For now we let him do what he said he'd do, and see what he comes up with. Maybe he will ferret out what we've missed. And maybe he will show us who he really is."

Loki's gaze landed on me and a chill ran down my back. *If Coop turns out to be someone from law enforcement, what will he do?* And how would I deal with it if he chose death?

CHAPTER ELEVEN

Cooper

I approached the office marked Financial Advisor and knocked on the door. The blonde woman who'd been sharking the pool tables last night looked up from her computer and pushed her glasses closer to her eyes.

"Can I help you?"

"Hi, are you Oriana Hunter, the woman they call Numbers?" I paused at the door, trying to appear harmless, though I suspected every new man she met wouldn't be able to pull that off.

"Yes." She didn't offer anything else as she regarded me with wary attention.

"My name's Coop DeVille and Loki hired me to investigate the other places where Eisenburg stashed the Concrete Angels' money."

She scowled. "Why?"

I shrugged. "He said you'd found all but three million and I offered to look in places you either couldn't see or hadn't thought of."

"I assure you, Mr. DeVille, I've searched everywhere, and I'm quite capable of thinking despite having blonde hair."

Damn, this woman was prickly, but I shoved my frustration aside and turned on the charm. "Yeah, I can see that. Karma said you're a former FBI agent and a damn good forensic accountant. I'm not here to critique your work, Ms. Hunter."

"Then why are you here?"

To find out if the Concrete Angels are conspiring with Backlog or just being used by them.

"I'm here to pick up where you left off and see if my friends in low places have any clues where the rest of the money went." I kept my voice even. "Two people with experience will get farther than just one, right?"

She studied my face with those sharp hazel eyes and I realized she could probably see more than most people gave her credit for. *And if she's former FBI, she's been trained like me to see what people are hiding.* Shit. That meant I'd have to be extra careful.

"All right, Mr. DeVille. I'll show you what I've found on Eisenburg's accounts and we'll go from there."

I gave her a relieved smile. "Great." I stepped into the office and left the door open as I snagged the chair and sat down. "I know Eisenburg was undercover FBI. Did you ever find out who his handler was?"

She shook her head as her fingers flew over the keyboard, bringing up windows containing her work. "Not that I'm aware of, but I was just following the money. I don't know if his handler knew about his embezzling and helped him with it or was completely ignorant. But I can show you what I found."

When she brought up the spreadsheets full of information, she went through everything she'd located and the codes Eisenburg, as Roy, had used. Some of them were easy to figure out and she'd traced those to the various accounts overseas, but others were more obscure with weird acronyms. We worked at it for a couple of hours, writing down on a pad of paper each abbreviation and what it might mean as referenced from other records.

"Damn, he had fingers in a shit-ton of pies." I scanned the list, hoping something would jump out at me, but they kept blurring together.

"Yeah, he did." She sighed and rubbed her neck. "I've been over it a thousand times, but I can't figure out to where he siphoned the money."

I nodded, looking again. There had to be a clue. Undercover or not, Eisenburg had still been a cop and they were lousy at hiding money. *But Ms. Hunter found all the personal accounts.* I frowned. There had to be some sort of record of how Eisenburg funneled money to Backlog.

"Personal accounts."

"What?"

"Eisenburg's personal accounts." I pointed at the paper and then at the screen. "Did he put anything down in his personal accounts that seemed weird? Some sort of annotation or mark that stood out?"

She shook her head. "No, they were pretty straight forward."

"What about the amounts? You said you're missing three million dollars. Did the amounts deposited and withdrawn match with what's currently in the accounts?"

"No, that's how I know we're missing the money. But I can't see where it could've disappeared." She blew her out her breath with frustration. "I've checked, re-checked, and cross-referenced. I got nothin'."

I scowled and dropped my head onto my hands, supporting my chin as I looked over the records. "Can you show me the original hand-written records?" When she shot me a narrow-eyed look, I held up my hands in surrender. "I just want to see what kinds of notations he put in his notes. I might recognize some."

Oriana sighed and clicked something on her screen. The printer in the corner hummed and spat out a couple of pages with markings on them. I rose and collected them before sitting down again.

"He did have a strange short-hand." She pointed to the symbols on the paper. "I've figured out most of them. That means 'paid in full,' and this one shows what the product was. But there are a few that don't seem to have a translation."

She moved her hand down the page to a squiggle that looked like a V with a tiny o at the vertex, like a TV with an oversized antenna. *Cute little alien steals money?* Yeah, I could understand why Oriana might find it puzzling.

The second symbol looked like someone had taken a capital T and laid it on its side, making the crossbeam vertical. It would be incomprehensible to anyone looking at it for the first time. It was for me. But I'd seen that symbol before.

"Fuck."

"What?" Oriana raised her eyebrows. "What's wrong?"

"I know what that one means."

"The sideways T?"

"Yeah." I nodded, biting my lip. "That's the symbol for the Backlog."

She frowned. "What's the Backlog?"

I met her gaze and debated what to tell her. She was smart and the minute I revealed what I knew, she'd figure out what I really was. I might be an investigator, but I wasn't private. A P.I. wouldn't know who Backlog was, not unless they were investigating local LEOs.

I got up and closed her office door before I returned to my chair, chewing on my lip. The question became how much to reveal to get what I needed but would still keep me alive. I had no illusions of what the Concrete Angels would do to me. Two FBI agents were dead after tangling with them.

"You're telling me you don't know about Backlog?" I met her gaze.

Oriana shook her head. "Never heard of them."

"And you're sure Loki, Michael and the others don't know about it?"

She frowned. "I can't speak for them, but they hired me to look for their money and they couldn't find it before I came along. They definitely couldn't read Eisenburg's notes. And Loki was adamant about finding who was stealing from him."

I nodded. "A couple of years ago, I was contacted by a source"—*me*—"inside law enforcement who'd noticed some odd shit going on. Evidence disappearing or being tampered with, suspects escaping or being ignored, captured funds diminishing, witnesses getting killed, stuff like that. He hired me to take a look and find out what the hell was going on."

"And this was only in his agency?"

I shook my head. "Not just his. I started noticing trends in other agencies. FBI, ATF, U.S. Marshal Service, police departments all over the country. The incidents were too numerous to be just random, and they all seemed to have one common source. The Backlog."

"How did you find out the name?"

"I started seeing that sideways T and hearing things like people couldn't get evidence back because of the backlog or DNA results were put on hold because of the backlog." I shrugged. "At first, I thought it was the usual. Funding is tight and people are overworked. But after a while, what I thought people were attributing to a backlog of work, they were actually attributing to a shadow organization that had infiltrated all the agencies of law enforcement. My source didn't know who to trust and he wanted me to find out just how high and deep it went."

Oriana tapped her chin with a pen. "What do the Concrete Angels have to do with this?"

"Through my investigation, it became clear that Backlog needed a way to launder the money they stole and get more." I rubbed the back of my neck as the frustration with Backlog returned. "From what I could tell, they'd hire or coerce other groups to help them. Inner city gangs, mafia groups of various kinds, motorcycle clubs. Anyone who society could write off as the bad guys and Backlog could hide behind. None of the illegal stuff would be traced back to them."

"You thought the Concrete Angels were part of this shadow organization?"

I spread my hands. "I couldn't know either way. Some of the groups are definitely in on this scheme and happy to help. Others, it's less clear. I had to know if the Concrete Angels were willing participants or just pawns. From what I've learned, I'm pretty sure Backlog was using you to get shit done."

"And Agent Eisenburg was a mole or plant, steering the club to benefit Backlog."

"Yeah, looks that way." I nodded with a grimace as she scowled. "Part of the reason I'm here is because Agents Dirk Hopkins and Arnold Eisenburg were part of the Backlog organization. I'd tracked funky payments and actions by them that were later covered up and the evidence disappeared. When they ended up dead, I wondered if they'd gotten too sloppy and Backlog killed them to cover their tracks. Or whoever they were infiltrating got wind of them. But I had to be sure the Concrete Angels weren't really in the know and on the take."

"So, you're saying you think the Concrete Angels have been used by Backlog to do their dirty work, and their mole was both inside the club and the FBI. You're saying part of the skimming Eisenburg did sent money back to Backlog, and that's what that inclined T represents."

"Yeah."

"And you're saying you came here to investigate all this to be sure we weren't in on it, but you've used Karma to get inside?" Oriana's expression was carefully neutral, but the storm brewed in her eyes and I swallowed hard.

"Yes, ma'am, that's correct."

She narrowed her eyes and scanned me, and I knew I'd fucked up. The question became how much.

"You're a cop, aren't you? You're not a private investigator, you're a real one." She sat back in her chair and looked me over. She hadn't reached for her phone yet, but it wouldn't take long. "Is all this for real or were you just trying to find your way into Backlog?"

I blanked my expression and shook my head. "It's for real and I want to dismantle Backlog. They're a blight on law enforcement and they make things harder for regular people."

"Regular people. Are the Concrete Angels included in that?"

"Yeah, they should be, under the law."

She nodded slowly, but her expression didn't change. "Which agency do you work for, Mr. DeVille?"

I kept my mouth shut for a few moments, considering the possibilities. The question became, who did I trust? The Concrete Angels weren't exactly Kindergarteners who did nice things for people, but they also weren't involved in supporting Backlog. On the other hand, the people meant to protect the public and uphold the law where neck-deep in Backlog's pockets and would kill me without hesitation for poking around. I weighed my loyalty to the U.S. Marshal Service against the reality that it had been infiltrated and corrupted by a group far worse than the motorcycle club, a group with no code or honor.

"I'm a U.S. Marshal, but I'm officially on leave. Only my boss knows where I am so if you kill me, no one will really know." I shrugged at her raised eyebrows. "You're former FBI, Ms. Hunter. You know how it is."

"I don't have any loyalty to the FBI."

I nodded. "I figured after what happened there and their support of your rapist. But here's the thing: I'm ninety-nine percent sure that was the Backlog's doing, too. Hopkins was a high-ranking FBI agent on Backlog's payroll. They couldn't have him thrown out of his position. So they made it harder for you to stay. They had to get rid of you to keep Hopkins in play."

Anger rolled over Oriana's face, but I wasn't sure it was at my deception or Backlog's actions to keep Hopkins employed. I just hoped she wouldn't pull a gun and shoot me for telling her. When she met my gaze, I shivered with the fury I read in her eyes.

"How did you recognize that symbol?" She pointed to the inclined T.

"I'd seen it from my investigation on papers and ledgers of cops and agents who'd let shit get past them in terms of suspects, evidence tampering, and money. I started to put together the backlog they were worried about wasn't the work they hadn't gotten done, but the organization at large." I pointed at the symbol. "See how the T is tipped over? The crossbar is "back," like a backstop, and the stem is "log". Backlog. An easy way to show something that no one will know if looking."

She nodded again and I could see the wheels turning. "So, now you know the Concrete Angels aren't part of this organization, at least not willingly, and you know that Eisenburg was skimming from the club to fund Backlog. What will you do now? Leave? Turn the Concrete Angels over to the cops?"

I shook my head. "I promised to help you find the three million dollars Eisenburg stole from you. I'm not going anywhere until I've done that."

"Right. And does Karma know you're actually an undercover U.S. Marshal just here to find out if her club was involved in the Backlog and the killings of two FBI agents?"

The question hung in the air between us and my gut curdled with guilt.

"No."

Oriana sighed and dropped her chin, her lips tightening. "Karma is my friend and I don't tolerate men fucking around on my friends. Did you lie to get into her bed, too? She might be just a biker chick to you, but she's a person and deserves honesty. She definitely doesn't deserve to be used just so you can get the information for your investigation, Mr. DeVille."

"I know. And I'm going to tell her, but I had to be sure the Concrete Angels weren't part of Backlog."

"Fuck you. That's an excuse and you know it. You just wanted some free pussy while you worked."

My anger kindled at her accusation. *Yeah, because you know she's right.* "No, thanks, you're not even my type. And as I understand it, you're taken."

"Listen here, you entitled prick, 'cause I'm only gonna say this once. When you leave my office this morning, you better go straight to Karma and lay it all out, or just walk the fuck away from the Concrete Angels entirely. Don't even bother telling Loki goodbye. This club, as repugnant as you might think we are, is still a family and built on trust, experience, and a remarkable amount of honesty and integrity. So, if you can't uphold that shit, I'll give you a head start before I tell the rest of the members who you really are. Got me?"

I nodded, anger still humming in my veins. "I got you. But you better remember what it's like to be an agent of the law heading into an unknown situation. I might not have gone about it the best way, but there was no way in hell I'd give away who I was until I was sure your club wasn't part of the organization trying to stamp out interference. I've lost friends trying to find out about this. Friends I cared about who had families, experience, honesty and integrity, and they were either fired or killed for it. So don't get on your high horse over me playing it close to my chest."

"That high horse you're referring to centers around

horny men who believe themselves to be entitled to free sex without paying the price of honesty. It doesn't excuse what you did, and I remember what it's like to be an agent in the unknown. Probably better than you."

I couldn't argue with that. She'd been raped and turned out by the FBI, then brought to the Concrete Angels. I didn't know the full story behind how she'd gotten there, but they'd evidently earned her respect and loyalty since then.

"Fine. We both know where we stand and I'll tell Karma as soon as I'm done here. In the meantime, I got one last question for you. Can you tell from those symbols where the money has gone now or do you need more of my help to track it down?"

She scowled and I suspected she wanted to shoot me, but she turned her attention back to the ledgers and scrutinized the symbols there.

"All of these are Backlog deposits, but then there's this other symbol on almost all of them." She pointed to another V with a straight vertical line between the uprights, like an arrow but the straight line didn't top the uprights of the letter. "See? It's been going back about…" She clicked through the images on the screen. "Eight months or so of the ledger."

I rubbed my chin, grateful Oriana was still willing to work with me. "Eisenburg must have had a key somewhere. Some sort of legend that mentioned what the coded symbols are."

"If he did, we haven't found it. He might have destroyed it when we caught on to him."

"Did anyone search his residence off-site? He must have had a place to live before he became Roy."

"The police probably did, but if what you say is true, Backlog probably got rid of anything tying them to him." Oriana shrugged, but then she paused, her gaze unfocusing. "Wait. Roy left the compound in a hurry and didn't take all his stuff. We cleaned out his cabin and found a few things that seemed really random. He had a bunch of pop culture figurines, like Star Wars, Harry Potter, and Assassin's Creed."

She rose and came around the desk without looking at me. Curious, I followed her out of her office and down the hallway to a door marked "storage." Originally, it had probably been the room where the hotel would've held luggage after people checked out and waited on taxis to the airport. Now it seemed to contain a Lost & Found bin, some old Army surplus camping gear, and random boxes full of knickknacks and loose electrical cords.

Oriana grabbed one of the boxes and rifled through it, pulling out Pez dispensers, Matchbox cars, random dolls' shoes, even a handful of Lego bricks.

"There it is." She reached in the box and produced an old figurine from one of the Sci-Fi shows aired in the 1990s. As I recalled, the character had been the chief engineer on the starship and he wore some weird kind of headband spray-painted gold over his eyes. The figure stood on a little plastic dais to keep it upright, but Oriana turned it over to look at the bottom. I expected it to be hollow, but it contained a battery compartment to allow it to make sounds.

"Please tell me that thing doesn't sing Christmas carols."

She snorted. "I have no idea. It wouldn't surprise me." She pried open the little battery box and sighed with pleasure. "Eureka." She held up a tiny flashdrive with a grin. "Let's see what's on this little baby."

She shoved the flash drive into her pocket and tossed the figurine back into the box, adding the rest of the junk on top of it. I followed her back to her office, something bugging me. It couldn't be that easy, could it?

"Do you think he'd really leave that behind if it had anything important on it?" I crossed my arms over my chest. "I mean, if you're trying to get out of here, you wouldn't leave incriminating evidence where anyone could get a hold it."

"I wouldn't, but he might not have had enough time to grab it. Or he only took the stuff that was *really* important." She sat back down and pulled out a tablet and a USB adaptor. "He probably figured no one would look at his toys and it would be safe until he could either retrieve it or get someone to bring it to him. And if he died, no one would know."

"How did you know to look there?"

She plugged the USB adaptor into the tablet and the flash drive into the adaptor before she met my gaze. "I had one of the original figurines from a popular video game about spies back when I was a kid. Each figure came with a stand that had a secret compartment for messages you could leave for your friends who played the game to find. At the time it was done by mail because email wasn't a thing yet. I used to hide all sorts of things in there, dreaming about being a spy."

"Before you plug that into your tablet, you better make sure you don't have anything on it you can't lose. It might hold a virus or worm." The last thing Oriana needed was Backlog getting a hold of the Concrete Angels' information. *Or more than they already have.*

"Sit down before you hurt yourself, junior." She shook her head. "This tablet isn't connected to any network or the internet. And if it clears the hard drive, I can have Neo rebuild it."

She plugged in the drive and tapped the tablet, bringing up the directory. I didn't look over her shoulder, but I definitely wanted to know what she found.

"Holy shit, we definitely hit pay dirt." She flipped the tablet to me. "Check out the little key to Mr. Squiggles' diary."

The list of symbols with explanations weren't in a

specific order, but they'd been clearly written down and scanned into the digital realm. In addition, there were what looked like account numbers and a list of names with locations and agency designations. *Holy shit, this was his insurance backup.* Eisenburg had compiled a list of info on other members who'd been connected to Backlog and where they worked.

"Apparently, Eisenburg didn't trust his bosses any more than he trusted you. Can I get a copy of that list of names?" Oriana raised an eyebrow and I held up my hand. "Just the names and agencies so I can know who's on the take. I don't need to know where the money came from or where it went."

She tilted her head. "I'll give it to you on one condition."

My mouth flattened into a line. "What's the condition?"

"You tell Karma the truth, warts and all, and let her make decision on what she wants to do about you."

Panic hit my gut and sickness followed it. I could lose Karma with that admission. *But I've already lost her if I can't be honest.* Fuck in a bucket. I'd heard of those 'damned if you do, damned if you don't' scenarios in movies and books, but I'd never actually lived one until now.

I cleared my throat. "And if I don't?"

She shrugged. "Not only do you not get a copy of the list, but I'll broadcast to the whole club who and what you are. The choice is yours."

Yeah, I was afraid of that. Of course, she wouldn't be worth her salt if she didn't threaten me.

"Got it. I'll go talk to Karma." I could lie to her and not do it, but we both knew I wasn't. That list of names was too important. *So is Karma.*

"Good choice. Give me a chance to isolate the list and I'll print it out for you."

"Thanks." I planned to wait for the list, but my phone rang and Battlebourne's ringtone, Rhapsody in Blue, trilled through the small space.

"George Gershwin?"

I smirked and shrugged. "It's a joke. I'm gonna take this and I'll be back for that list."

I ducked out the door again as I answered the phone. "DeVille."

"DeVille, you gotta come in. The higher-ups are starting to ask questions about why you're taking so much leave." Battlebourne sounded tense and harried.

"Yeah, give me a minute to get somewhere private." I scanned the clubhouse, but there were people everywhere, including the women the members called honeys. I didn't see Karma, but at the moment, I really didn't want to. Instead, I pushed through the front doors of the clubhouse and headed for my car behind the barn. I almost missed my silent shadow, the guy who'd been watching me the night before, as he stood just inside the workshop entrance, but I nodded to him. Surprisingly, he nodded back.

"Yeah, okay, I'm clear. What's going on, Battlebourne?"

"It's the Assistant Director. He's been hounding me to find out where you are and why the hell you've been gone so long. You have to wrap this up soon, son."

I nodded, but grimaced at the same time. "I just need another few days and I'll have all the answers I've been looking for." And I'd know if the Assistant Director was part of the problem. I ducked down to check my car for more listening devices but I didn't see any. "I'll tell you this, though. The Concrete Angels aren't involved in…the organization."

I still couldn't say Backlog's name aloud on the phone to the U.S. Marshal's office. I didn't trust Battlebourne's phoneline.

"Are you sure? They were the last ones to see

Eisenburg and Hopkins alive."

"I'm sure. But I thought Hopkins died in Searchlight, Nevada."

Battlebourne hissed. "That's where they found the body, but it had been dumped. Down a 400-ft deep mine shaft."

"Shit. They figure out a cause of death?"

"Nope. But the corpse was desiccated damn near beyond all recognition. They had to use dental records."

"Hell. Okay, I can't prove the Concrete Angels had a hand in his death. From my research, none of their local members were anywhere near Nevada in the time frame. But I can prove that Eisenburg was embezzling money from them and sending it somewhere other than the FBI."

"The organization you mentioned."

"Yup."

"You got records and confirmation?"

"Yup."

"Well, hot damn, son. Bring it in."

"Just give me a few days and I'll have everything I need." I hoped. "I don't want to expose the Concrete Angels to the organization."

"They already have been if Eisenburg was in there."

"Not like this. They might have some dubious motives, but they don't deserve the shit the organization brings."

"Fuck. Someone's coming. Look, hurry up and get that information, then get your ass back to work."

Battlebourne hung up and I stared at the phone in my hand. I'd damn near run out of time. I shoved the phone into my pocket and turned around to head for the clubhouse to get the list. *Then I have to face Karma.* Yeah, I was looking forward to that as much as a prostate exam. Except if I was coughing, it would be because she'd kicked me in the balls.

I reached the doors of the clubhouse and pulled them open, stepping through out of the sunlight. There wasn't a breath of sound and my gut told me to be careful. I glanced around for enemies, but the room was empty. *Odd.*

I strode to Oriana's office and glanced inside. She wasn't there. The computer showed its dancing screensaver and all the papers sat in neat piles on the surface. The tablet and flash drive were gone, but the computer sat alone and unattended. Some folded pieces of paper with my last name inscribed on them sat on the edge of the desk. I picked them up and opened the fold.

Mr. DeVille,

Here's the list of names you wanted from Eisenburg's files. Now, go make good on your promise to talk to Karma.

Oriana Hunter.

I stared at the note before I folded the pages again and shoved them into the waistband of my jeans at my back, flipping my t-shirt over them. I glanced at the computer, considering if I should try to find more, but Oriana had given me what I wanted and anything else would be a violation of trust. *And probably would get me killed.* Yeah, not on the list of my long-range plans.

Instead, I turned around and retreated to the main room of the clubhouse. A few people had come in and sat watching one of the big screen TVs hanging on the wall. I caught sight of Attila standing with the woman named Dollhouse, and both of them watched me go by. I waved, but they didn't wave back and my gut flipped over. Had Oriana told everyone who I was? *If she did, I'm probably a good extra for The Walking Dead.*

I just hoped I could talk to Karma before all hell broke loose, but I wasn't holding my breath.

CHAPTER TWELVE

Karma

My phone chirped and I glanced down at it despite Loki's glare of disapproval. I caught the text message from Coop and my heart rate went up. Why was it that even a little message from him could make me happy? I swiped the screen and read his words.

Got some info I need to run down and calls to make to contacts. Will try to get back tonight, but if not, may I come back tomorrow, Ma'am?

I smiled as a thrill of joy zipped up my back. He'd not only asked permission but he did it with the agreed upon honorific. Damn, that was sexy. But I wanted to test him anyway.

You will come back tonight so I can be sure you are safe and well taken care of. Besides, I'd like a dance since you didn't come to the party last night.

There, that should get a response of one kind or another. I shoved my phone into my back pocket as I returned my attention to what Neo had found so far. Coop might be hiding something about himself, but he'd come through after talking with Numbers. Not only had he helped her identify some of the symbols in Eisenburg's ledger, but he'd also clued her into the key to the rest of the symbols. We'd discovered a wealth of information.

My phone vibrated against my ass and I pulled it back out.

I don't really dance that well. Does swaying to the beat count?

I snorted in humor and started typing.

No. You're gonna have to do better than that. But I might be willing to train you if you ask nicely.

My finger hovered over the send key and I bit my bottom lip. Domme's didn't use the word "train" unless they meant something far more intimate and long-term. If I sent the text as it was written, would he know what I meant? And did I mean it that way? Was I offering to train him to be the sub who held my heart as well as my attention?

Sweet Goddess, it's true. I want him to be mine, forever and ever. I hit send on my phone, my heart pounding with the implications of the words I'd used. I held the phone in my hand, sweat popping out on my forehead as I waited for his response. Would he understand? And if he didn't, would I just let it go?

The seconds passed in excruciating slowness as I waited for him. *Can't he type faster?* But I took a deep breath and tried to keep myself calm. When the phone vibrated again, I couldn't swipe fast enough.

Please, Madam, would you train me to dance with you?

I let out my breath with a sort of soft whimper that had Michael shooting me a raised eyebrow, but the grin I offered must have satisfied him because he didn't do anything else.

I will happily train you to dance with me. You must be here at 1900 sharp and wear a pair of cowboy boots, preferably black.

Cowboy boots? Do I need to bring a matching

hat?

I snorted softly. Do you have one?

Yes, Ma'am. Stetson and everything.

Oh, be still my thundering heart. I could imagine Coop wearing his faded jeans that hugged his ass and thighs, a black Stetson, and his black boots crossed at the ankles as he leaned against his cool car. *Fuck, that's a sexy image.* And I could have the real thing.

Hell yeah, bring the hat.

Will do. I'll dress for you any way you like, Ma'am, but we definitely need to talk tonight. I got something important to tell you.

And just like that, the sexy fantasy popped. I hadn't known him long enough to hear his voice through text, but "we need to talk" wasn't a phrase to be handed out lightly. *He could be thinking of proposing.* Yeah, and I could be a fully human woman with ancestors in the English Monarchy, but neither were likely.

See you at 1900.

"You want to join us again here, Karma?" Loki's voice intruded as I shoved my phone into my pocket.

"Yeah, yeah, I'm here. Say something really important and I'm all over it."

"I'd think a shadow organization infiltrating law enforcement agencies and manipulating us to do their dirty work would be riveting." Loki raised an eyebrow, a dangerous move for most of the members.

"Yeah, that's pretty bad. Thank the Goddess Coop was here to decipher that for us." I nodded at Numbers who scowled. "But I'm pretty sure Numbers found the rest of the key to Eisenburg's symbols so how 'bout we let her talk rather than you and Neo? I think you've flapped your gums enough."

Loki blinked and Neo's eyes grew wide while Michael chuckled. Numbers allowed a faint smile to curl her lips until Loki shot her a look.

"Okay, so what I've determined is this V with a straight line between the uprights isn't a down-arrow, it represents a brothel or prostitution den. V for a woman's legs, line for…well you get it." Numbers shook her head. "In any case, all the payments that went to the brothel also had the symbol for the Backlog, according to Coop. I didn't find the Backlog's symbol in Eisenburg's key, but when I added up all the entries with that little inclined T, the sum equated to our missing money. Three million dollars' worth."

"So, if Coop's right, Eisenburg was getting paid by the FBI to infiltrate our club, he skimmed from us to set himself up, and he sent a little somethin'-somethin' to Backlog to…what? Keep up his membership dues?" I shook my head. "It's a good thing he got the karma coming to him."

"Somethin'-somethin'." Neo's eyes narrowed. "Let me check something."

We waited as his hands flew over the keyboard and the trackball that looked like a glowing crystal ball with swirling liquid inside that changed colors. It was mesmerizing and I kept my gaze on his screens.

"Yup. Bingo. Look at this." He displayed two documents with lines of information. A few lines were highlighted in pale rose and they blinked together to show coordinating info. "You said to look for places where FBI Agent Hopkins and Eisenburg had other connections beyond the FBI. Turns out they were both big fans of paid sex, but they were cheap bastards. They didn't go to the high-end brothels or escorts. They visited this place."

He put up images of a warehouse in the industrial side of Fort Collins, near the railroad tracks where freight could be easily offloaded without anyone noticing. *Freight like human cargo and trafficking.* Anger kindled in my chest.

"What the hell is that?" Michael's growl surprised me, though it shouldn't. His intolerance for injustice eclipsed my own.

"That is a warehouse being used as a whorehouse for women and girls someone has stolen. They're deposited there for crooked cops and agents to get their rocks off." Neo's voice held a banked fury. I'd never seen the man angry and given that voice, I really didn't want to. "Hold up, I think there are boys there, too. From what I can tell from the records and Hopkins' financials, he got a discount. That could be because he had a membership with this Backlog group."

The Concrete Angels weren't saints by any stretch of the imagination, but we drew the line at women and kids. Anyone weaker than us needed to be defended, not harmed, and those who preyed on them were fair game to anything we decided to pull on them.

"So we find this place and rescue the people inside. What do we do with them once we take down the brothel?" I crossed my arms over my chest.

"I know a few shelters that can help them." Numbers raised her chin. "I'll make a few calls. When are we doing to do this?"

"Tomorrow." Loki's voice filled with finality. "That'll give us time to determine who runs that place and make sure they're there to be dealt with."

"And if they're not there?" I raised an eyebrow.

"Then we'll hunt them down."

A chill ran down my back. Loki wasn't kidding and he could be ruthless when eradicating problems.

"Mr. DeVille has Eisenburg's list and I suspect he'll be running down the names on it." Numbers pushed her hair behind her ear. "It looks like most of them are FBI agents and cops from Denver and Fort Collins PD. But there are a few other names who didn't have designations and I don't recognize them from the Denver office of the FBI."

"I'll look into them and see what I can dig up." Neo took the copy Numbers held out. "We'll figure out who runs the whorehouse and find them. Can you get me a list of shelters where we can take the victims?"

"Yeah, I'll do some research to find out which ones are still in operation. I used to know them a little better before I left the FBI." Numbers grimaced. "I'll refresh my knowledge base."

"Good. Let's talk more tonight, *ja*? Then we make a plan for tomorrow." Loki nodded to everyone and strode out the door, the conversation over.

I checked my phone to see if Coop had responded to my last text, but no notifications lit up the little device. I shoved it back in my pocket as I headed out of Neo's lair, but Numbers called my name before I'd gone very far.

"Wait up, Karma. I want to talk to you." She hurried after me.

"Come to the buffet with me. I want some coffee. You want anything?"

"I'll get some tea." She followed me to the sideboard and we doctored our drinks.

Once we had what we wanted, she led me over to the fluffy chairs set closer to the front window set in an intimate arrangement for privacy. She sat down, setting the file beside her as she cradled her tea mug in her hands.

"Did Mr. DeVille talk to you yet?"

I raised my eyebrows. "No, I haven't seen him since breakfast. Why?"

She pursed her lips and shrugged. "Yeah, I guess that makes sense. You were in the meeting with Loki when I came in." She sighed and sipped her tea. "I promised I wouldn't say anything until after he talked to you, but he has something important he needs to tell you."

"And you can't tell me?"

She shook her head. "You need to hear it from him. And I promised. I try not to break my promises because then I end up feeling like shit. But if he doesn't talk to you by tomorrow, I'll tell you what I know."

My gut sank and my blood chilled. "Is it that bad a thing?"

She gave a one-shouldered shrug. "It could be if he doesn't talk to you about it. It comes down to trust and if he's being intimate with you, you have to be able to trust him." She rose with a troubled look. "I don't want to say more. Just let me know if he doesn't talk to you."

"Oriana." She stopped and met my gaze. "Are you sure you can't tell me?"

She nodded. "Just let me know. Give him a chance to explain it himself. Then come to me if he doesn't."

With that, she headed back to her office, leaving me with that insecure, scared feeling coiling in my gut. What the hell could be so important about Coop that Numbers felt the need to ensure I knew?

****

Cooper

I grinned as I shoved my phone into my pocket and headed for my bedroom. Karma wanted me to wear boots and my Stetson? Damn, if it made her smile, I'd wear those and nothing else. *In private.* No point in showing off the goods to anyone but her. But I didn't have a pair of boots or clean clothes. Part of the reason I left the Concrete Angels' compound after talking to Oriana Hunter was to do laundry.

And to figure out how to tell Karma I'm a damn Marshal.

The list of names mocked me from my pocket, calling me to take a look and see who I recognized. I suspected most of the names would be FBI agents since Eisenburg would've had the most interaction with his own agency. But he wouldn't have been much of an investigator if he hadn't found other members of Backlog in other agencies.

I considered what his reasons for compiling the list might have been while I did laundry. *Blackmail? Insurance? A way to recognize his fellow crooked cops?* Whatever his motivation, I was glad he'd kept the list. It would help me find out who might be part of the group in the Marshal Service.

And then what? What would I do when I figured out who they were? I scowled as I yanked my clothes out of the dryer. I couldn't exactly bring those assholes down by myself. Hell, even with my boss, we wouldn't be enough to disrupt a nation-wide organization. Especially if they had members in every law enforcement department and agency. They might have even secured crooked judges on their payroll.

Fuck.

I carried my clothes back to my apartment and took a shower, trying to relax enough for my mind to come up with some answers. No such luck, but the warm water felt good. I hurried to finish and dressed with the intent to get my chores done before I returned to the compound that night. I packed up a few things, grabbed my black Stetson, and headed out to my car. I felt my pocket for my phone and the list Oriana had given me, relieved they hadn't disappeared while I did my chores. I refused to leave it anywhere. I hadn't bothered to scan my apartment for bugs, but I wasn't prone to talking to myself so my secrets remained my own.

But when I settled behind Rosé's wheel, I noticed a silver Chevy Cruze parked on the road outside the apartment complex. Normally it wouldn't be a big deal. The only cars that ended up on that side of the road were junkers or vehicles for purchase. But this car looked like it was in pretty good condition and it didn't sport a for-sale sign in the window. I tried to get a good look at the tag, but it was too far away. It could be nothing

Right, and I could be a faery princess.

I put Rosé in gear and headed for the road, playing the unconcerned driver. Fortunately, the car in question happened to be on the way toward I-25. I drove past it and memorized the Colorado tag. The vehicle looked empty but I grabbed my phone and had it out when I hit the first red light, tapping out the plate numbers. *I'll be keepin' an eye out for you, buddy.*

I headed up the freeway to Cheyenne, Wyoming, to visit their big western store in downtown. I'd always liked the small-town feel to one of the biggest cities in the state. Granted, it paled beside Denver or even Fort Collins, but at 65,000 people it had one of the largest populations in Wyoming. I decided to park Rosé in the depot plaza and walked to the big store on the corner. Along the way I noticed a silver Chevy Cruze parked on the main drag on the opposite side of the street. The tag number matched the one I'd seen across from my apartment.

Ah ha, so you are watching out for me. Much obliged. The question was, why were they keeping an eye on me? Had Backlog gotten wind of what I was doing? Or were the Concrete Angels checking up on my movements?

I shook my head as I stepped in the doors of the Wrangler. The motorcycle club would have someone on two wheels following me, not in four. So, who was my shadow?

I headed for the boot section of the store and a pretty, young sales lady helped me find the right pair of black boots for my date that night. She helped me try different brands to find the one that fit my feet best, and even then, she suggested I put on the socks I was likely to wear with them and soak the leather boots in the bathtub.

"What? Why would I do that to good boots?"

"Because if you do that and let 'em dry on you, they perfectly mold to the shape of your feet and you don't get blisters." She gave me an amused smile. "Beats waitin' for them to mold the regular way, and uses far fewer

145

Bandaids."

I still thought she was crazy to put such expensive leather boots in the tub, but I thanked her and left the store with my new Ariat boots. I scanned the street before I stepped outside, but the Cruze with the Colorado tags had moved from its spot across from the store. I didn't see it on the cross streets or in the plaza, but didn't think they'd given up. I checked my phone as I sat in the front seat of my car. No texts or messages, and still plenty of time to get back to Longmont before heading to the Concrete Angels' compound.

I pulled out the list of names Oriana had given me, keeping my peripheral eyes aware of any movement around me. I caught sight of a silver Chevy Cruze, but it had Wyoming tags and I let it slide out of my awareness.

Most of the names on the list didn't mean anything to me. From what I'd been able to gather from Eisenburg's symbol key, the names showed their association with the Denver office of the FBI. A couple others showed Denver PD, Fort Collins PD, some county sheriffs, and one ATF agent. But the last three names made me grit my teeth.

Three fuckin' U.S. Marshals in the Denver office. Sonuvaprick.

One guy was my level, part of the rank-and-file Marshals, but the other two were supervisors, and one was my boss's boss. *Fuck-a-duck. No wonder Battlebourne has been nervous.* The names had no symbols beside them, which probably meat Eisenburg hadn't known which agencies these names had worked for. But I knew them.

The only good news was my partner, Anna Fitzsimmons, wasn't on Eisenburg's list. *That doesn't mean she isn't part of Backlog, just that he didn't know her.* But Anna had always struck me as down-to-earth and honorable. I couldn't imagine her being on the take. *But then, I couldn't imagine the Assistant Director of the U.S. Marshals' Denver office being crooked either.*

I took a picture of the list with my phone and emailed it to my personal email account so I'd have a backup should anything happen to the list or phone. I stuffed both items into my pockets and started the big Caddy's engine. Rosé rumbled to life with a throaty purr and satisfaction rolled through me. I loved this car and her power, but I didn't need a tail. As I headed for I-80, I noticed another silver Chevy Cruze. This one also had a Wyoming tag and I cursed as I realized two more cars around me were the same. *Dammit, what is it with Wyoming residents and the damn Chevy Cruze?*

My trip back down to Longmont was uneventful, but I picked up my tail again when I closed in on my exit. *Ah, there you are. Shoulda stayed in Cheyenne where you blend, buddy.* But that made me think. Talk about blending. Rosé stood out like an ostrich in a flock of flamingos. She wasn't likely to hide anywhere. I'd have to leave her at home and take my less visible and more fuel-efficient Toyota. I sighed and patted the dashboard.

"Sorry, honey, but you're just too gorgeous this time."

I drove back to my apartment and parked in my front parking spot. I gathered my bag, my Stetson, and my purchases and returned to my apartment just in case the silver Cruze followed me home. Then I left out the back entrance where I parked my other car. It was black, sleek, but otherwise unremarkable in the Colorado motor-scape. I checked my phone. I still had two hours to get up to the compound, but I'd need all that time if there was any traffic or I had to lose another tail. I grinned at myself in the rearview mirror. *Let the games begin.*

CHAPTER THIRTEEN

Karma

"Hey, Karma. Get a load of this." Dollhouse's voice brought me to the front windows of the clubhouse. "Is that your man coming in driving a boring car?"

I raised my eyebrows as I peered out the windows. "I have no idea. I've never seen that car before."

The black Toyota sedan pulled into the spot Coop's Caddy had occupied earlier that morning and parked. I left the clubhouse at a fast walk, wondering who it was. Logically, I understood it was someone we knew if he'd come in the gates, but I couldn't reconcile the car with the man.

I almost took a step back when a tall man wearing a black Stetson, Navy blue button-down shirt, and black leather cowboy boots under faded blue jeans got out of the car. Coop had been sexy and handsome before, but holy shit. He damn near melted my panties off my ass right there.

"Well, howdy stranger."

"Ma'am." He tipped that hat and my heart fluttered. Seriously, it fluttered. I didn't think that was a real thing, but I was fluttering. "Sorry for the confusion with the vehicle. I was gettin' followed around town and Rosé is kinda noticeable. So I switched her out for my old reliable here and went out the back way."

My gut cramped and my eyes narrowed. "You were followed?"

"Yup." He nodded as he pulled his bag out of the trunk. "All the way up to Cheyenne and back."

"Why would anyone follow you?"

He shrugged as he locked the car. "I think it probably has to do with my investigation. Speakin' of which, I need to talk to you about that. You got some spare time before things get rockin' around here?"

"Yeah. We can talk in my cabin. Grab your stuff and we'll talk there." I gestured for him to precede me so I could watch his sexy ass in those butt-hugger jeans. I'm all for serious conversations and things that need to be fixed, but I wasn't about to give up on ass-watching for it.

He smirked as he sauntered past me, leading the way to my cabin. I caught Loki's and Dollhouse's speculative gazes as I followed Coop, but I ignored them. Whatever was coming I'd weather it like I had the rest of my human existence. I got to the cabin behind him, slid my hand over his ass, and unlocked the door.

"Come on in, cowboy."

"Thank you, Ma'am."

He sauntered, just like a damn cowboy, in the door and I followed after him like a horny bitch. He set his bag down on the chair, rather than in the bedroom, and waited for me to close the door as he removed his hat and held it in his hands. He looked so uncomfortable, I wanted to wrap him in my arms and tell him it would be okay. But something about his energy suggested he didn't want to be comforted at the moment so I settled into my favorite fluffy arm chair to wait him out. I probably looked like a queen on her throne, but it gave me comfort when my own unease ramped up.

"All right. What did you need to talk to me about?" I tried to keep my voice level and my expression calm while my heart rate increased with every moment he stood silent.

Coop cleared his throat and slid the hat between his fingers, turning around and around as he organized his thoughts. "So, you know I talked to Ms. Hunter, Numbers, this morning and I'm sure she filled you in on who stole your money."

I nodded. "She said you identified some of the symbols in Eisenburg's ledger. She said you knew the name of the group he was working for while undercover for the FBI."

Coop nodded with a grimace. "Did she tell you why I knew their name?"

"No. I figured it had to do with your investigation into our missing money."

He sighed and glanced down, still turning his hat. "Yes, and no." He chewed on his bottom lip, a habit I'd learned meant he was nervous about something. "I knew the group from my investigation, but not from this one. Not from trying to recover the money stolen from the Concrete Angels."

"Okay..." I still didn't understand why this was a big deal.

"I've been investigating Backlog for around two years because their membership is made up of people within all branches of U.S. law enforcement. I suspect many judges and possibly some law enforcement groups outside of the U.S. are involved, too."

"That makes sense. What does it have to do with me or the Concrete Angels?"

He set the hat upside down on the table and rubbed the back of his neck, another nervous gesture. "Backlog has been known to either hire or use groups like the Concrete Angels to do their dirty work so it can't be traced back to them. They hide in plain sight and don't want to lose their position to allegations." He paused to see if I'd figured out what he was trying to say, but I just nodded to let him continue. "If they can't get the groups to work directly for them, they insert a mole."

"Like Eisenburg."

Coop nodded. "Yeah, exactly. You already knew Eisenburg was undercover FBI. But he also worked for Backlog, funneling money into their coffers that the FBI didn't even know about. I knew he was Backlog. I'd been tracking him for a while. Hopkins, too. But what I didn't know was if the Concrete Angels were in on it or just pawns in the game…"

He paused, waiting for me to catch up with what he inferred. It took me a few moments. "You were investigating the club. You approached me because of that, not because you wanted me specifically."

"Yeah—well, no, not quite." He had the grace to wear chagrin on his face. "I saw you first. I was watching the compound from up on the hill, and I swear you looked at me."

I remembered that day. The itching between my shoulder blades of someone watching me had been a constant thing. Just before I'd stepped into my cabin, I'd looked up on the hill above and seen the guy in the hills watching us. *Watching me.* He'd jerked when I winked at him and that perversely made my day. *No wonder Coop came looking for me. I basically gave him an invitation.*

"So, when I saw you leave the compound, I sort of followed you to see where you went. And then I made sure to bump into you." He didn't smile as he met my gaze. "I could've followed anyone, but I really only wanted to get to know you." He sighed and rubbed the back of his neck again. "It doesn't excuse what I did. I wasn't completely honest with you and I was investigating how much involvement the Concrete Angels had with Backlog. I now know your club was being used to hide their activities, and probably launder money, but I didn't tell you everything."

He stepped closer to me and knelt down, resting his fisted hands on his knee. "I was investigating the club, but when I met you, all I wanted to do was be with you and forget the investigation. Nothing I said to you about me or my feelings was fake. I had to be sure the club wasn't with Backlog, but I'm sorry I didn't tell you everything."

His remorse was genuine and I could understand why he didn't tell me what he was really doing here. But it still hurt. "Is that everything? I'm not a big fan of surprises, especially when it comes to being intimate with someone."

Coop opened his mouth to answer when someone knocked on the door.

"Karma? It's Loki. We need to talk, *ja?*"

I sighed and rose. "Hold that thought." I moved to the door as Coop stood up, and I pulled it open to reveal our crazy-ass leader.

"What's up, Loki?"

He glanced in the cabin and caught sight of Coop watching him warily. "Oh, good, he's dressed perfectly, *ja?* Have you told him yet?"

"Told me what yet?" Coop raised an eyebrow.

"Uh, no, we were getting to that." I shot him a rueful grin as Loki nodded.

"What were we just getting to?"

"The strip show." Loki grinned.

Coop's eyes widened. "What?"

"She hasn't told you yet?" Loki tsked and shook his head, but his grin never slipped. "And you had him dress like a cowboy. We give him a mask and he'll be the Lone Ranger, *ja? Det er bra.*"

"What the hell is he talking about, Karma?" Coop crossed his arms over his chest.

"Yeah, so, um, every year, we do a strip show with detachable costumes and whatnot." I rubbed one arms with the opposite hand. "The first year, the strip show was women strippers, but a few of us complained that it was unfair. We'd like to see something like Thunder From Down Under. So Loki agreed that some years would be women only, some would be mixed men and women, and some would be men only. Guess what year it is this year?"

"Mixed?"

"Yeah, no. Men only. Would you, uh, well, would you be willing enter?" I shifted under his gimlet gaze.

"Me? Are you serious? What the hell do I know about stripping?"

"Come on, Coop. You'd be great at it. We'd call you Deputy Dick and give you a mask, *ja*?"

"Deputy Dick? Oh, you gotta be fuckin' kidding me." Coop scowled. "No. No way. This is insane."

"What if I told you to do it?" My voice changed, infused with some of my Madam tones. I liked the idea of watching Coop strut around on the stage in front of everyone. They'd be able to look and enjoy, but not touch. He was mine. "No one could touch you and you can keep the mask on your face."

He met my gaze, his unease warring with his need to obey his Madam. I was pushing him outside his comfort zone, but stripping was a minor requirement, just a little exhibitionism for me.

"Are you sure, Ma'am?" His gaze hadn't left mine, but I knew he really asked if I was okay with showing of what we both considered mine.

"Yes, I think it would be fun." I turned my gaze to Loki. "But only down to his skivvies. Anything under those are mine alone."

Loki pouted. "Aw, that's no fun. Perhaps an ass shot?"

"No. Down to the skivvies or not at all. Your choice."

I wasn't giving anyone that treat. Loki, Attila, and the other members of the Concrete Angels would just have to enjoy Coop's torso and legs. *The good stuff is mine alone.* I wasn't about to share my man with porn star proportions.

"Fine. Down to the skivvies." Loki sounded resigned

but his eyes twinkled. "The show starts at 2030 and he'll go on as Deputy Dick. See you soon."

Loki damn-near skipped out the door and I closed it behind him, not sure I should laugh or cry. Coop hadn't been with us for very long and he didn't know all the weird things Loki sometimes made his crew do. *Well, he's been watching us for almost two weeks. That's long enough to get a clue.* I turned to meet his gaze, enjoying the bemused expression on his face.

"Are you sure, Ma'am? I really don't know dick about stripping, if you'll pardon the expression." He stood with his feet shoulder-width apart and his hands loose at his sides, but his shoulders had tightened.

I strode up to him and grasped his chin, forcing him to look into my eyes as I soaked in his energy signature. I sensed anxiety, but also arousal and excitement as he thought of the possibility of stripping. I suspected he'd be easier with it if I made it a command of his Madam.

"You'd be doing this for my pleasure, Coop. I want to see that gorgeous body up there, slowly taking your clothes off." I gave him a slow grin but kept the steel in my voice. "You'll be so sexy everyone will want you. But you're doing this for me and my pleasure. Do you understand?"

He held my gaze and swallowed hard. "Yes, Ma'am."

"Good. Then we'll table our earlier discussion for later and I'll let you get ready."

He blinked. "Ready, Ma'am?"

"Yeah." I released him and strode into the bedroom as he trailed behind me. "When I said down to your skivvies, these are what I had in mind."

I held up some brightly colored manties in jewel tones with cutout sides in black elastic. He swallowed again. But the sense I got was he wanted to wear those for me even while wearing them for others made him nervous. *Aw yeah. My sexy private eye has an exhibitionist side.* And I was gonna enjoy the hell out of it.

CHAPTER FOURTEEN

Cooper

I'm gonna be a fuckin' stripper.

Of all the times I'd been undercover and had to do something odd, I'd never expected to be a stripper. But when Karma told me to do it for her pleasure, I couldn't get out of my clothes fast enough. Fortunately, Samurai, Sam for short, had a wide collection of stripper clothing for both men and women, and I found a pair of rip-away jeans that would fit over my ass well enough. He appraised my shirt and hat, and pronounced me ready.

"Now, all you have to do is go out there and shake your ass while you get undressed. It's pretty easy and no one will care if you aren't smooth." Sam didn't smile, but I swore he had a twinkle in his eye. "Just save the pants for last and rip 'em away with your ass facing the audience. That'll give 'em a thrill, Deputy Dick." He'd eyed my package while he said it and I suspected he'd like to see it as much as the audience would. "You sure you won't go down to skin?"

"Yeah. I'm sure."

He shook his head. "That's too bad." He shrugged. "You'll be dancing to this old 90s rock song. It's one of

Karma's favorites and she requested it." I hoped it didn't
have a fast beat because there was nothing sexy about
bouncing balls in a banana hammock. "And wear this on
your undies somewhere." He handed me an honest-to-glory
tin star that read "marshal." I damn near choked. "I suggest
you pin it to the front of your package, but make sure you
don't prick your dick."

He turned away and I held the star in my hand, afraid
to move. Did they know who I was? Had Oriana Hunter
already told them? Granted, I hadn't told Karma the whole
truth about who I was, but they wouldn't be this subtle
about letting me know they'd found out, right? They'd just
run me off or kill me.

"Need some help with that?" A gravelly voice with a
northern English accent cut through my thoughts and I
looked up to meet the eerie gaze of the balding man with
more scruff on his face than his head.

"What?"

"Your star. You need help with pinnin' it on, Deputy
Dick?"

"Uh, no. Thanks. I think I got it." I shook my head as I
pinned the badge on my shirt instead. There was no way I
was shaking my star for everyone.

"Suit yerself, mate." He shrugged into his cut and
matching leather tear-away pants.

I raised an eyebrow. "Who are you supposed to be?"

"The Schlong Ride." He grinned and winked as I
choked out a laugh.

"Accurate?"

His grin widened. "You'll just have to wait and see."

I laughed at his arrogance and shook my head, grateful
for the small moment of humor. I'd missed that in the
Marshal Service. With the infiltration of Backlog, everyone
had been edgy and withdrawn, me included. Laughter was
a thing of the past, and sharing it with a rough biker while
preparing for something as crazy as a strip show eased my

heart.

"All right, guys, get ready to strut your stuff." Sam nodded with approval at my outfit with the tin star on my chest. "We'll start with The Kilted Nutsack, followed by Firehose, The Schlong Ride, Deputy Dick, Pocket Rocket, Kiddie Pool Shark, Happy Hardon, Harry Longballs, and Wally Ballbanger. Go out there and shake your asses for the ladies and some of the gents."

Attila hadn't changed much, though he'd added a shirt under his cut and a pair of lace-up Roman style sandals. Sam made the announcement that the show was about to start and the feminine crowd went wild. Attila shot me a grin and adjusted his package before Sam announced The Kilted Nutsack. Then the big Scot sauntered through the door to what I'd discovered was a little movie theater with a raised dais. Apparently, the Concrete Angels had enough of these shows throughout their year that it was worth the up-keep. A biker named Gadget ran the sound and light boards, and she kept the projectors for the movies in top condition.

"Bad Romance" began to play through the speakers and Attila twirled onto the stage, his kilt flying around him like a pinwheel. Despite his size, the man was remarkably light on his feet and I tried to remember some of his moves for when it was my turn. The crowd seemed to enjoy it, high-pitched laughter and squeals echoing through the room. Attila soaked it up and he finished with a flourish, ripping his kilt off his body as he bent over and wiggled his ass, allowing his balls to swing between his thighs. The crowd went wild as he sauntered off the stage.

"All right, people, you sound all hot and bothered. Guess you're gonna need some cooling off. Say hello to Firehose!"

The next guy to get on stage wore a fireman's outfit complete with red suspenders and a helmet, but he moved with a sinuous grace that made my back ache. He used a chair as a pivot point to flip himself over and flash skin, and I thought I'd do the same. If nothing else, it would be a good way to show off my ass with my back to the crowd. Firehose danced to "Hot Hot Hot" and if I'd swung more toward the bisexual side, I would've found him sexy as hell. As it was, I found myself nodding to the salsa beat.

"Woohoo! I'm definitely feelin' hot, hot, hot, right ladies? But we don't want to get too worked up, so let's slow it down a little for The Schlong Ride."

The man in leather with scruff and the northern English accent headed onto the stage to the opening chords of "You Can Leave Your Hat On" and the crowd cheered. He moved with practiced ease in his stipping moves and I watched with my jaw dropping. He was impressive and I hoped I wouldn't disappoint my Madam with my lack of skill. When he ripped off his leather pants, he exposed his white mesh "manties", as Karma had called them. His cock and balls could be glimpsed behind the mesh, along with the crack of his ass, and the crowd roared its approval. He sauntered off stage with his cocky grin still in place.

"All yours, mate." He winked at me as the other guys pounded him on the back with, "Nice job, Friar."

Holy shit, I've been outdanced by a man of the cloth...or lack thereof.

I swallowed hard and grabbed the chair as Sam nodded to me before he headed for the stage to announce me.

"Oh yeah, did you enjoy your long, slow ride, ladies? Well, then, let's pick it up a bit in the "Wild Wild West" with our next guy. He'll take you back to the 90s, but he'll give you an easy ride. Give it up for Deputy Dick."

The drums and cowbell intro started and I sauntered on stage, setting the chair in the center of the space. I kept my back to the crowd and stood with my feet shoulder-width apart, bouncing one heel to the beat. I hadn't danced like this since I was in high school, but most of the moves came back to me. Of course, I'd never stripped while dancing, but I figured it wouldn't take much to modify the moves.

When the voice started, I spun around and swayed my hips, undulating my body as I skipped my feet across the stage. I looked out into the crowd, searching for Karma. She sat to one side with a smile curling her lips. I winked at her and rocked my hips, mimicking the motions of sex as I opened each button on my shirt. I yanked the tails out of my belted jeans and showed off my abs to the crowd. They cheered at the view and I worked the shirt over my shoulders, leaning back with my hips thrust forward.

I moseyed over to straddle the chair with my back to the crowd and pulled the shirt off, looking over my right shoulder with a grin. It was stupid and silly as hell, but the cheers and squeals of the people in the audience made me feel good and egged me on. I tossed the shirt to the side, relieved I no longer wore the tin star, and stood up, presenting my ass to the audience. I used the back of the chair to support my upper body as I wriggled a bit then dismounted like getting off a horse. It wasn't as smooth as Friar, but the crowd didn't seem to mind.

I strutted across the stage, unbuckling my belt. It didn't have a big cowboy buckle on it, but the act of pulling it out of the loops seemed to electrify the audience. I glanced toward Karma as I tossed the belt after the shirt. A big grin split her face and she cheered along with the rest. Her pleasure made my chest puff up and I strutted my stuff a little harder to the beat of the song.

In the end I damn near put my back out when I bent over and tried to rip the jeans off. I'd done everything Sam showed me to get them ready for the big rip, but they resisted my initial jerk. I had to roll over and do a full body plank, face up, to get the damn things to start the Velcro to release.

The only saving grace came when I rolled up onto my knees and pulled the jeans off from behind me. They finally split off my thighs and calves, revealing the jewel-toned,

cut-out side manties Karma insisted I wear. Just the thought
of her watching me had my cock filling out the pouch of
them with a decent hardon as I faced the crowd, left leg
bent, right hand on my hip, and left hand holding the crown
of my Stetson on my head.

The song ended and my chest rose and fell like a
bellows along with my abs, but the crowd seemed pleased
with my performance. Karma cheered just has loud and
hard as the rest and my heart damn near burst. I jogged off
the stage, collecting the chair and my clothes as I went.

The next guy after me only came up to my chest in
height and wore a sequined jacket against his dark skin. He
snagged the chair from me and headed out onto the stage as
Sam announced him.

"Damn, ladies, Deputy Dick got me hot and bothered.
I'm gonna need a cold shower. Whew!" Sam wiped his
forehead with the back of his hand and the audience
laughed. "But in the meantime, we got the Pocket Rocket
encouraging you to 'Come and Get Your Love.'"

Say what you want about the little guy, he could move,
and he was sexy as hell. The women in the audience were
very impressed. I laughed as I put my pants back on and
shrugged into my shirt with the tin star. It felt weird to wear
it because it fit me so well even if it was just a costume
accessory. None of the people around me knew how
accurate it was sitting on my chest.

You have to tell Karma the truth.

I bit my lip as Pocket Rocket finished to cheers and
Sam introduced Oriana Hunter's man, Scott, as Kiddie Pool
Shark. I laughed along with the crowd. The name fit him
considering she'd completely skunked him at pool. *Strip
pool.* So he belonged in the kiddie pool.

"Nice job, Coop." The man known as Firehose stepped
up to me and clapped me on the shoulder. "For a spur-or-
the-moment entry, you had some good moves out there.
Name's Torch."

Oddly enough, his praise made me feel pretty damn good. "Thanks. I learned from watching all the rest of you. Your moves were badass."

He snorted and I swear I saw tendrils of smoke rising from his nostrils, though I hadn't seen him smoking any cigarettes. "I've had a lot of practice over the years. Before I joined the Concrete Angels, I was a stripper at clubs all over the world. It was an easy way to make money and keep in shape."

"Didn't you catch a lot of flak for stripping from other guys?" I couldn't imagine my coworkers at the Marshal's Service being all that accepting of my recent endeavors.

Torch shrugged. "You can't stop the haters, you can only figure out how to react to them. I made a helluva lot more money than some schmo whose claim to fame was how many beers he could guzzle in a night and the size of his truck. I got paid and had women dying for sex with me. Don't really see the downside."

I laughed. When he put it like that, I couldn't argue with him. "Yeah, I guess that's a good point."

"If you want, I could show you some easy moves so you can keep up with us for the last number."

I blinked. "Last number?"

"Yeah." He nodded as he put on his firefighter gear again. "The finale is everyone on stage dancing in unison. I could show you a few easy steps to make it look more uniform if you want." He gave me a half smile. "What? Did you think you were gonna be a one-and-done?"

"Yeah, I kinda did." I straightened my Stetson. "Yeah, okay. Show me some easy moves." I just hoped I wouldn't trip over my own feet and knock the other guys down.

****

Karma

I laughed and cheered along with the other people in the audience. Most of us were women, but there were a few men who liked to watch the guys strut their stuff on stage. I knew Loki was pansexual and enjoyed a variety of sexual partners, and I was pretty sure many of the other Concrete Angels weren't stuck in the duality of societal gender bias. *That's because we don't really operate using mainstream society's rules.* And thank the Goddess for that.

Samurai announced that the dancer Hank Hardon would be dancing to our theme song and Flint strutted on stage. I clapped along with the crowd but my mind kept going back to the moves Coop had made. My pussy grew slick and my nipples hardened at the memory of him wiggling his ass to the music. Glory, he'd been hotter than the Mojave in July and I wanted more.

Fortunately, there were only two more strippers with the funny names of Harry Longballs, which turned out to be an accurate description of Gopher's man parts, and Wally Ballbanger, given to Indiana for his honest-to-Goddess gymnastic flips off the walls and chair. But I was waiting for the finale which would bring all the dancers back up to do a coordinated number. How Coop would keep up with the others after not practicing with them at all was a mystery, but I looked forward to it nonetheless.

Indiana sprang off the stage at the end of his show, his cock and balls swinging in the wind with impressive reach. I was sure there were a few of the honeys and the other club members who'd be hitting him up for an "evening ride" that night. Samurai trotted back out to where we could see him, giving the dancers a chance to get back into their outfits before the last number.

"Well, that should get your engines revving, huh? I know I got a little high off Wally's ballbanging dance." The audience laughed but I kept my eyes on the stage behind him. "Now, here it is, the last show before we let you go. Give a round of applause for the Concrete Rockin'

Cocks!"

I roared my approval along with the rest of the crowd as all our makeshift performers came back out and arranged themselves in a pattern where all could be seen from the audience. The lights went out and rotating strobes flashed white light around the room as the first strains of music started.

When a voice started, a spotlight lit each man up individually and I had to hand it to Gadget. The woman knew how to make things magical with a little light and timing. Despite all the sexy man-flesh to look at, my gaze fixed on the hot cowboy and when he raised his head, his gaze zeroed in on mine. My breath caught. There was no way he could see me with the spotlight on him, but he stared at me as if I was the only person he could see.

Maybe that's true. He was mine and I was his. The Goddess had guaranteed it. But some part of me feared this wouldn't be all rainbows and unicorns. Something was coming. Something I hadn't accounted for, and I suspected it would throw all my previous assumptions about love and the Goddess's choice of true mate into the crapper. But I refused to entertain the thoughts and shoved them away to watch my mate dance.

He wasn't as polished as Torch or Friar. Hell, even Hamster, who'd taken the name Pocket Rocket, moved with more confidence, but Coop stole the show for me. He remained in sync with the rest and when he removed his shirt, that tin star flashed in the light like an omen. It momentarily blinded me and made me blink, but when my vision came back, his gorgeous chest captured my attention.

Damn, he's sexy.

I made a mental note to make him strip for me again in the near future. I licked my lips as he spun around and wiggled his ass in those tight jeans. I wondered if Sam had picked a size too small so they'd show off all the muscles in his legs, but it didn't matter. He would've looked good in baggy jeans too.

Their final flourish had all the men ripping their pants off and rocking their hips to the beat. The guys who'd gone commando let their cocks harden, the tips thrusting upwards like spearheads. Coop's brightly colored manties caught my attention more than the naked penises of the others and again, he finished the song with one leg pent and one hand holding his hat to shadow his face. It was sexy as hell.

I launched to my feet and clapped until my arms ached as the guys cleared off the stage with a bounce in their steps (and their balls). Sam wrapped up the show with a final send off, but I was already moving toward the hall outside the theater room to meet up with my hot and sexy cowboy. I was gonna ride him hard and put him away satisfied.

The crowd pretty much had the same idea I did and the hallway filled up with boisterous spectators. Gopher and Hamster came out together, which cracked me up when I thought of their road names, and were immediately surrounded by honeys. Flint stalked out by himself and ignored everyone as he headed for the yard. His expression never changed, but his gaze flicked to me and he nodded once. Evidently, he'd keep an eye on Coop tonight like always.

Attila and the Friar came out together, teasing each other as only a Scot and a Sassenach could. They'd buried the hatchet between them years ago and only ribbed each other good-naturedly. They were followed by Indiana and Scott, though the first man headed for another group of honeys and Scott peeled off to look for his old lady, his expression hungry.

Looks like I'm not the only one getting some tonight.

The hallway had cleared out by the time Coop came out with Torch, the two men laughing like they were old friends. Normally, I'd be suspicious of such behavior from someone who'd only been with the club for a few days, but Torch didn't make friends easily. That he interacted with Coop this way made me relax even more.

"Hey, Cowboy. You up for showin' a girl a good time?" I tilted my head with coy invitation.

Coop bumped knuckles with Torch and they parted ways with mutual appreciation. It warmed my heart that he'd found a friend in the club beyond me.

"Hell yeah, Ma'am. I'm all for showin' you a good time. Do you wanna do it in the clubhouse or somewhere a little more private?"

"Oh, I've shared you enough today. It's time for you to give me a private show, hot man." I trailed my fingers over his chest until I slid them into his open shirt. "Think you can pleasure your woman when no one is watching?"

He raised an eyebrow. "That depends. Did I managed to pleasure my Madam when everyone was watching?"

"Oh, hell yeah, you did." I grabbed his hand and shoved it between my legs so he could feel my panties. "Feel how wet you got me?"

"Holy fuck." He licked his lips and swallowed hard. "Yeah, I feel it, Ma'am. Let me take care of that for you. I promise to make it good."

I laughed a throaty laugh dredged up from my arousal. "Oh, Marshal DeVille, I know you will."

Despite my playful tone, he stiffened and his eyes widened as he searched my face. "What did you call me?"

"Marshal DeVille. You know, because of the tin star you wore in the show." I frowned. "Why? You had the stripper name Deputy Dick but Marshal fits you a lot better."

"Oh." He laughed nervously and rubbed the back of his neck. "Oh yeah. Yeah, I forgot about that. You really think Marshal fits me better than Deputy?"

"Oh yeah. You'd definitely be the one in charge rather than a lowly deputy in town." I leaned into him and took his mouth in a sensual kiss. Glory, he tasted so good, like hot man and sexual desire. "Now, Marshal, take me back to my cabin and make love with me until I scream your name. And if you're a good man, maybe I'll let you ride me like a trick pony."

His eyes gleamed though I sensed a little unease. "Ma'am, you're not a trick pony. You're more of a wild mustang who needs to be gentled rather than broke."

"You think so?" I winked at him as I stepped back and took his hand. "Show me what you've got, Marshal."

"Yes, Ma'am."

To my surprise, he lifted me up into his arms and carried me all the way to my cabin door like the hero from an old Western. The self-assured look on his face mixed with the sexy hat made my nipples harden and I cuddled closer to his chest, enjoying the irony. The Concrete Angels' badass Enforcer played damsel to this hot Colorado cowboy.

I gave him my keys and he opened the door, kicking it shut behind him before he let me down. Then he knelt at my feet and worked at pulling off my ankle boots. I didn't stop him as he skimmed his hands up my thighs until they rested at my hips. But he didn't get to his feet. He just knelt there, looking up at me with adoration and desire.

"May I help you undress, Ma'am?"

The deference in his tone and his patient confidence turned me on more than I expected. I fell deeper in love with him with each moment he waited on my answer. His raging hardon pushed at the front of his jeans, but he looked like he could wait all day on whatever I wanted to do.

"Yes, you may, Coop." He moved to undo my pants but I stilled his hands, waiting for him to meet my gaze again. "You may undress me and pleasure me with a pussy licking tonight, Coop. But before I let you between my legs, I want to see you strip slowly for me, and I want you to hold back long enough to make me come on your face and your cock. Can you do that for me?"

The slow, cocky smile curling his lips damn near curled my toes. "Yes, Ma'am."

I nodded and he resumed his sensual removal of my clothes. He started with my pants, unfastening the button and sliding the zipper down. He licked his lips as he inhaled in front of my open fly but managed to push my pants and panties down to my ankles without doing more than enjoying my aroused scent. He carefully lifted my feet to step out of my clothes then kissed my thighs low enough to not push my instructions.

"Come, Ma'am. Let me pamper you tonight." He pulled my shirt off and moaned in pleasure at the sight of my breasts not held by a bra. "You're gonna kill me, Ma'am. Do you walk around all the time without a bra?"

"Most of the time."

He groaned as he threw his head back. "Damn, I'm gonna be hard all the time knowing you're not wearing one."

"That's good to know." I winked at him as he ran his hands over my skin, the rough calluses on his fingers tightening my nipples even more.

"You're diabolical." He lifted me again and carried me to the bed, setting me down gently. "Now, you wanted me undressed before I lick this pussy, is that right, Ma'am?"

"Yes, that's right." I nodded. "But I want you to leave the hat on. There's something sexy about a man eating pussy hidden by the brim of a nice hat. Gives a whole new meaning to "keeping it under your hat." Get me?"

He threw back his head and laughed as he unbuttoned his shirt and peeled it off his shoulders. "Oh, yes, Ma'am. And I'll definitely be keepin' it under my hat from now on."

I squirmed on the bed at the thought of his tongue on my pussy lips but I enjoyed the sight of him getting naked in front of me. He pulled off his belt and unbuttoned his jeans, but paused before he bent to take off his boots.

"You want the boots to stay on or not, Ma'am?"

"Off, please. The only hard thing I want on your body is your cock."

He grinned. "Yes, Ma'am. I definitely have that covered." He yanked off his boots and jeans, and wrapped a fist around his porn star-sized shaft. My mouth watered with the idea of him sliding that weapon into me, but I wanted his face between my legs more.

"I want you, Coop. Come feast on my pussy. You've earned this reward for being such a great stripper, Marshal."

Again, he stiffened at the title and I wondered why it bothered him so, but he crawled onto the bed and settled on his belly between my legs with a grin.

"You sure you want me to keep my hat on, Ma'am?"

"Oh, yeah. Show me what you got, Coop."

"Yes, Ma'am."

He lowered his head and his breath brushed across my wet nether lips. Just the caress of warmth sent more cream to my pussy as he inhaled deeply.

"Damn, Ma'am. You smell so sweet and juicy. I'm gonna enjoy this." Then he slid the flat of his tongue over my sensitive flesh.

I groaned and tightened my hands in the bedsheets as I glanced down my body. I couldn't see anything around the brim of that sexy hat, but I could feel him tickle my labia with his hot, wet tongue. The erotic sensation of his sensual touches mixed with my inability to see what he was doing turned me on so much. I loved the idea of me sitting at a table somewhere in public with Coop under its tablecloth, eating out my cunt without anyone the wiser. The effects of that hat while he feasted on my pussy were the same.

He laved my pussy lips, working the tip of his tongue between them to stroke the individual folds. Each slide of his hot flesh against mine ratcheted up my arousal, sending sparks of pleasure across my vision. I whimpered and rocked my hips against his mouth as his hands cupped my buttocks.

"Oh, glory, Marshal. Let me ride your face. Lick my pussy so good."

Coop hummed against my flesh as he pulled my clit into his mouth and sucked hard. More sparkles flashed across my vision as pleasure began to build toward my orgasm. Wet, slurping sounds came from between my legs, but his black Stetson hid the sight from me and drove my arousal higher.

I tried to rock my hips harder, but his strong arm slid over my thigh and held me still while the other snaked between my legs, caressing my inner thigh. I wondered what he was up to until he thrust a finger into my aching pussy, making me gasp and moan.

"Oh, glory, that's so good, Marshal. Eat your Madam's cunt."

He hummed his agreement and licked my folds like a kid with a melting ice cream cone. He slurped and groaned and added a second finger into my cunt, massaging my G-spot with pinpoint accuracy. I whimpered and tried to increase the friction of his motions, but he held me down and took his time. The sounds I made had turned into pleading whimpers as I writhed on the bed until I couldn't hold back any longer.

"Sweet glory, Marshal. Make your Madam come. Make me come hard."

He thrust a third finger into my pussy while sucking hard on my clit and my release blew through me, shooting me out into the cosmos of pleasure, the sparkling erotic stars my only company.

He lapped at me, letting me fly for as long as possible and cleaning my release from my pussy and thighs before he looked up at me. I settled back into my body as I watched him languorously lick my cum off his hand and it stoked the fires of arousal again.

"You're so fuckin' gorgeous when you come, Ma'am." He caressed my thigh with his clean hand as he gazed at me. "I could eat you out all day and never get tired of watchin' you hit your release."

"Come up here and kiss me with that mouth." I grinned at him as he moved his body over mine, settling his hips into the cradle of my thighs. "And you can take your hat off now."

He paused long enough to toss the hat into the chair before he leaned down to give me his lips. They were hot and firm and smelled like me. When his tongue slid into my mouth, I dragged mine over it with ravenous intent. Damn I wanted him to fuck me more than I'd wanted anything in a long time. This was my true mate and I needed him inside my body where I could hold him safe and sacred.

I pulled back and looked up at him, making sure I had his complete attention.

"You're mine, Cooper DeVille. You'll always be mine, come hell or high water, and I won't give you up for anything. Do you understand me?"

"Yes, Ma'am."

"Say it. Tell me you're mine."

He swallowed hard, but arousal and yearning flared in his eyes. "I'm yours, Ma'am. I'll always be yours, no matter what." Then he leaned forward and kissed me again as if sealing the deal.

"Very good, Coop. Let's make it more official, shall we?"

He pulled back, his eyebrows raised as I sat up and reached toward the bedside table.

"Open the drawer for me and pull out what's inside."

He snorted and leaned over. I'm pretty sure he thought I was asking for a condom or lube or something of that nature, but he frowned and tilted his head as he pulled out a little elegant velvet pouch.

"Open it."

He pulled open the draw strings and dumped the glittering jewelry into his palm. Sturdy chains with small links connected to a hinged pendant with a dangling pink cultured pearl. He held it up and turned it around in his hands.

"What's this?"

I smiled as I took it from him. "This, my sexy Marshal, is a gift for you from me. It's a sign that you're mine and belong to me. Scoot up here and show me your cock."

"My cock?"

He obeyed, but his eyes widened as I unhooked the chains from the pendant and fitted them around his testicle sac and the base of his shaft.

"See? It fits around your scrotum and penis so it won't impede peeing or a hardon, and it's adjustable to make the perfect fit." I stroked his softening cock and it perked up again. "I want you to wear this as often as possible so I know you're mine. It's a little reminder of who you belong to and who will bring you your pleasure. What do you think?"

He looked down at himself covered in my glittering gift and his cock flexed with his arousal as he glanced up. "You want me to wear this all the time?"

"As much as possible." I nodded. "It's a secret that no one will know except us, and yet it will proclaim you as mine."

I held my breath. It was a big step for me to make this kind of overture toward anyone, and even my favorite jeweler in Fort Collins had raised an eyebrow at the specifications of the piece. But my gut said it was something I needed to do and he looked sexy as hell in the cock jewelry.

Coop raised his gaze to meet mine as he crawled back between my thighs. "I love it and it turns me on, Ma'am.

But are you sure you want me to make love with you in it? I don't want to hurt you."

"Oh, you won't. This was designed with sex in mind, and the pearl is there to stimulate my clit when you thrust." I grinned at his widening smile. "So if you're all right with it, I'd like you wear it always, especially when we make love. Can you do that?"

"Yes, Ma'am."

"Good. Now I want you to ride me, Marshal. I want you to make me come hard around your cock, and I want you to come with me. Do you understand?"

"Yes, Ma'am. Do you want me to ride you slow and easy like a gentle canter or do you want me to ride you hell-bent for leather?" He grinned his amusement with the turns of phrase.

"Tonight, I want you riding me hard, hell-bent for leather, and I want you screaming your Madam's name." I squeezed his hips between my legs. "Come on, Coop. Make me proud."

His deep brown eyes gleamed just before he thrust hard into my pussy, his cock filling me all the way up. We both moaned when he stopped, balls-deep, savoring our connection. I loved the thick, hard intrusion. The hard nub of the pearl pressed against my clit and I knew I wouldn't last long.

"Oh, glory, Ma'am, you're so tight."

I flexed my inner vaginal muscles, rippling them over his shaft and he closed his eyes in pleasure.

"I'm tight for you. Now fuck me hard and keep your eyes on me. I want to see you when you come. I want you to call my name."

"Yes, Ma'am."

He did as I ordered, rocking his hips back and snapping them forward with single-minded intensity. My primal arousal rose with his motions and meeting his gaze had to be the most intimate thing I'd ever done. There was no hiding my emotions or reactions when he stared into my eyes, and I could read his as well. This was my mate, my man, and he wore my jewelry on his cock. Just the thought of that pushed my desire higher.

Pleasure built in a rising wall as he slammed his cock into me, over and over, like rutting stag. It drove my arousal higher. I held his shoulders, digging my fingers into the skin of his deltoids and urging him on with my whimpers.

"I want you, Ma'am. I want you always in my life." He thrust harder and faster, his gaze filling with yearning and a touch of desperation. "I've never felt this way about anyone before, but I need you, Ma'am. Let me stay with you forever, come hell or high water."

"Oh, glory. Yes, Coop. Ride me hard and give yourself to me. Come for me, Marshal." I squeezed down on his cock as my orgasm broke over me.

"Karma!"

He roared out his own release as he thrust into me hard and fast. Hot semen filled my pussy as I rocketed out into ecstasy, his shuttling cock bringing more pleasure with each stroke. It was perfect. It was sudden. And it was so right. Something had shifted since the first time we'd made love. I didn't know what it was, but I felt the change and the deepening of our connection. I was bound to him in ways I hadn't discovered yet, and I suspected it was the same for him.

At last we came back down from our heights of pleasure and he collapsed beside me, pulling me close to his body as he caught his breath. I loved the scent of our combined releases mixing with the heat of our bodies. It was perfect and I never wanted to give it up again. Coop was my true mate, a mate meant to be loved, fucked, and protected. I'd do everything I could to make sure of it and I'd never let him go.

CHAPTER FIFTEEN

Cooper

My phone ringing with George Gershwin's "Rhapsody in Blue" yanked me from sleep and made me open my eyes to the late morning light. I struggled to find coherency as well as consciousness as I rolled over to look for the phone. Karma and I had made love more times than I could recall and my cock and balls were tired, even after sleeping in.

I didn't move fast enough and the phone stopped ringing. I cursed under my breath as I scrambled out of the bed and headed for my jeans, stopping when something dangled over my flaccid cock. I glanced down and caught my breath.

Karma had given me cock jewelry, and it was surprisingly comfortable despite being made from metal and chains. She'd said it was to show I belonged to her and the idea not only turned me on, but brought me a sense of comfort and homecoming I'd been missing in my life.

I glanced back at the bed where my Madam slept in a delicious disarray of sex-mussed hair and relaxed features. My heart swelled with aching love for her and I almost climbed back into bed to gather her into my arms again.

But my body reminded me I'd been in bed long

enough and had to pee as well as take Battlebourne's call. Even if he didn't call back, I'd need to find out what he wanted. I grabbed my jeans as I headed for the bathroom, hoping I wouldn't wake Karma if the phone should ring again. The cock jewelry brushed against my penis and thighs, and the little pearl pendant bounced with each step, reminding me of Karma's ownership.

And how much of an asshole I am.

I sighed as I closed the door behind me and glanced at the mirror. Karma had repeatedly called me Marshal last night and it had reminded me of my deception. I hadn't told her who I really was and now she'd given me the gift of possession and trust. I closed my eyes and sighed as I took care of business. The rattle of the chains around my dick and balls only reminded me of what I hadn't told my Madam and gut-deep unease clattered inside me.

I gotta tell her. Over coffee.

I pulled on my jeans over the cock jewelry and headed out to the kitchenette just as Battlebourne called again. I silenced the phone and closed the bedroom door before I answered the call.

"DeVille."

"Hey, DeVille, how's it going on that vacation of yours?" Gary's voice held forced amusement.

"Uh, good. Good. What's new with you, boss?" I moved into the kitchenette and started working on making coffee for Karma.

"Oh, you know, same-old, same-old." Again, my boss didn't sound like things were going as usual. "Hey, I wanted to know if you have an ETA for getting back at it? A lot of stuff has come up here lately and we need all hands on deck, so-to-speak."

Oh, shit. That had been our catch phrase for when things heated up too much to keep the investigation secret much longer. If Gary was using it, the wolves were closing in and the heat was rising. I thought about what I needed to do before I came back in and bit my lip as I poured water into the coffee maker.

"I'll be back tomorrow."

It killed me to say it, but I couldn't stay hidden in the Concrete Angels forever. I was a U.S. Marshal and I had to get back to work in the real world. I had most of the answers I was looking for with regard to the club's involvement, and I could check them off the list of possible co-conspirators.

But I didn't want to leave Karma to return to my empty life. Until she'd offered me a place as her lover, I'd been living in a gray existence full of just about nothing but the job. And the job had me investigating my coworkers for involvement with a shadow organization. Not a fun place to be. *I don't want to go back.*

"I'll be back home tonight and come in first thing tomorrow morning."

"Great." The false joviality came across the line. "It'll be good to have you back, DeVille. I'll see you tomorrow."

"Yeah, see you tomorrow, boss."

I ended the call and shoved the phone into my back pocket, hating the upcoming conversation with Karma. I hadn't been completely honest with her and she'd offered me everything I could've ever wanted.

I'm the worst kind of asshole.

I ground the coffee and spooned it into the machine, but not even the delicious smell of the brew could shake the unease gripping my gut. Karma was one of the Concrete Angels' Enforcers and she'd do what needed to be done when it came to my deceit. Oriana Hunter had kept her word and hadn't said anything. And I'd tried to explain to Karma.

Until Loki busted in with the strip show thing yesterday.

I bowed my head over the counter and tried to figure out a way to break the news to my Madam. Every way I came up with ended with her telling me to get the fuck out of her life forever. There had to be a way to salvage the new relationship we had despite the dishonest beginnings to it.

I'm going to have to tell her straight out and let the chips fall where they may.

I clenched my jaw and squared my shoulders as the coffee machine dinged with its completion. There wasn't any other way around it. I just hoped I hadn't lost it all before I'd even had a chance to enjoy it.

****

Karma

I woke to the delicious scent of coffee brewing and stretched luxuriously. My body felt as if it had gone through a helluva workout and my pussy ached with sensual use. It had been a long time since I'd felt anything so strong and I reveled in it. Coop was a fantastic lover and my little gift to him made the sex even better. My clit was still sensitive from the rubbing it had gotten from the pearl pendant.

"Hey, Ma'am, I brought you some coffee."

Despite the warmth in Coop's voice, I detected an undercurrent of resignation and sorrow. I frowned as I met his gaze, trying to determine from his expression what could be wrong.

"Everything okay?" I took the coffee and held the mug beneath my nose as I watched him.

Coop nodded and settled on the bed beside me with his own cup, his expression withdrawn. Unease slid through me as I waited for him to say something, but he kept his silence as he sipped the hot beverage. My connection to him told me he was agitated, but I couldn't tell from what it stemmed. He seemed calm enough and his body remained relaxed beside me, but something was off.

"Are you going to tell me what's going on or are you going to make me guess?"

Coop shot me a guilty look and grimaced. "I'm trying to figure out the best way to say it and I'm not impressed with any of the options."

I nodded slowly. I'd been in a few situations like that and it was never fun.

"In my limited experience, it's been better to just come out and say it. Like ripping a bandage off, it's better done quickly." My gut sank. *This is where he tells you he's not into the BDSM lifestyle and you're just too weird for him.*

"Yeah." He snorted. "I don't think that'll improve things this time."

I didn't know what to say to that so I turned my attention to my coffee as the unease increased, fear worming its way through the wonderful feelings I'd woken up with. What had I done to make him wear that expression? I tried to think over everything that had happened the night before and never once did I get the impression he'd been upset by anything. He'd even laughed about the strip show and flaunted his stuff with confidence and good humor.

So what the hell happened this morning?

Before either of us could say anything, someone knocked on the door of my cabin.

"I'll get it. You get dressed and I'll see you out there." He rolled off the bed and out of the room before I could even think to move.

I slid out of the covers and headed to the closet to find clothes. Something about the day suggested I needed my armor around me so I put on jeans, a t-shirt that read "Don't Fuck With the Big Dog" and Anubis on it, and my cut over that. I gathered my hair behind my ears and added pearl drop earrings, a set that matched the cock jewelry I'd given Coop. *Sad irony there when he doesn't want to be with me anymore.*

That hurt more than I was willing to admit and I turned my attention to whoever had come to my door. I heard Coop offering them coffee and stepped out into the living room to see Torch waiting with a steaming cup in his hand.

"Hey, Karma. Loki says we gotta get ready to roll. He wants to go in before anyone but the victims are there." Torch grimaced and took a sip of coffee as if to wash the bad taste out of his mouth.

"Shouldn't we just hand this over to the cops? I'm sure they'd love to bust up a prostitution ring." I sighed as I headed over to the door to grab my boots.

Coop shook his head. "Backlog has the cops in their back pockets. They'd just lose the report or downplay what's really going on. If there's any hope to rescuing the people in that makeshift brothel, we have to hit them ourselves. And if we do it during the work day, there'll be fewer of the Backlog members there to identify us."

I nodded with a grimace. "I take it we'll be killing anyone who's there, right?"

Torch shook his head. "No. I think Loki wants you to do your thing."

My thing. My thing was bringing about their accumulated karmic debt a lot faster. It often ended in the death of the person and I didn't sentence anyone to that very often. It was hard on me and hard on the families of the person experiencing it.

Yeah, and how hard is it on the victims of forced prostitution?

I sighed. This day wasn't going to get much better if all the omens could be believed. Coop sent me a searching glance when I bowed my head over my boots.

"Okay. Let's get a handle on what's really going on and we'll see how much of my thing I'll have to do. Are we leaving right away?"

Torch nodded, sympathy in his gaze. "Unless Michael

says otherwise, that's the plan."

"Okay. We'll be right out."

Torch shot a look at Coop but nodded again before stepping out. I raised my gaze to the man I'd fallen for and hoped I hadn't made a mistake that would cost me more than my usual disappointment. *Who am I kidding? It's gonna hurt a helluva lot worse.* Coop was my true mate and if he ran from me, I was screwed six ways from breakfast.

"I'm gonna get dressed."

Before I could say anything more, he'd ducked back into the bedroom. I nodded though he couldn't see me and headed for the locked weapons chest behind the loveseat. I put it there to keep it out of sight while still remaining accessible. Opening the combination lock, I took a deep breath and lifted the lid.

Rows of gleaming knives lay in black foam and two small derringer pistols went into my shoulder and ankle holsters under my clothes. More than likely I wouldn't need any of them, but as the Enforcer, I might be required to remind people what I did when the chips were down. I closed the lid and locked up the chest just as Coop returned to the main room.

"Ready?" He eyed my position in the room but didn't ask anything else.

"I am. Are you planning to come with us?"

He nodded. "I want to get pics of what was being done and any of the players. It'll help the investigation." He hesitated. "Should I ride with you or take my car?"

"You can ride with me. A lot less conspicuous if you're on a bike rather than a car." I headed for the door and held it open.

"Yeah, okay." He followed me out and I locked the door of the cabin.

"Hey, are you okay?"

"Yeah. You know, just still trying to figure out how to tell you that thing." He stopped, chewing on his lower lip.

"Karma—"

"Hey, Karma. Let's scratch gravel!" Michael's voice conveyed the urgency and I headed for my bike in the barn.

"Yeah, I'm coming!" I shot a look at Coop. "Can this wait until after we get back? We gotta go."

"Dammit, this is important." He trailed after me, unease pulling the corners of his mouth down.

"Yeah, I get that, but I don't have time to concentrate on it right now." I straddled my bike and turned the key, feeling the rev of the powerful engine between my legs. *Not unlike Coop's cock.* The thought made my smile. "Jump on or follow along."

"Karma."

I sighed and looked back at him. "What?"

"No matter what happens, I love you."

I frowned despite the fluttering excitement that bubbled up at his words. *He loves me!* "Great. We'll talk about it more when we get back."

His lips moved as he swore up a blue streak I couldn't hear over the roar of the bike engines and darted toward his car. Part of me clenched in disappointment that I wouldn't feel his arms around my waist and his chest against my back, especially after his declaration.

He loves me!

But I forced myself to focus on something else now. The scooters held the gates open for us to roar through and Scott said he'd hold down the fort with Numbers while we did the work. Michael drove our van just in case there would be victims to transport.

I got a sick feeling in my gut. If there were victims, there'd be hell to pay, and I planned to cash in everyone's karmic debt. I hardened my expression and followed the rest my crew onto the road.

CHAPTER SIXTEEN

Cooper

I didn't have much time to get into my car and follow the Concrete Angels out of their compound. I yanked open the door of my Toyota and slid behind the wheel, cranking the engine. I wanted to check if my Glock was still in the lockbox under the passenger seat, but I didn't have time. I shoved the car into reverse and spun out of my parking spot before throwing it in gear and peeling out after the crew.

My heart pounded as we headed down into Fort Collins. This could get ugly fast, though I suspected the Concrete Angels would avoid violence if they could. But the huge chest behind the loveseat in Karma's cabin gave me pause. It was chock full of weapons and she appeared to be proficient with all the ones she pulled out of it.

She's an Enforcer. She does what needs to be done.

My gut sank at the thought as I followed the bikers into the industrial portion of the small city. We skirted the warehouse I'd seen in the photos and parked behind one of the other derelict buildings nearby. Despite being the middle of the day, the streets remained relatively empty and I suspected the cops didn't make regular trips to that part of town.

Despite the loud engines on the bikes, no one seemed to notice our arrival. I grabbed my Glock and checked to see if it was loaded. I had a full magazine. I took a deep breath, wishing I could wear my vest, but it had big yellow letters screaming "US MARSHALS" on it. Not exactly the way I wanted to tell Karma. I shoved the gun into my waistband at my back and locked the car.

The Concrete Angels fanned out around the warehouse and I joined the group going in the front. Attila took another bunch to the back entrances and Loki led the crew in the front. I followed along, keeping my head down and my steps silent. I left the gun at my back, hoping I wouldn't need it. *Please, Goddess, make it just be the victims, not the johns or pimps.*

Loki counted down to three on his fingers before pulling open the warehouse door and slipping inside. Someone had oiled the hinges into silence so no one could hear our entrance and I thanked our lucky stars. We surprised the first guard wearing an old Uzi, the Friar grabbing the guy from behind and cutting off his airway. Despite the manic expression on Friar's face, he let the guard down gently. Dollhouse came behind him and used zipties to secure his hands and feet.

The warehouse had been partitioned in to several rooms, though none of them were soundproofed. I could imagine this place on a Friday night. Men and women grunting as they fucked the unwilling whores. I swallowed against bile and brought out my phone, documenting everything I could see, including the downed guard.

Turns out we'd come in the back way, through the "rooms" for fucking. All but one were empty. The one occupied room had another guard pumping into someone underneath him, his white, hairy buttocks flashing with each thrust. The person under him was too small to see from behind, but they made high pitched, painful grunts as if each intrusion hurt. My lips pulled back from my teeth and I swallowed my snarl as I moved to yank the guy away.

"Hey, what the fuck!"

He tried to throw me off, but I slammed my knee into his wilting cock and balls, before I decked him to the floor. Gopher moved in, his face more serious and focused than I'd ever seen it, and he bound the guy's limbs. I turned to see who he'd been fucking and almost threw up.

The girl on the floor couldn't have been more than sixteen, her body bruised and emaciated. She'd rolled up into a ball and scooted to the back of the pallet on the floor, her eyes wide and wary.

"It's all right. We're here to help." I crouched at the other end of the pallet with my hands out.

"You don't look like cops."

Her voice was low and scratchy, like she'd been sick or coughing. I smiled and shook my head. "Not cops, just concerned citizens."

She didn't look convinced but I wasn't about to give her the 411. "Are there more guards?"

"Why?"

I raised my eyebrows. "Why what?"

"Why are you really here?"

"We're here to put a stop to this." Karma appeared over my shoulder and the girl's gaze shifted upwards. "We'll make sure you get home after this, but we need to know how many guards we're likely to meet. Can you tell us?"

She took her time considering and I gritted my teeth against the urge to shake her.

"There are five or six guys who watch us all the time. Sometimes they use us when they think no one is looking."

Karma growled and I concurred. "Okay, stay here. This is Dollhouse. She'll be hanging out with you." The smaller woman stepped in the room and handed me the zipties as we shifted out of the nasty room.

Holy fuck, Backlog is gonna pay for this. Hopkins and

Eisenburg had been siphoning money into this enterprise and it made me want to kill them all over again. I knew they were into all sorts of shitty things, but underage prostitution sickened me. Decorated FBI agents, my ass. I photographed the room, making sure I never got the girl's face, and followed Karma deeper into the warehouse.

From what I could tell, it had been split roughly in half, with the rooms and kitchen in the back, and the greeting area and a prison cell in the front. All the people the Backlog had kidnapped or captured were in a large cage near the front entrance behind one last partition. *Oh, look, they made a foyer for their coats and boots.* And possibly weapons.

The cage sat to our right and held about thirty people ranging in age from about ten years old to somewhere in the late twenties, male and female. The wary and solemn expressions on the victims told me they didn't trust this new influx of armed people anymore than they did their jailers. I couldn't blame them as I snapped more pictures.

Shouts and gunshots erupted in the foyer as the guards realized something was wrong. Karma darted past ratty old couches and chairs in the open space just as the guards boiled into the main room. And that's when the shit hit the fan and broke it.

Her face solidified into an otherworldly mask of anger and intensity, her skin turning reddish in the dim light of the warehouse windows. She threw out her hands at the guards, tossing knives at them without looking, as the other Concrete Angels swarmed into the space.

But I was looking, and those damn knives curved mid-air to strike at the guards' most vulnerable spots, even when they ducked. One guy caught one in the neck, right over the jugular vein. He yanked it out and dropped like a stone, his blood sheeting across the floor. Another guy miraculously missed her knife but his foot caught the strap of his automatic rifle, tipping the muzzle upwards, and he ended up shooting himself in the head.

Karma spun and caught a guy at the throat, lifting him off the ground with one hand. My Madam wasn't a very large woman, but she held this guy like he weighed no more than a sack of leaves cleared from the garden. He struggled and writhed, clutching at her hand with both of his as his eyes bulged, but she just kept squeezing until his eyes rolled up and he went limp in her grip. Then she dropped him and kicked him out of her way.

Holy shit.

I stepped to the side as the rest of the clubmembers took over. I hadn't taken any images of Karma doling out justice, but my knees shook along with my hands. What the hell had I just seen? There had to be some sort of scientific explanation for what I'd seen her do, but nothing in my experience came close to making sense.

"Oy, Coop, are you gonna take your shots?" Friar waved a hand in front of my face and I blinked up at him.

"Uh, yeah. Yeah. Right." I nodded as I clicked my phone, but my mind wasn't on the mess of the warehouse.

Something's wrong with Karma. That's the only coherent thought I had as I photographed the cage of people and the conditions of the make-shift brothel. Michael shot me worried looks periodically as he organized moving the victims from the cage and into groups. Another biker, Nightingale, checked over all the people in the cage with careful attention, offering first aid and medicines to get them stabilized before they were taken to a shelter.

I photographed what I could and had almost finished when Loki sauntered up to me, his expression unusually grave.

"This place is an abomination." Anger coursed through his voice and I was glad it wasn't directed at me.

"Yeah, it is." I zipped up all the photos on my phone and sent them to a secure folder in Dropbox where Battlebourne could get to them should anything happen to me. "Hey, Loki. What the hell was going on with Karma? I swear I saw shit that doesn't make sense."

Loki snorted and shot me a half-smile with no humor in it. "What doesn't make sense to you, Marshal? That she came in here and killed some of these dritmongers or that these dritmongers would do such a thing to other humans?"

"Both, honestly, but did you see what she did with the knives? They curved mid-air. And she didn't look...normal." I swallowed hard, my words sounding crazy when said aloud.

Loki barked a laugh. "By normal, you mean 'human,' *ja*?" His eyes twinkled as he grinned. "That's because she's not human, Marshal Cooper DeVille." When I widened my eyes, he nodded. "Oh, *ja*, I know who you really are. I've known for a long time. Shall I tell you a secret? Karma *is* karma, the energy of retribution. I tempted her into a physical body to give her a taste of what it's like to be amongst those she affects. Now she's here and you love her, right? *Det er bra*, Marshal."

Then he sobered and an odd golden light shone at the backs of his eyes, like a hunting cat at night. "Don't fuck this up, man. You've been given a chance of a lifetime and you don't want to miss it. Got me?"

"Let me guess. If I do fuck it up, you'll kill me." I shot him a dry look.

"Oh, no, man. Not me." He turned and nodded back toward Karma where she helped the girl we'd found in the room toward the entrance of the warehouse. "She will. Energy of retribution and consequence. Remember?"

He clapped me on the shoulder and strode away, taking my confidence and reality with him.

****

Cooper

The rest of the clean up and dismantling of the make-shift brothel happened faster than I thought possible. Nightingale triaged all the people forced into prostitution, some of them so young I could barely keep my breakfast down. She led them out to where Michael waited with the van to take them to the shelters Numbers had suggested.

I stood back out of the way, only helping when someone needed some brut strength. In addition to the victims, we found caches of alcohol and drugs, some prescription strength, meant to keep the whores pliable. Attila had scowled and asked Torch to destroy it all. The big green-eyed biker grinned and took the contraband out to the parking lot behind the warehouse to set it ablaze.

All the while I kept my eyes on Karma and Loki. Both of them appeared normal now, but the idea that she wasn't human set my teeth on edge.

And you didn't tell her the truth about who you are.

Yeah, there was that, too. And after what I'd seen her do to the guys in the warehouse, I didn't think it would go easy between us.

"Fuck."

"What's wrong, Marshal?" Torch appeared next to me and I jumped. Where the hell had he come from?

I rubbed the back of my neck and glanced around. He was the only one near me as we finished the cleanup.

"You ever have one of those moments when you realize you've screwed up so badly there might not be any way of coming back from it?"

His gaze sharpened on mine and my gut dropped. *Oh shit, he's not human anymore than Loki or Karma.* But a grimace ruined the otherworldly effect and he nodded.

"Yeah. Been there, done that, got the t-shirt. Why? What did you do?"

I scowled. "It's more what I didn't do and it's gonna bite me in the ass so bad I might forget how to walk."

"Hellwinds." He shook his head as he glanced toward

Karma. "Does this have to do with your relationship with Karma?"

"Yeah."

He hissed a breath and it sounded just like the vicious warning of a dragon. It unnerved the daylights outta me. Smoke even rose from his nostrils for a moment.

"Here's the thing, Coop. Karma has my respect and loyalty. It's a Concrete Angels thing." Torch met my gaze and his eyes shimmered with peacock green sparkles. "But I like you and I think you're an honorable man. When you finally get the balls to tell her whatever it is, you won't lose my respect or my friendship. And I'll back you up if I can." He paused and tilted his head. "Is this about you being a U.S. Marshal undercover?"

"Fuck!" I gaped at him. "How the hell do you know that?"

"I heard you talking to Loki. I got damn good hearing." Torch gave me a smug smile.

"And you're okay with it?" I narrowed my eyes.

"Yeah. I'm not sleeping with you, so it's not that big a deal. You could've just asked us if we were involved with Backlog."

"Oh, right. That's exactly how undercover investigations work. You just come right out and ask and the people you're investigating are totally open and honest about things." I shot him a dry look before I sighed. "The good news is I figured out pretty fast you weren't working with Backlog. But I don't know if that'll save my ass with Karma."

"Yeah, no, probably not." He clapped me on the shoulder. "I totally get why you didn't say anything. But you should've said something before you slept with her."

I should've said something before I fell for her.

"Good luck, Marshal. You're gonna need it." He shot me a sympathetic glance before he strode off to finish the clean up of the warehouse. I took one last look around before I headed back to my car, wondering how the hell I was going to tell Karma who I really was. I still didn't know.

But one thing I did know. I truly loved her and I meant it when I told her. The question was if it would matter after she found out my profession. I scrubbed my face as the world lit up with a huge *whoosh* and heat blasted past me. I jerked around to see flames licking the sky from behind the warehouse just as the rest of the Concrete Angels came out to their bikes.

"What the fuck was that?" I yelled the words to Attila as he jogged up.

"Och, just Torch gettin' rid of the contraband and the bodies." He shrugged as he swung his leg over his bike. "It'll get the pigs' attention and bring 'em here to check things out. We'd best be well away by then, aye?"

"Damn. Yeah, I'd say so."

I slid into my car and started it, waiting for the rest of the club to head out. Karma strode out and shot a look toward me, but she didn't hesitate to climb on her bike and start it up. I swallowed hard as I remembered what Loki told me. *Karma is karma, the energy of retribution.* I'd always known this job was going to be full of bad karma, but I hadn't thought I'd be the one cultivating it. I'd just been trying to find the bad guys. Unfortunately, I'd hurt people along the way, and there was more than a good chance it would hurt me back, tenfold.

My phone rang with Rhapsody in Blue as we drove back to the compound and I hit speaker phone. "Yeah, DeVille."

"Holy shit, DeVille, what the hell did you upload there?"

"A make-shift brothel, deep in the sex trade, and funded by the organization via Hopkins and Eisenburg."

"Dammit. You're sure? You got evidence?"

"Yeah, and I got a list of all the people Eisenburg

190

knew were working for the organization. At least in the
FBI, local PDs, and ATF. There are even three from our
office, but there might be more. He didn't have contact
with the Marshals as much."

"Nice. Okay, you're really comin' back tomorrow?"

I sighed. The last thing I wanted to do was bug out
after this discovery, but there was no help for it.

"Yeah, I'll be back tomorrow. Maybe some of the
people on the list will lead us to the rest of our own moles.
I just gotta finish one thing and then I'm out."

"Good. Then I'll see you tomorrow. Good work."

"Thanks, boss. Later."

I knew I'd done the right thing in this investigation, but
I still felt like shit and it didn't ease when I pulled in
through the gates of the compound behind the bikes. I
parked in my usual space behind the barn and girded my
loins for the coming conversation. *Hopefully she won't kick
the shit out of me. Literally.* Karma scared me in more ways
than one. But in particular, I was scared I'd lose her over
this one detail. *Yeah, the most important detail.* She'd said
BDSM was all about trust, and I'd violated hers.

I got out of the car, locking behind me as I headed for
her cabin. *Lucky number thirteen.* I found the door open as
if she expected me to walk right in.

"Karma, Ma'am? May I come in?" I stood outside the
door, my shoulder blades prickling with unease.

"Yes."

Her answer was short and her voice sounded angry. I
swallowed hard and pushed the door open so I could step
across the threshold. Karma stood in the middle of the
living room with my duffle bag at her feet. She held
something in her hand, the knuckles turning white from the
strength she exerted on the object. I met her gaze, reading
anger and betrayal on her face before I dropped my gaze to
what she held.

Oh fuck.

"I found your 'tin star,' Marshal." She held up the gold star in the leather wallet that had been tucked away inside the duffle. "Is this real? Are you really a cop?"

How the hell did she find that? I didn't leave that lying around, not while undercover. Must have been bad luck. *Or bad karma.*

"Sort of. Karma—"

"Sort of? What the hell does that mean?"

"It means I was trying to tell you last night and again before the raid. It means that I never meant to hurt you. It means that I was conducting an investigation of Backlog and how deeply they've compromised every law enforcement agency in the US." I stopped and rubbed the back of my neck.

"Which one, Coop?"

"What?" I raised my eyebrows.

"Which law enforcement agency are you from?" She waved my badge at me.

I sighed. "The U.S. Marshals."

She barked a laugh that sounded more like a sob, and tossed the badge into the open duffle bag. "Perfect. Just fuckin' perfect. You gave me all the clues, I was just too arrogantly blind to see them. Hell, even Samurai gave hints of who you were at the strip show." She kicked the duffle to me. "Take it."

"Karma—"

"Take it and get out." She pointed at the door behind me and my gut sank.

"Ma'am, please—"

"Get. Out. Of. My. Space." She advanced on me and I got another glimpse of her wicked 'death angel' appearance that I'd seen at the warehouse.

I grabbed the duffle and backed out of her cabin into the yard. She followed, her expression thunderous and I had serious doubts about whether I'd make it out of the compound alive. She slammed her cabin door shut and kept advancing, driving me toward my car. The other members of the Concrete Angels paused what they were doing to watch the unfolding drama. It made me grit my teeth and stop.

"Wait, Karma. Hear me out." I dropped the duffle at my feet and held up my hands. "Please. I should've told you long before today. Hell, I tried to tell you last night. That's no excuse. It is what it is, and I can't change it now. I should've made more effort and when we started this, I didn't know you. But I know you now and I'm not hiding anymore."

"Oh, I can see that, Marshal DeVille." She stopped in front of me, her eyes glittering. "And now I know who you are." She smiled, dark secrets in her eyes, and I shivered. "The question is, do you know who I am?"

I licked my lips and swallowed hard. If anyone had asked me two weeks ago if I believed karma existed, I would've agreed to the abstract concept of retribution for actions rendered. But after what I'd seen today with the men in the warehouse who'd lied, cheated, and killed just to make a little money, I realized Karma was *the* karma, just as Loki had said.

And I've fallen in love with her.

That might have been the most unsettling idea of all. I'd always believed in karma, I just hadn't counted on an actual being. But I'd made love with her, laughed with her, danced for her. She watched me with those wise and unusual eyes, waiting for my response, and I wondered what my future would hold, what kind of karma I'd accrued based on my actions.

And on my lies.

I wanted to say they weren't actual lies, just omissions of the truth. But that equated to splitting hairs. I'd lied to the Concrete Angels about what I did, and I'd lied to Karma about why I was in the area above Fort Collins.

"I need to tell you something, and I'm afraid it's gonna

193

piss you off." I wanted to grab her hands to keep her from walking away from me—or me from her—but I tightened mine into fists. "I wasn't honest when I first talked to you at the lake." I rubbed the back of my neck. Why was it so hard to come clean? "As I told you, I didn't just stumble across you at the gas station. I followed you there."

She'd lost her smile and slid into her stoic, inhuman mask. She hadn't gone all 'death angel' on me yet, which I counted as a damn good thing, but she wasn't all warm and human-looking either. My heart rate sped up.

"So the full truth is I'm a U.S. Marshal investigating the disappearance of FBI Agents Dirk Hopkins and Arnold Eisenburg. The last report we had, they'd been here with the Concrete Angels, so I needed to get into the compound to find out what part you all played in their disappearances and their actions with Backlog."

Karma raised her chin. "Dirk Hopkins left here without a scratch on him. He was alive the last we saw him. As for Arnold Eisenburg, I have nothing to say about him."

What I saw in her gaze made my blood go cold. She was telling the truth. She wouldn't say how Eiseburg died, but she knew something about it.

I nodded slowly, aware of the fine line I was walking. "Hopkins and Eisenburg were subjects of my investigation, not just because they died in suspicious circumstances. But also because they were members Backlog."

"I know this, Coop. What's your point?" She tilted her head and anger glittered in her eyes.

I grimaced. "The point is, I came up here to find out if the Concrete Angels were working with Backlog. In that time, I've figured out that the club was being used."

She narrowed her eyes. "Are you telling me this because you don't like lying to me, or because you don't want bad karma to come to you?"

CHAPTER SEVENTEEN

Karma

The question hung there between us and Coop opened his mouth to say something. But he closed it again without a word and my heart contracted with his silence. Pain, anger, and fear flooded my system as my gut sank. My breathing grew labored as the emotions rose to choke me. This was my true mate, and his only fear consisted of consequences from his actions, not from hurting me.

"Both."

I tried to take solace in his answer, but I'd gotten to know him pretty well over the last few days and knew when he hedged his bets. There was more to his answer than he was saying, but I couldn't tell which direction he leaned.

"And what have you concluded from your investigation while pretending to care about me?" My voice came out cold and hard, and my hands tightened into fists.

"Let me address all the issues in your question before you cut me or my balls off." He swallowed hard and met my gaze. "I suspected that the Concrete Angels had a hand in killing Arnold Eisenburg, aka Roy, but I can't prove it. I know he didn't die in the wild fire, but that just shows he

195

was killed and dumped. Not by whom."

I tilted my head and raised an eyebrow, waiting for him to save his ass or die trying.

"I can't show any evidence to support a connection between the Concrete Angels and the death of Agent Dirk Hopkins. None of your members, not even your nomad Luke Everfall, were present in Searchlight, Nevada around the time of Hopkins' death, and whatever killed him aged him damn near beyond recognition. The ME said he was a mummy when they found him, but the last time he was seen on camera was in a Vegas casino. There's no way that kind of desiccation happens by natural causes."

Of course, he wouldn't find evidence for Hopkins. Karma didn't work like that. Retribution came, but not necessarily from those Hopkins had wronged. We'd made sure of it, especially by having his body dumped down a 400-foot mine shaft by a contractor. As for what killed him, I didn't know that. Loki said he'd take care of the means, I just helped by upping the timeline.

"I also found out that Backlog was using you through Roy to siphon money from your endeavors straight into their coffers, and using your contacts to make sure their agenda was promoted and achieved." He dipped his chin to show his earnestness. "The Concrete Angels weren't collaborating or colluding with the Backlog. Any apparent collusion occurred because of proximity, not a direct contract.

"Hell, Roy was even siphoning money from the FBI with help from Dirk Hopkins, but both of them were doing Backlog's dirty work."

Anger kindled in me over Roy's betrayal, but I calmed myself with the knowledge that he'd received his dose of karma and the matter was settled.

And that's not really what's pissing you off. No, what really pissed me off was my true mate was an undercover U.S. Marshal and I'd only met him because he hoped to indict my club for murder.

Coop stopped and licked his lips. "And I never pretended to care about you, Karma. I always did. I knew from the moment I met you, you were someone special and magical, I just didn't understand how magical. I never hid my feelings for you and I never intended to lead you on or hurt you."

"No?" Anger shivered off of me and I shook with trying to contain it. If I got too angry, people were made to pay for their actions a helluva lot faster and harsher than necessary, and I ended up exhausted for days. "Instead you just fucked me while you milked me and my friends for information. And you weren't honest with me about it. How the fuck am I supposed to trust you ever again, Coop?"

I stopped and widened my eyes. "Wait, is that even your name? Or is that your carefully constructed alias, meant to distract and deflect?"

"Cooper DeVille is my name. The story I told you about Rosé was true." Pain tightened his lips and the skin around his eyes. "And I told you I was an investigator."

"You said you were a private investigator, not a U.S. Marshal. You said you'd help find the money stolen from us, but you did it to uncover our complicity with Backlog. You said you loved me…" I trailed off as the cold reality hit home. "Given your previous half-truths and outright lies, why should I believe you?"

"Oh, glory, Karma." He took a step toward me but I kept the distance equal by taking a step back. The wounded look on his face pierced my chest, but this was his fuck-up, not mine. "I'm shit with words. My ex always told me that, but I'm also shit at hiding my true feelings. My boss told me that. I fell for you the moment I met you, I just hadn't recognized it for what it was, which is why it took me so long to verbalize it. I loved you then, I love you now. I'll love you forever."

"Stop." The pain and agony his words extracted from me felt like torture. "Stop. Those are just pretty words. You don't mean them. Because if you meant them, you wouldn't have lied to me, hidden who you are. You would've come clean."

"I *am* coming clean. I'm telling you now."

I shook my head and tears slid down my cheeks. I had no idea I could cry, but apparently that came with the physical body.

"You're only telling me because Loki and Torch figured out who you really are. You wouldn't have ever told me as long as your cover story held up." My breath caught in my chest as sobs robbed me of clear speech. "You would've lied to me forever…just…so…you could…keep…fucking…me."

"No, Ma'am, I was trying to tell you…"

I shook my head and backed farther away. "Get away from me. Get…out of…here and leave…me…alone."

Sweet glory, I'd never hurt this badly. I'd lived a long time in this form, but I'd never felt that kind of agony. I'd had gunshot wounds and been stabbed, but the new pain took those and multiplied them a thousand times until the betrayal equated to someone jabbing needles into every joint in my body.

"Karma, wait…"

I couldn't look at Coop and see his anguished face. I couldn't take that he hurt, too, because someone had to pay for this loss and action. Someone had to reap the consequences and experience the karma from it, and I'd paid with my heart. A very human heart despite my inhumanity.

I shook my head and turned, bolting for my cabin. The other Angels had gathered to watch our confrontation and I slammed into Torch and Viper, stumbling hard enough to knock them back a few steps.

"Karma, honey…" Viper tried to catch me.

I broke free and headed for my sanctuary, trying to find a place to retreat and hide from the pain. So much for the big, badass Enforcer. Coop called my name again but I didn't look back as I fumbled to get my keys in the door. It took me three tries and one bloodcurdling scream of frustration before the door opened and I spilled into the dark interior.

I tried to catch my breath and stop the sobs raking my body, but the more I forced myself to calm, the harder the emotions whipped through me. I couldn't find reason or serenity, and I couldn't find solace. I scrambled to the bedroom and grabbed a pillow to muffle my wails. But it smelled like him, my true mate, and there was no holding anything back.

****

Cooper

Oh, that went well.

I couldn't have fucked up any more than if I'd tried. I should've made the effort to tell Karma even when Loki interrupted us. I should've tried again that morning. I stood in the middle of the yard with my duffle at my feet and my heart bleeding out inside my chest as Karma walked away. I watched her fumble to get into her cabin and I wanted to help, but the forbidding faces of the other clubmembers made me hold my ground.

I shifted my gaze to them and met a wall of anger, disgust, and hostility. The woman beside Torch looked like she'd flay me alive. Torch, though, gave me a look of sorrow and compassion. Why he thought I was worth his sympathy, I had no idea, but at least he didn't outright hate me.

I shook my head and picked up my duffle, turning to walk to my car. Out of nowhere, a tall, feminine body hit me and shoved me against the vehicle, anger in every one of her movements. I rolled with it and braced for impact again until I recognized Oriana Hunter's angry face.

"What the fuck, DeVille? I told you to tell her. I told you not to hurt her."

I wanted to spit in her face and defend myself, but there wasn't anything I could say that would change the present. Instead, I nodded.

"Yeah, you did." I gestured back to the yard behind her. "And you saw. I told her. But it doesn't matter now. She knows who I am and so do the rest of you. But for what it's worth, I'm glad I helped you find your money and I'm glad I came here." I paused and met her hazel gaze. "Take care of her for me, will you?"

"Better than you."

I nodded again, taking the venom in her voice as my due. "Yeah, I suspect you will."

I turned away and got into the car, closing the door behind me without another word. There wasn't anything I could say that would repair the damage I'd done. I started the car and backed out, heading for the gate. No one tried to stop me or shoot me, for which I'd always be grateful. Even Gopher wore a look of sad disappointment rather than disgust. I counted that as a good thing.

I drove out of the compound and the gate closed behind me, locking Karma away from me with a finality my heart couldn't take. I'd resume my life as Marshal Cooper DeVille and I'd turn my attention to taking down Backlog. But my heart screamed its agony the farther I drove from the Concrete Angels, and tears overwhelmed my eyes, sliding down my cheeks to soak my shirt. I didn't cry often, but it hurt bad enough to override my stoicism.

So this is what it's like to have loved and lost. Lucky me. I squared my shoulders and drove home, hoping the investigation would help distract me from the damage I'd done.

CHAPTER EIGHTEEN

Karma

It took me a few days to come out of my cabin, and even then it was because my physical body actually needed to eat. I'd survived on coffee and tea, but I'd grown shaky and needed sustenance to continue living.

Why exactly do I need to go on living?

With the pain so overwhelming, I considered using up all my life years and fading back into the nebulous energy of consequences that was my true self. I'd never felt pain until I got the physical body and at the moment, it seemed like a much better option than the agony and betrayal hounding me.

I struggled to leave my cabin, but I couldn't hide forever. Someone would come looking for me and force me back into the world of the living. *I just wish it would be Coop who comes looking.* Except he was a liar, only here to get information out of me and the others. Anger flared again and I damn near sagged against the doors of the clubhouse. Instead, I pressed my hand against my gut and pushed through. I'd somehow survive because my body stubbornly refused to die.

It was midday according the clock over the bar and not

many people were in the clubhouse. I had no idea what day it was or what all the club had planned, but it seemed remarkably deserted. Grub had set lunch out and he'd made something fancy I didn't even know the name to. I served it onto a plate and sat down at one of the empty tables, trying to find interest in eating.

My mind ran around in angry little circles as I stuffed the food in my mouth, but I couldn't taste a damn thing. Thank goodness none of the foodie members of our club were nearby. *And Goddess help us if Grub finds out.*

I don't know how long I sat there trying to choke down the food before I noticed someone standing near the table. I only realized they were there because smoke drifted past my face, smelling of charred meat and molten rock.

I glanced up and met Torch's peacock green gaze. "Hey Torch, what's up?"

"Mind if I join you? I didn't want to get my ass handed to me, karmically speaking." He gestured to a chair at the table and I nodded. He sat down, his gaze narrowing. "Thanks. How are you doing?"

I didn't bother to answer as I shoved more food into my mouth. I hadn't showered in at least two days, I still wore the same clothes, and I'd barely slept.

"How do you think I'm doing?"

"I suspect you feel like ground up dog shit with a side of death warmed over. You pretty much look like that." His voice held banked amusement, but I sensed concern underneath.

"Thanks."

"He tried to tell you who he was."

Pain rose up in my chest, damn near choking off my breath. "I don't want to talk about it."

He nodded. "I know. But I gotta tell you I think he was good for you."

This time I did choke. "You think a deceitful liar is good for me?"

"Cooper DeVille isn't a liar, Karma. That's just your anger talking." Torch sat back in his chair. "He was an undercover cop trying to get answers and he hadn't intended to get close to anyone. Then he met you and the parameters of his investigation changed. He just couldn't switch gears fast enough."

"He is a liar, Torch. He could've told me the truth."

"And then what? How would you have reacted when he did that?"

I stared at him sullenly, not liking the answers to that question.

"Not good enough? Okay, how about this." He crossed his arms over his chest. "What would you have done in his shoes? Same situation, but you're the one investigating and you found a man you wanted above all others."

"I would've finished my investigation and gotten out so I could connect with him when I could be honest."

"Bullshit. You would've done exactly as he did. Okay, sure, you might have told him who you were a day earlier, but you'd enjoy him as much as you could before breaking the news." Torch shook his head. "This is an easy fix, Karma."

"How, Torch? How is any of this easy?" I dropped my fork and pointed at him. "He's my true mate and he lied to me. How can I trust him to tell me the truth? How can I know any of it is real?"

He snorted and more smoke drifted up from his nostrils. "Real? You want to talk real? Okay, when did you tell him you weren't his species? When did you tell him that the creatures he thinks are imaginary—dragons, angels, gods, gargoyles—are actually real and live around him? He's human and we've hid from them since the dawn of time. When did you tell him you weren't like him?"

I opened my mouth to refute his words but I couldn't find an argument that didn't sound petulant.

"Exactly. You weren't honest with him, either. I figure

that makes you both even." Torch leaned forward, his eyes sparkling. "But he tried to tell you, and if I had to guess, I'd say Loki did his best to draw this out as long as possible. You know the kick he gets out of watching people squirm emotionally. It's like an aphrodisiac to him."

I thought back to all the times Coop tried to tell me something and sure enough, Loki was there, distracting, insisting on something else to shift my focus. I raised my gaze to the dragon shifter sitting beside me.

"Did he send you that morning when we went to the warehouse?"

Torch nodded. "Yup. He didn't want to give Coop a chance to say anything that would derail you from what needed to be done."

"That unbelievable bastard."

Torch snorted. "Count on it."

I dropped my head into my hands and closed my eyes. Torch was right. Neither Coop nor I had been honest with each other. At least he'd had a legitimate reason to hide the truth. I was just scared. Scared he wouldn't want the embodiment of the energy of consequence. *And since we're being honest, who would really want to be involved with a person who judged your every action in the grand scheme of things?* It didn't matter that I didn't do it on purpose.

"Look, I've lived a long time and I've watched the humans. They might be short-lived, destructive, and stupid as hell sometimes, but they learn from their mistakes far faster than the Elder Races ever do and they often love more fiercely. He knows he screwed up and I'd lay odds that he's beating himself up over it. Give him a chance and talk to him."

"I don't know what to tell him." I met Torch's gaze miserably. "I'm scared."

He laughed, a deep rumbling sound that would be really creepy in other circumstances. Like a deep shadowed cave in the earth.

"Good. That means you're on the right track. Love wouldn't be worth a damn if it didn't scare you once in a while." He grasped my hand and squeezed gently. "Give yourself time to get your shit together, and for the Goddess's sake, take a shower."

I swiped at him and he grinned momentarily before he sobered. "But don't wait too long. I got the feeling he's gonna need you sooner rather than later." He rose from the chair, giving me a solemn look.

I raised an eyebrow at his enigmatic response. "Can you see the future, Torch?"

"Not as often as I'd like." He winked and sauntered out of the clubhouse.

I watched him leave, going over everything he'd said. Coop hadn't been completely honest with me, but he didn't have the monopoly on half-truths either. The question became, was I too scared to take the chance on him seeing past my otherness? Or would I step up and grasp the courage humans seemed to carry with them when it came to love?

The answer was easy. I wanted Coop and I wanted to try, and as far as honesty was concerned, we were on equal footing. I stood up and took my plate to the dish bin before heading back to my cabin, my head up and my mind clear. I'd take the day to figure out how to approach the problem with Coop and I'd go looking for him the next day. I needed a shower, clean clothes, and a plan.

And after I got him back, I'd be talking with Loki. He owed me, big time, and God of Mischief or not, he'd have to pay up. For the first time in days, I grinned.

****

Karma

I woke with a start, trying to get my bearings before I

did anything drastic. My heart pounded in my chest and I panted as if I'd been running. Something had been chasing me in my dreams and I jerked awake just before it caught me.

I frowned as I sat up, taking in my bedroom. Everything sat quiet and serene. But the panic in my heart was real. Except nothing was happening where I sat in my bed. I shot a look out the window and the half moon cast wan light over the ground. I couldn't see the actual satellite from my window, but the ground glowed with its silvery light. Again, everything sat silent and calm.

Something's wrong.

I knew it in my gut just as clearly as I knew when someone needed their cosmic bill collected. I shook my head, trying to ferret out the feelings and emotions associated with my gut instinct, but nothing came to me. I frowned. *Must have been a nightmare.*

Except I never had nightmares. As the physical manifestation of karma, my dreams weren't full of fear. They always consisted of setting things right and the satisfaction that came with it. I glanced at the bed and realized I lay on one side of it, as if making room for the person who wasn't there.

Coop.

Sorrow and pain rose in my chest, but they weren't as sharp as they'd been the last few days. *Thank the Goddess for Torch.* Who knew a dragon could be so wise in the ways of the heart? *Especially since he's single.* Maybe he'd made similar mistakes. I wasn't sure how old Torch was, but he was old enough to shift shape. I'd heard dragons had to be five hundred to do that.

Taking a deep breath to calm my heartbeat, I lay back and closed my eyes, trying to coax my stressed body back into relaxation. It had gotten harder and harder to do since Coop left. *I'm gonna fix that first thing tomorrow.* Pretty words for sure, but I didn't know if I'd have the courage to do it in the daylight.

I settled finally and let my mind go back into that twilight area between waking and sleeping. At first, everything swirled around my awareness and I swirled with it, not focused on anything. But the eddies of mist took shape and I found myself standing in the shadow cast by a building in an industrial part of a city. The walls had graffiti in large light-colored loops that were vaguely reflected in the puddles of the alley floor. Dumpsters created a strange obstacle course into the darkness and small mammals—probably rats—scurried away from any light presented.

Like the set of headlights on the vehicle at the mouth of the alley.

Rhythmic thumps came from behind one of the Dumpsters along with grunts and moans of pain. At first, I just listened to them, but after a while I could feel the impacts of each blow and pain filtered into my awareness. Agony seared through the ribs on my right side and my left hand screamed with pain at each beat of my frantic heart. My face had grown numb from all the blows it had sustained and one eye had swollen shut.

What the actual fuck?

"All right, Kinsley. That's enough."

The beating stopped and from my place in the shadows I saw a cop with a nightstick step away from the Dumpster. It took me a few moments to realize Officer Kinsley had been beating someone on the ground. The man who'd spoken shifted in front of one headlight, his silhouette a stark, black smear against the light. He wore a fedora hat and actually held a walking cane. *Now all he needs are black-sided spats and he's got the whole Chicago Mafioso thing going.*

Fedora Guy tilted his head to take in the body on the ground. "So, Marshal DeVille, have I gotten your attention now?"

Marshal DeVille? My blood chilled and my gut clamped into a painful spasm. I had to get closer to see if the name fit the man I knew.

"F-f-fuck off." I recognized the voice, but it sounded haggard, tired, and resigned.

Fedora Guy shook his head, tsking with disappointment. "Not the best response, Marshal. Kinsley?"

The uniform moved in and dealt several more blows, DeVille moaning with each impact. I felt them on my own body and bit back the screams as pain swelled in a crescendo. At last, Kinsley stopped and stepped back once more. I crept closer, trying to get a better view, but my chest tightened into immobility, the pain making it hard to breathe.

"Now then." Fedora Guy leaned forward on his cane. "I'll say this again. Have I gotten your undivided attention, Marshal?"

"Y-y-yeah." Anger remained in DeVille's voice, but it had been banked.

"Very good." Fedora Guy nodded and straightened before he tilted his head. "You know, all that blood looks good on you. It really brings out your eyes. Of course, you were much prettier before Kinsley got to you, but such is life." He shrugged. "So here's the deal. You need to stop looking into Backlog. Don't dig into us or our money. Don't talk to anyone about it. Don't even mention it to your pretty, darkie girlfriend."

Coop made a sound in the back of his throat and Fedora Guy nodded.

"Oh yeah, we know who she is and how to get to her, so keep that in mind." Fedora Guy motioned to Kinsley. "Give him back his gun."

The uniform set the gun on the ground near Coop, but far enough away that he couldn't get to it quickly.

"This is how it's all gonna play out. You forget about the Backlog. Stop researching where the money goes or who the players are, and you go back to your life as Marshal Cooper DeVille." Fedora Guy waved at someone else and the engine of the car started, the headlights flickering with ignition. "If you don't, we'll come back to finish the job we started tonight. And we'll make sure your girlfriend is collateral damage. Are we clear?"

"Y-y-you s-s-stay away f-f-from her or I'll f-f-fuckin' kill you."

Officer Kinsley barked an ugly laugh. "You hear that, boss? He's the big man givin' orders now." He aimed a kick at Coop and I marked him for death in that moment.

"Hey, Marshal DeVille, the choice is yours. Your girlfriend won't know a thing if you let this all go. Simple as that." Kinsley slammed his boot into Coop's side and I growled. "Stay away from Backlog. Got me?"

Oh, I got him. They'd just pissed off karma and I'd go Full Metal Bitch on their asses. From what I could tell, all the men surrounding Fedora Guy, him included, were due for some retribution. But Fedora Guy and Officer Kinsley had harmed my true mate, and while Coop and I had some issues to work out, no one harmed my mate and lived to tell about it. Fedora Guy and his crew were tagged for death. I'd see to it personally.

Once the car had backed out of the alley, I crept to the Dumpster and crouched beside my downed mate. From the wheezing in his chest, they'd broken some of his ribs and done damage to his lungs. *Shit-oh-dear, he can't breathe.* I reached out to touch his forehead and damn near jumped when my skin touched his. *Holy shit, I'm really here now.*

"K-K-Karma?" Coop opened his one good eye, blinking rapidly. "Is that you?"

"Yeah, Coop, I'm here." I tried to give him a warm smile.

"I'm so sorry, Ma'am."

My heart broke at the anguished words and at his use of my honorable title. "It's all right."

"No, Ma'am. I wasn't honest enough for you and I've lost you because of it." He blinked and a tear slid down his cheek. "It doesn't matter anyway. I can't go back to you or Backlog will hurt you, and that's worse than not having your trust. Can't let them hurt you. Love you."

He closed his eye as he lost consciousness and panic surged in my gut. If he stayed out there without help, he'd die. Humans weren't as tough as the Elder Races, and they didn't heal as fast.

"Coop? Coop. Stay with me. Come on, sweet man. Open your eyes."

But he didn't move again and his breathing sounded watery. *Oh fuck.* I glanced around the alley, trying to figure out where in the world he'd been beaten. I rose and took a few steps away from his body, hoping I wouldn't lose whatever connection that made this possible.

The world of the alley remained stable as I moved closer to the cross street ahead. I kept glancing back to be sure I hadn't lost Coop, but I managed to reach the road and glanced around. It was late so very few cars moved about. I tried to focus on landmarks to tell me where he was, but the buildings were too high and too close together. *Shit. Shit. Shit.*

What could I do? I didn't want to leave Coop and it was getting harder and harder to breathe. I moved back down the alley to his side and looked him over. If he didn't get help soon, it wouldn't matter if Backlog threatened to hurt me. I dropped to my knees and pawed through his pockets, trying to be careful while I searched for his phone. The face was spiderwebbed with cracks, but it powered up and let me dial 911.

"Nine one one, what's your emergency?" The man on the other end sounded calm.

"Oh my gosh, I just found this guy on the ground here and he's been beaten pretty bad. He's not breathing too good." Neither was I, but that helped with my scared young woman persona.

"Stay calm, ma'am. Where are you located?"

"I-I don't know. I went for a walk and got all turned around." I glanced at the Dumpster beside me and found the street name and number on the side. "I think he's in the alley behind 1455 W. Prospect Boulevard."

"Okay, I'm alerting the Emergency Services nearest you. They should be there in just under five minutes. Stay on the line with me, okay?"

"Can't you just track the phone or something with the GPS thingy?"

To his credit, he didn't laugh. "Yes, ma'am, that helps us narrow it down. But I need you to stay on the line until the police get there. Can I have your name please?"

"Carmen." I injected more fear into my voice as Coop's wheezing got worse. "Please hurry. He's having trouble breathing and it sounds awful."

"EMS is on the way and say they are about two minutes out. You should be able to hear the sirens soon."

Yeah, I could hear them. I'd have to drop the phone and fade out soon, but I didn't want to leave Coop's side. The idea that he could die when I wasn't looking made me want to throw up. But I couldn't stay. I wasn't sure I was even really there anyway.

I carefully set the phone down in his hand and leaned close to him, hoping the 911-worker couldn't hear me.

"Hang on, Coop. Help's on the way and I want to see you again. You hear me? I need to talk to you so you hang on until I can. This is an order from your Madam. You will live until we can talk."

"Yes, Ma'am."

I blinked, looking at his lips, but they hadn't moved. But I swore he'd answered me. I had to take solace in that as the flashing red and blue lights of the ambulance and police cars filled the alley. I stood and hurried back the way I'd come, letting go of my physical essence just as the headlights of the ambulance illuminated the alley. I looked back and met the gaze of the lead EMT before I faded back to my bedroom. He called out but the silence of my cabin cut off the sound.

I drew my knees up to my chest and dropped my head on them, hoping they'd arrived in time. *Come on, Coop. Hang in there just a little longer.* I hoped the Goddess heard my prayer because I had planning to get done. Fedora Guy and Officer Kinsley had some karmic debts to pay.

CHAPTER NINETEEN

Cooper

Everything hurt. Even my hair and my fingernails.
Why the hell does everything hurt?
I focused my mind to bring back the last thing I
remembered. I'd left the Concrete Angels' compound and
made it home. I noticed the silver Cruze was back out on
the road in front of my apartment but I didn't worry about
it. I went back to my usual routine of going to work in the
Marshals' Denver office and tried to forget about Karma.

I snorted and a spike of pain when through my chest.
Fuck, I know heartbreak is bad, but this seems extreme. I
wasn't going to forget about her anytime soon.

I opened my eyes and looked around, listening to the
soft beeping coming from my right. A heart monitor
chirped along steadily as I took in the details of the room. *It
looks like a hospital.* A pale blue blanket covered me from
the chest down and the IV in my elbow ran to a saline bag
hanging from the rack to my left. I was alone although
there was another bed in the room.

How the hell did I get here?
I frowned. I'd gone to work and everything seemed
normal, but I kept getting the feeling I was being watched.

My partner, Anna Fitzsimmons, had been more reserved than before, but I figured it was because I'd left her with our caseload. I couldn't tell if she was Backlog or not, but it didn't matter because she seemed to avoid me. *Maybe she's avoiding Backlog, too.*

But four days after I'd come back, I got jumped on my way out to my car. Two guys threw a bag over my head and shoved me in the back of a police car. I could smell the piss, sweat, puke, and nervous desperation of the suspect seats. Plus the cold weight of the handcuffs clinched it.

I didn't remember how long we drove and no one talked. But when we stopped, they dragged me out into an alley and ripped off the hood. There were five guys and the big boss in a fedora, holding a walking cane. I recognized a couple of the guys from the names on Eisenburg's list in Fort Collins PD uniforms, but the big boss looked like a businessman straight out of Chicago. *Yeah, well, I'm probably not going to be able to nail him for tax evasion.*

"Do you know who I am, Marshal DeVille?" Damn, he even had a Chicago accent.

I'd shaken my head.

"My name's Daniel Ainsworth and I'm the Police Commissioner for Fort Collins. I understand you've been poking around in things you shouldn't. Care to explain yourself?"

I'd given him my best blank look. "I don't know what you're talking about."

His mouth had flattened into a thin line. "I don't have time to play games, DeVille. We need you to stop snooping in business that isn't yours."

"Uh, I'm pretty sure you've got the wrong guy. I really don't know what you're talking about. Seriously."

Ainsworth had sighed. "Oh, DeVille. I'm gonna have to get your attention, then. Officer Kinsley, jog his memory."

I didn't remember much after that except impacts and

pain, but I did recall Ainsworth and Kinsley threatening to hurt Karma if I kept up with my investigation, and I think I'd threatened them right back, but my memory grew hazy.

Then Karma had been there. I frowned and closed my eyes. *That doesn't make any sense.* Karma wouldn't come near me with a ten-foot pole. Why the hell did I think she was there? But I could see her, her face creased with worry as she leaned over me. I wanted to tell her I loved her, that I was so sorry for betraying her trust, for not being honest with her. But I couldn't get the words out and she wasn't there anyway.

I shifted my legs under the sheets and realized something was missing. Panic rose through my chest along with renewed pain as I tried to push the blankets back. When they wouldn't move, I shoved one hand under them to feel my cock and balls.

Oh no, it's gone. I felt around as best I could, but my hand came up with nothing but skin and hair. *Where the hell is it?* I moved my hand under my hip and ass and I'm sure I looked like I was feeling myself up, but there was nothing on the bed, either.

Oh, glory, it's really gone.

Karma's last gift, her beautiful cock jewelry and her mark of possession, was gone. I'd worn it every day we'd been apart, trying to hold on to the memories and love I'd experienced with her. I couldn't be near her and feel her touch, but the jewelry had kept me grounded enough to go on despite our breakup.

And now that's gone, too.

Tears leaked out of my eyes and dripped onto the pillow behind me. I wasn't used to being so emotional. Hell, I hadn't cried at all when I broke up with my ex. But losing Karma drilled a hole straight through my soul. Worse, since Backlog was aware of her, I couldn't go back even if I wanted to. Which I did, desperately.

To protect her, I'd have to walk away.

It was probably for the best. After all, I must have cashed in some of my karmic debt to sustain the beating I got from the Backlog members. I wondered, sullenly, if she took any pleasure in exacting retribution for hiding who I was from her, but I chided myself for the whiny thoughts. She'd been heartbroken, I could read that clear enough on her face when she'd bolted for her cabin.

I'm really sorry, Karma. I was, especially because I wouldn't be able to serve her or comfort her. I'd be walking away from the woman who held my heart and soul. Yeah, okay, she wasn't human, but my heart didn't care.

I cleared my throat and closed my eyes, trying to focus my energies on healing all the hurts. I hadn't seen the doctor yet, but I'm sure they'd be along to tell me all the damage. *And then I'm coming for you bastards.* I'd figure out a way to keep Karma safe and take them down, because I was done being nice.

****

Karma

I didn't talk to anyone for a couple of days after Coop was taken to the hospital. I didn't want to. I know Torch and Loki kept a weather-eye on me, but they left me alone. I left the compound every day, taking my time to find out where Officer Kinsley and his motley crew of assholes hung out. He was easy enough to find, being a beat cop, but I didn't want to catch him on duty. I needed to study and understand him before I set his karma in motion.

Turned out, he liked to visit this one diner on the south end of Fort Collins and he often met with the other members of his beat squad. If I hadn't been looking for him, I probably wouldn't have found the other guys who'd been there the night they assaulted Coop. I kept an eye on the diner and planned how I'd get close to the cops who surrounded Kinsley.

The morning I set my plan in motion, he was stuffing his face with a heart attack on a plate. The temperature had grown warm so I'd chosen to wear the fringed leather top that tied behind my neck and back, and my tight low-riding jeans. I'd put on my low-heeled booties with matching fringe and I strode into the diner for scrambled eggs and bacon. Kinsley sat with three of the other guys from the assault on Coop and in a moment, I had their Karmic Dossiers scrolling through my mind.

I gave a low whistle as I swung my hip onto a counter stool. *This is going to be easier than I thought.* They had more things to account for than an embezzling hedge fund manager. I settled onto the stool and thanked the waitress for the coffee. I was pretty sure every man in the place had his gaze glued to my ass. When I wanted to look good, I usually turned heads. But I'd be taking them instead.

I sat at the counter, showing them my hip bones and back. Their eyes and lust slithered over me like cold syrup. I ordered a breakfast sandwich and listened in on the conversation behind me.

"So, are the Marshals finally on board now that the snoop's gone?" The guy who spoke had been the driver of the car at the alley.

Kinsley shook his head. "Not yet. Ainsworth thinks there are a couple more who're makin' waves and will have to be ferreted out. But at least DeVille is shut down. I'm pretty sure he's more worried about his darkie girlfriend than getting more dirt on us. But we'll keep an eye on him for a short time. We fucked him up pretty good."

Anger kindled in my chest and I gritted my teeth against doing anything rash. Instead, I let his Karmic Dossier fill my mental screen. The pathway to the repayment of his Karmic Debt unfolded in my mind and I mapped it out.

The waitress trips, accidentally pouring hot coffee into

Kinsley's lap. He shrieks and gives her hell, but he and his buddies leave the diner.

Kinsley must go home, but his car has a flat. Checking for his spare, he finds it's flat, too, from the last time he didn't bother to get it repaired. Swearing, he checks his phone for the nearest tire repair shop and finds one a few miles north.

He calls one of his breakfast buddies and they come to get him, loading up the two tires.

Their drive takes them through a neighborhood where they almost hit some school children and the traffic cam catches their plate, calculating a school-zone ticket.

By the time they hit the freeway, Kinsley's pants are wet and cold, freezing his balls and he looks like he's pissed his pants. His buddy ribs him on it, laughing too hard to see the drunken truck driver who plows into the car, flipping it over and over into the median.

The driver is pinned by the concaved door, dead on impact. Kinsley's neck is broken and he has internal bleeding that kills him before the paramedics arrive.

I nodded sharply. *Works for me.* I flicked my wrist a little, nudging the energy of the waitress to stumble as she headed to refill the mugs on the cops' table. She threw her hands out and the coffee shot out of the carafe, pouring a hot, brown stream into Kinsley's lap, making him scream.

"Sonovaprick! What the fuck is wrong with you, lady?" He lurched to his feet to get away the saturated cloth on his lap as I kept my head down, watching out of the corner of my eye.

"I'm so sorry, sir. It was an accident. Let me get you a towel."

"No, I don't want a towel. Get the fuck away from me." Kinsley pushed out of the booth and threw some money down on the table. "You can forget about a fucking tip."

He stalked out as the others dropped money on the

table and followed him, scowling and grumbling. I figured they wouldn't be back to this diner, but that would be a saving grace for the other customers. Kinsley and his crew needed to pay the piper, so-to-speak, and the deposit window was open.

The waitress came back to the counter, her expression a combination of bewilderment and chagrin.

"You all right?"

She turned and nodded before shaking her head with dismay. "I don't know how I managed to trip. The floor was clean and smooth."

I shrugged. "Must have been karma."

She snorted. "Mine or theirs?"

I tilted my head with a half-smile. "Maybe a little bit of both. The question is, what can you learn from it?"

The waitress snorted and shook her head. "Clocking out on time instead of waiting for the last possible tip from guys who didn't pay it."

I nodded. "Sounds like a plan. Here's thirty bucks. That should cover my tip and theirs."

"Oh, you don't have to—"

"Nah, I insist. Hopefully, it'll make your day a little better after those jackasses." I waved at my breakfast sandwich. "Can I get a box for this? I gotta get going."

Some of the tension left the woman's face and she brought me a box, adding a little slice of apple pie along with my sandwich. She gave me a wink and a smile. "For your sweetness."

I left the diner with a huge grin on my face as I settled onto my bike. I caught sight of Kinsley scowling at the flat tires in front of him as I drove away with my sandwich and pie. It was shaping up to be a pretty good day.

CHAPTER TWENTY

Karma

It took me the better part of a week to make sure all the guys from Kinsley's crew had paid their Karmic Debts in full, and all the resulting deaths had been ruled accidents. I just had to get the ball rolling. The only one I hadn't found was Fedora Guy, but I suspected he was the "Ainsworth" Kinsley had mentioned at his breakfast meeting. I'd find him eventually and give him his due, but in the meantime, I had to talk to Coop.

"You gonna be okay?" Torch's voice pulled me back to the present.

I shot him a look from the passenger seat of the Concrete Angels' moving van. Was I okay? Kinda. Sorta. Not really. I was afraid to face my true mate who lay in the building just beyond the passenger door.

"Yeah. Yeah, I'll be okay." I nodded even if I didn't feel like the words were true. "You'll wait here for me to come back out, right?" I tightened my hand over the bag at my feet as I met his gaze.

"Yeah, I'll be here. Whenever you're ready. Just text me and I'll come to the doors."

I nodded again before I pushed the door open and got

out. "Thanks, Torch."

"No problem. Go get 'im, Tiger."

I snorted. "Yeah."

I closed the door and he drove out to park the van. He'd done me a huge favor bringing me there with nothing but a vague plan and hope, but Torch told me he liked Coop and could see he was important to me. He wasn't wrong. I took a deep breath and headed for the entrance.

I stopped outside of the hospital doors and fidgeted with the handles of the duffle bag I carried. I hated hospitals. They often sat full of people who'd experienced my dubious gifts in a spectacular way, and facing their suffering wasn't fun.

Like Coop.

Although, I wasn't sure if it was his karma he'd experienced or my own. He lay in the hospital bed upstairs because I told him to leave the Concrete Angels' compound, and the guys from Backlog found him. They beat him nearly to death. I made them experience their karma far faster than they would have normally, but I wasn't waiting around for them to pay for harming my true mate.

Even if it was kinda my fault.

Taking a deep breath, I stepped through the sliding doors and headed for the elevators to the fourth floor. Most people ignored me despite my fluffy hair, my denim jacket with the arms cut off, and my tight jeans, but I wasn't there for them anyway. I slid past the nurse's station as if I was meant to be there and found Coop's room.

Again, my courage damn near failed me at the door. Would he want to see me after I'd pushed him away and refused to answer his phone calls and texts? I bit my bottom lip and stepped into the room, setting the bag down on the chair inside the door.

Coop lay in the bed, slightly propped up and covered with a light blue blanket. His head was tilted toward the window, his eyes closed, and my breath stilled in my chest. Horrid blue and purple bruises marred the cheek I could see and probably the one I couldn't. His left arm hung across his chest in a cast and sling, and I'd learned they'd installed pins to help the bones knit. I'd taken another one of those dream walks into the hospital and overheard the nurses talking about Coop. They'd discussed his broken ribs, a bad concussion, and a punctured lung. He'd received surgery quickly enough to correct it, but he'd be hurting for a long time.

I wanted to pull him up from the bed and hug him close to my body, promising to take care of him forever. Which I could, being who I was. But it wasn't who he was. U.S. Marshal Cooper DeVille was the kind of guy who'd run toward danger just to save a few innocents, including members of his own law enforcement club. He was a rare breed.

"Hey, Karma." My breath stopped in my throat as his cracked voice washed over me. "What are you doing here?"

I barked a surprised laugh that came out too close to a sob. "I'm checking up on you to find out how you're feeling."

Coop grimaced, one eye swollen shut. "Pretty much everything hurts, but at least I can breathe again. How are you?"

I sighed and rested a hip against the end of his bed. "Miserable and lonely, but that's pretty much par for the course, so I'm fine."

He nodded. "Yeah, I guess being the physical manifestation of retribution can be pretty rough." He frowned as he shifted his body in the bed. "I take it this is my payment for lying to you?"

"What?" I gaped at him. "You think I had this done to you?"

"No, or not directly." He gave a tired shrug. "I'm sure it's just my karma from actions in the past."

222

I wanted to deny it, to insist that I had anything to do with it. But karma was always working whether we believed in it or not, and his actions had brought the attention of Backlog onto him. *Yeah, but he didn't have to be alone when they came for him.* No, I could've been there. Hell, all the Concrete Angels could've been there to back him up.

But we weren't because I'd told him to go and leave me alone.

"I'm sorry, Coop."

He raised an eyebrow. Probably. It was hard to tell with the swelling and bruises. But he didn't say anything and let me squirm through my apology.

"I'm sorry I told you to leave me alone. I'm sorry I didn't take the time to listen to you." Tears started to roll down my cheeks, but I couldn't stop them any more than I could stop the pain in my heart. "And I'm so sorry I wasn't there when those guys cornered you and beat you all to hell. I should've been there. I should've stopped them. I should've had your back." I didn't tell him I had been there, just not in my physical form.

Coop said nothing, watching me cry and squirm at his silence. I didn't know what he was thinking but I could guess it was something along the lines of a day late and a dollar short. And he was right. I'd let him down when it counted and nothing could change that.

"I'm sorry. I know I said some shitty things to you because you didn't tell me who you really were. It was wrong of me to hold it against you since I didn't tell you who I really was, either." The tears kept rolling and I kept talking. "In that, we're pretty much even. I was afraid you wouldn't believe me, or worse, you would and run screaming from me. I guess that's pretty much what kept you from telling me, right?"

He said nothing to my question. I shrugged and rubbed the back of my neck. "I've never had a long-term

223

relationship with anyone who wasn't like me. You know, not human. But I've also never met anyone like you, and according to the Goddess, you're my true mate. My one-and-only. The happily-ever-after everyone reads about in romance novels."

I waited for him to respond, but he only turned his head to look outside.

"I know, it's a lame excuse, and I should've tried harder. I get that, now. And I want to try again. With you. On equal footing. No more secrets about who we are between us."

He said nothing. He didn't even turn his head to look at me, and the very real fear that I would lose him entered my mind. *Sweet glory, don't let it be so.*

"I'm so sorry, Coop, and I don't want you to leave. In fact, I want you to come back to the Concrete Angels with me. And hey, I'm trying to have a conversation with you. Could you please look at me?"

"I can't." He didn't move.

"You can't look at me or you can't come back with me?"

Now he met my gaze. "I can't come back with you."

So, this is what it feels like to have a sword in my gut. The swirling, piercing pain just about made me double over and sink to my knees. I'm pretty sure my face drained of color because the skin on my head tightened hard enough to make my cheeks and eyes ache. I'd experienced a broken leg once, and it didn't even come close to the agony in my chest at the moment.

"Okay." I had to swallow a couple of times before I could find my voice again. "Fine. Yeah, good. Good."

He grunted. "Aren't you going to ask me why?"

"I'm trying to subtly avoid it."

He snorted and I thought it might be with laughter. "Fine. But I'm gonna tell you anyway."

I swallowed hard. "Okay."

He grimaced as he tried to get into a better position, but he gave up after a few moments of painful movement. I rose and moved to his head, rearranging the pillow behind him so he could meet my gaze without straining.

"Thanks." He settled back as he gathered his breath. "I can't go back with you because Backlog will come after you if I survive. I'm not going to give up on bringing them down. There are too many people they can hurt and that's unacceptable. But just because I'm putting myself in harm's way doesn't mean I have to drag you down with me. So I can't go back with you. You'll be safer without me around."

I wanted to tell him he was full of shit. No one could kill karma, not even Loki, the God of Mischief. But I'd known Coop long enough to read resolution in his voice and body language. Nothing I could say would sway him from what he perceived he had to do.

I nodded slowly, my heart breaking into shards of cracked ice. But I changed the direction of my head, swiveling it into a shake. *To hell with it.*

"No."

"What?"

"I said no."

"What do you mean no?"

I raised my eyebrows. "Is there some part of 'no' you don't understand? It's a pretty direct answer."

"I mean, I don't understand what you're saying no to."

"Ah." I gave him my best disagreeable smile. "No, I'm not going to be safer without you. And even so, I refuse to be without you."

"Karma—"

"Nope. I made the mistake of being without you for the better part of two weeks and that turned out to be a shit decision on my part. So, I'm not about to do that to myself again."

He sighed. "Short of my death, I won't ever be safe.

And neither will you. Immortal goddess of retribution or not, I can't put you in that kind of danger." His resigned expression told me he wouldn't be convinced in the usual ways. "I won't put any of the Concrete Angels in that kind of danger."

"Even Gopher?"

He cracked a sad smile. "Yeah, not even him."

I nodded. "Okay. Then we'll just have to kill you."

His one eye opened wide. "What?"

"We'll just have to kill you." I grinned. "That way the Backlog guys will think the problem is solved."

He eyed me for several seconds. "You're serious."

"Yup."

Coop's brows came down over his eyes. "Why does that make you grin?"

"Because I've always wanted to try something like this."

He swallowed hard. "Try something like what?"

"Try making someone disappear. It's like WITSEC, only sexier."

"You've gotta be kidding me."

I shook my head. "Nope. Come on, Coop. I'll help you up and get you out of here. Then we'll work on your disappearing act."

"Karma, I'm in the hospital, recovering from a collapsed lung and a concussion, plus I have pins in my arm from where it was broken in three places. I can't just leave."

I snorted. "You can, and you will. Come with me to the Concrete Angels' compound and let Nightingale look after you. I guarantee her infirmary is far cleaner than this place, and you'll be way more comfortable. Plus, I'll be there."

I moved toward the bed to start unhooking the IV and heart monitor, but he held up his good hand to stop me.

"No, stop. You have to get away from me. I can't let

them hurt you, Ma'am. I couldn't go on if you got killed because of me. I don't matter, and if I stay away from you, you'll be safe. I have to do this because you're more important than me."

"See, that's where you're wrong." I leaned forward until we were nose-to-nose. "You're mine and I take care of what's mine. It's my job, remember? I'm the Enforcer and I take care of what needs to be done. And right now, you need to come home with me where you'll be safe until you heal completely. Hear me?"

He stared at me a long time, taking in my words and my expression, and I prayed to the Goddess that he wouldn't fight me on this. I couldn't be without him any more than he could be without me. But if he insisted I leave, I'd have to take his wishes into account. I might be his Madam, but he was the one in control, and ultimately, he made the choices.

His jaw bunched before he drew in a deep breath. "Do you love me, Ma'am?"

I blinked, excited and afraid all at once, but there was no question in my answer. "Yes, very much."

"Even if I'm a U.S. Marshal?"

I nodded. "Yes, very much."

"And will you allow me to keep trying to bring Backlog down?"

"Yeah, hell yeah. I'll help." I smirked as I turned off the heart monitor. "A lot of those assholes have some karmic debt to repay and I'm looking forward to cashing in." I stopped, making sure I met his molten chocolate gaze. "Making sure you're protected is my first priority, though. Which means the local group of Backlog who knows who you are will have to be taken out."

"You mean, they'll have to be killed."

"Probably, yeah." I didn't tell him most of them were already dead. I was the Enforcer, after all. "They have karma coming and they upped the ante when they attacked

227

you. Challenge accepted."

Coop grimaced as he slowly sat up. I helped him move his feet to the floor and handed him the bag from the chair. I knew he didn't like killing people as a solution. He was a good guy, a cop, and bringing people to justice was his schtick. But in this case, Backlog had infiltrated the system and didn't play by the rules. Maybe someday there'd be enough judges and cops and agents who could override Backlog's insidiousness, but until then, I would protect Coop from them with more permanent solutions.

"I brought you one of Torch's t-shirts, an extra-large sweatshirt, and sweatpants, and some athletic slides. That'll help you get out of here without anyone really noticing." I also handed him a Colorado Avalanche ballcap to cover his head. "Will you be able to walk, or should I get a wheelchair to help you out?"

He nodded. "Yeah, a wheelchair might be a good idea if you actually want me out of here."

"Okay, let me help you get dressed and I'll go find one."

I helped him get out of the hospital gown and had to bite back an exclamation over the bruising on his torso. Anger flared at the visible damage on his beautiful body and I reached out to steady him with one hand. As soon as I touched him, I released some of my life years, pumping the energy into him before I could stop myself.

What the hell?

I'd never given my energy to anyone, ever. Hell, I didn't know I could do that. But the power flowed into his body, fixing the punctured lung, knitting the ribs, and repairing the damage from his concussion. For just a moment, he glowed with returned vitality and health, and his eyes widened as he stared at me.

"Holy shit, what the hell was that?"

I released him and stood back, waiting for the feeling of being drained to swamp over me. But it never came and

I blinked back at him.

"I dunno. I've never done that before, but I think I just gave you some of my physical life energy. Maybe. Sort of." I grimaced. I didn't know how to explain. "Maybe it's because you're my true mate."

"What? True mate? What does that mean?" He blinked at me and already the swelling around his eye had reduced to almost normal, his face only slightly lopsided.

I wanted to blurt out the whole thing, but I didn't know who else might be listening or watching so I gave him a neutral smile. "Let's get you dressed and out of here. I'll explain everything in the car."

There was a lot of grunting and hissing while we got him dressed, and none of it was in the good, porn sort of way. But at last he wore the sweatshirt that read, "Colorado Avalanche" and the matching sweats over the t-shirt. I'd snipped off the tags, but he still looked like he'd just gone shopping at a sports gift shop.

"All right, come with me and keep your face turned down and to the left while we find a wheelchair. I don't want to leave you here in case a nurse or someone comes in."

Coop nodded without a word and I inserted my shoulder below his armpit as I wrapped my arm around his waist to help him out the door. No one seemed to notice our exit though it probably looked weird to have a small woman helping a tall man down the hall. But Coop kept his face away from the cameras and we found him a wheelchair to make it look more natural.

"Come on, honey. Let's get some fresh air."

I set the duffle bag gently in his lap as I pulled out my phone and texted Torch to bring the van to the front doors. Then I pushed him to the elevators, trying to look bored and casual. I didn't want any of the nurses or doctors asking where I was taking Coop.

I'd brought a brimmed slouch hat to cover my hair and

face, and left my cut at home so I wouldn't be as easy to identify should anyone look at the security cameras later. The elevator apparently had a lot of stops to make because by the time the doors opened, I was sweating bullets.

The car held a couple of nurses with clipboards and a visiting family. The family got off and sauntered past us, but the nurses stayed in the elevator. I swallowed back my unease and backed the chair into it.

"Excuse us." I gave them an apologetic smile as I settled in to the back. *Please, Goddess, get us get out of here before they notice he's gone.*

No one spoke in the elevator but as soon as the doors opened, I made a break for the front doors. We were half-way across the entry when Coop stiffened and swore under his breath.

"What's wrong?"

"See that doctor with the nurse?" He nodded toward a pair of people carrying paper to-go cups of coffee as they headed toward the elevator.

"Yeah." I pulled the wheelchair to the side out of the flow of foot traffic.

"That's my doc and the head nurse on my floor. They'll recognize me."

Fuck. I bit my lip and glanced around. The doc and the nurse were headed straight for us so I ducked from behind the chair and stood in front of Coop, bending down to talk to him. I figured if they were gonna look at anything it would be my ass in my blinged-out jeans rather than the man in the chair. Plus, my wide hips managed to completely block their view of his face.

"So, here's what we're gonna do. I'm going to get you into the van that Torch should be bringing and we'll disappear. How much stuff do you have at your apartment?" I kept my body in between the chair and the medical professionals taking their damn sweet time to get to the frickin' elevator.

Coop frowned. "What are you talking about?"

I sighed, wishing the elevator doors would open soon as I stepped back behind the chair and turned him to face away from the people waiting to get on. "You have to disappear, Coop. That means you have to clear out your place. Unless you want someone else to take your stuff?"

He scowled. "You think we have to hurry to do that? I'm not dead yet." We'd almost made it to the front doors and I could see the van waiting in the covered pickup area.

I shrugged even if he couldn't see it. "Not necessarily, but when they realize you're out of the hospital, that's the first place they'll look for you." I bit my lip. The next piece of info was going to hurt. "And we're gonna have to get rid of your car."

"What?" Yup, I could hear the outrage and disbelief in that one word.

We pushed through the sliding doors and I wheeled him over to the curb before locking the brakes on the chair. I grimaced as I met his gaze.

"That Caddy is the most recognizable car in Colorado, Coop. If they see it, they're gonna know it's you."

I offered him my hand to get out of the chair, but he didn't take it. My unease rose as he waited. The hospital staff would be checking on him soon and we were running out of time to get away.

"That car represents a new beginning in my life, Karma." He said the words quietly but they were no less powerful.

"I know. I know it's important to you. But it could also represent the end of your life if they find you with it."

He got out of the chair without a word and I hurried to open the van's sliding door for him. He didn't look at me as I helped him climb in and my heart quailed in the face of his hurt. I rubbed the back of my neck as I met Torch's gaze.

"I'm gonna take the chair to the nurse's station. I'll be

231

back."

Torch nodded, his gaze full of sympathy. Coop was losing so much. His life, his job, his car, all because of Backlog and their willingness to do damage to people. I didn't want him to lose so much, but maybe changing who he was on the outside would free him to do a lot more to take Backlog down. And with karma on his side…

The painful laugh worked its way up from my chest as I parked the chair and returned to the van. Still, I needed to do something nice for Coop when the dust settled. He wasn't a biker, he was the Dude with a Cool Car. I'd have to figure out a way to let him keep that description.

CHAPTER TWENTY-ONE

Cooper

My chest felt like someone had taken a mace and swirled it around inside. It might have been from the punctured lung or the beating I'd experienced. *Or it might be more about the loss of Rosé.* When Karma told me I'd have to get rid of my car, it felt like she'd finished the job the Backlog thugs had started.

She was right, of course, but that didn't mean it felt good.

They'd taken me to my apartment and I'd directed them to what they could pack and what they could leave. There wasn't much there. I was a confirmed bachelor and I hadn't spent much time at home after my divorce. Karma drove Rosé up to the compound and I'd sat in the front seat of the van beside Torch, stewing. None of this was fair, but then, I'd already learned the hard way that life wasn't.

I wanted to rail at life, fortune, the universe, venting my rage at Backlog's grip on my life and those of my colleagues trying to make things better for the public. It wasn't fair that I had to go into hiding, lose my home, my job, my friends, and my car just to keep myself and Karma safe.

And that's the thought of every person in WITSEC.

The Marshal's Service oversaw the program to protect the innocents from criminals bent on killing them. Most of the time it was for a trial, but in other instances, it was forever. The irony of punishing the innocent for daring to speak up against the malignant and guilty. *No good deed goes unpunished.*

Was it better to be alive and someone/something else? Or did it make more sense to stay who I was and put a target on my back, ending with my death? *And am I more upset with losing the life I've built or a damn car?*

I was still chewing on those questions a few days later after I'd recovered in Nightingale's infirmary. Karma had been right. It was much cleaner, smelled better, and been a lot more personal than the hospital's care. Plus my nurse was a helluva lot sexier.

I'd slept a lot, but Karma had come in often to tell me about the planning sessions going on to help me disappear into the woodwork. Viper and Neo were working on my new identity documents and Torch and Calhoun, a sarcastic woman with sharp eyes and a British accent, had worked out how we'd "kill" Marshal Cooper DeVille in his 1962 Pompeian Red Cadillac. My heart ached at the loss to come.

I wanted to contact Battlebourne and Fitzsimmons to tell them I was okay but would disappear, but that defeated the purpose of WITSEC. Maybe I'd take a drive to California and write them a postcard without my name on it, just mention something only we'd shared. I'd have to wear gloves to protect my prints, but it might be worth all the trouble to let them know.

Thanks to Grub's good cooking and Nightingale's expert care, I could walk and move about pretty easily. I hadn't heard where I'd be staying—or if I'd be staying. Scott, Attila, and some of the others had voiced their concerns over having me stay. *Voiced. Ha. More like railed and shouted.* I'd heard some of it from the infirmary.

Scott was the loudest until Karma pointed out he'd hooked up with a former FBI agent. He'd argued that they'd known who Numbers was before she came onto the compound and I'd been hiding my true purpose, lying to everyone. I'd tuned out after that. Scott was right and I couldn't change how it all had turned out anyway.

"If your face gets any longer, you're gonna look like a hound dog." The woman known as Dollhouse rested her hip against the observation chair as she crossed her arms over her chest.

"Thanks. Nothing like a dog reference to perk someone right up." I hadn't meant to sound so sullen but my heart apparently was taking the lead at the moment.

Fortunately, she laughed. "Yeah, it wasn't meant as a compliment." She tilted her head and squinted. "Though maybe you are kinda like a dog that's been kicked and doesn't know who it can trust or if it will find another good home. You feelin' kinda adrift?"

I shot her a dry look, but bit back the acidic sarcasm trying to break free. Did I feel adrift when my whole life, friends, and car were being taken from me? *Let me just think on that a moment.* But I didn't have the energy to fight the truth so I nodded.

"Yeah."

She nodded as well. "Yeah, I figured. My brother doesn't like or trust you, says you're still playing us. But Karma's smarter than he is and she says you're on the up-and-up. And I know what it's like to lose everything and have to start over."

"Thanks. I think."

"Yeah. I don't have to tell you if you fuck things up with Karma you'll have a helluva time here, but you aren't without friends. Torch vouched for you, too."

"Torch?" There was a surprise. I'd liked the guy the moment I met him, but I hadn't expected him to back me up in front of the others. "Wow. Good to know. And yeah, I know I'm on thin ice here. But at this point, I'm no longer a Marshal."

"Actually, you are." She held out some papers to me and I picked them up. "It's nice to meet you, Eric Marshal, Dude with the Cool Car. Turns out you were born in San Antonio, Texas, and you have three brothers in the Armed Forces. Two have been killed, of course, one in Iraq and one in Afghanistan, and the third is comatose in at the Coronado Medical Center in California."

"Holy shit."

I had a new license, social security card, and even a birth certificate. According to everything, I was Eric, no-middle-initial, Marshal who'd been born in San Antonio thirty-eight years ago. Parents deceased, brothers mostly deceased, and never married.

I glanced up at her. "Why would you do all this for me?"

Dollhouse shrugged. "Karma loves you, and she knows how important taking down Backlog is to you. She can't save your life, but she can give you a new one so no one else has to lose theirs."

"What happened to the real Eric Marshal?"

"Died a few weeks after birth from a heart defect, I think. Neo would know." She headed for the door. "Sounds like we're gonna make this official tomorrow night. Karma just needs a little more time to find the head guy who had you beat up."

"Who, Ainsworth?"

"You know the guy's name?" Dollhouse paused at the door.

"Yeah, Daniel Ainsworth, Police Commissioner of Fort Collins."

Dollhouse whistled. "That should make it a lot easier. I'll tell her and she'll be back with a plan."

"Why didn't she come to bring this to me herself?" I

couldn't hide the hurt in my words.

"I think she's giving you time to come to terms with the change that's barreling toward you, knowing she's the cause."

"Backlog's the cause."

Dollhouse nodded. "Yeah, that's what I told her. Maybe you want to reinforce the idea the next time she comes in."

"Hey, Dollhouse?"

"Yeah?"

"Tell Neo and the rest thanks for me."

"What should I tell Karma?"

"To come see me. Anything I have to say to her I want to tell her myself."

Dollhouse smiled. "Excellent plan. I'll pass the message along." She ducked out of the room.

I hoped she would, but I didn't want to be flat on my back when Karma came to see me. I slid my feet onto the floor and prepared to get up. I couldn't remember what all Nightingale had done while I'd stayed in her infirmary, but I hadn't had nearly as much trouble breathing as when I first arrived.

As if my thoughts had conjured her, the Nurse Practitioner strode into the infirmary and studied me with her dark and wise eyes. I couldn't tell how old she was— her face remained unlined and there was no silver in her black hair—but she knew her stuff and gave me the sense that she'd been around the block a time or two.

"Where do you think you're going?"

"I think I'm ready to join the land of the living again." I stretched gingerly to make sure I didn't pull on anything I shouldn't.

"Humph, that remains to be seen." She came to me with a critical look before she pointed at my shirt. "Take it off. Let's see how your body is healing."

I carefully tugged my shirt off and set it aside as she

studied my body. Most of the bruises had healed to become ugly green and yellow blotches on my torso, but the surgery scars showed up as pink lines. Her cool fingers touched me here and there, testing for tenderness. I hissed a few times as I moved my arm still in the sling, but otherwise I didn't feel too bad.

Must be the drugs.

Speaking of drugs, they must have been good ones because my arm sat in a light brace slung across my body. It didn't feel broken despite the doctor's report Karma had photographed with her phone. Nightingale ran her hand over my arm, her eyes closed as she hummed for a few moments. Heat penetrated down to the bone and some of the background pain receded.

"There, that's a little better, isn't it?" She glanced up at me and I swore her eyes glowed with golden light. But when I blinked, it was gone. "I think the pins are going to have to stay, but I suggest you pick up some calcium to help repair the bone around them. It'll provide a lot more stability. From what I can tell, your ribs have knitted quite nicely and you should be moving and breathing much easier."

"Yeah, I am. Thanks. How'd my arm heal so fast?"

She shrugged, her smile a lot like that of the Mona Lisa. "You must have good genetics and have gotten enough rest. But don't push it for the next week or so. If you do, you won't reach your full health for a lot longer."

"Yeah, okay, I will."

She narrowed her eyes as she looked me over. "Don't make me chant a geas over you to make sure you rest. Ask Loki if you don't believe me."

Something about the way she said it made me think her chants were a whole lot more powerful than just singing in another language. I nodded and promised to heed her words as I dressed. The last thing I wanted to do was ask Loki just about anything.

It wasn't until I had all my clothes on and had gathered my bag that I realized I had nowhere to go. Karma had brought me to the infirmary barely functional after they'd packed up my apartment. I had no idea where they'd put my stuff, or if they'd simply brought it to a Goodwill and dropped it off. Did I even have a place to sleep?

Will I be able to stay with my Madam? Does she want me to?

"Problem?" Nightingale raised an eyebrow as she started stripping the bed I'd used.

"Yeah, no, I just don't know where to go from here. They cleared out my apartment and made me disappear, but except for this bed, I really have nowhere to go."

She nodded as she pulled the pillowcase off and tossed it into a linen hamper. "I'm going to go out on a limb here and suggest that maybe Karma wants you to stay with her."

I shrugged. "Maybe."

She also wanted to get rid of my car. She was right about it being the most visible vehicle in Colorado, but its loss meant more than just my ego. Rosé had given me new purpose when my life went to shit the first time. *And it's going to shit again.*

"Didn't you tell Dollhouse that it wasn't Karma's fault?"

"What?"

"You said Karma hadn't caused this rough spot in your life when Dollhouse told you the news."

"Yeah, that's right."

"So why are you holding the loss of your car over her? She's trying to protect you and give you a chance at bringing Backlog down." Nightingale pulled the sheets off and threw them in the hamper. "She's also trying to apologize for exposing you to Backlog and leaving you vulnerable. Maybe you could cut her a little slack. It's just a car, Eric. It can always be replaced. Karma? Not so much."

Eric. That was my new name for my new identity. When I'd helped other people start new lives, I'd never understood the difficulty of giving up who they'd been to have a chance at who they'd become. I faced the same challenge.

"Yeah, I know. It's just hard to let go of who I've been, the person I thought I was."

Nightingale shot me a compassionate smile. "I understand. The question is, is that the person you were always meant to be, or is there someone far stronger, smarter, and better out beyond this change?"

I frowned. "What do you mean?"

She shrugged as she gathered up the hamper to take out of the infirmary. "The only thing constant in this world is change, and if you refuse to do so, you could stagnate and die. Evolution isn't just in biology and paleontology. It's in sentient beings' development, too. You have to adapt. There are plenty of people who've died long ago but they're still walking upright. They were too scared to make the effort to change. You have a second chance, Eric. What will you choose to do?"

She left me standing there with my mouth open. I'd thought Rosé and the Marshals were my second chance at a better life. But what if I had a third chance, and this time I had a partner to back me up? Someone who made the bad guys quake in the boots they didn't know they had?

The questions rattled around in my head as I stepped out into the clubhouse. Music played and voices came from the main room where people lounged in the chairs or against the walls near the TV. I skirted around them and the pool tables, not meeting anyone's eyes. I was pretty sure most of them wanted to hang me from the nearest tree and I couldn't blame them. I didn't really have a crew, a family, backup or an agency.

And I don't have anywhere to go.

I had Rosé, but she was pretty damn visible. At least

she could get me somewhere if Karma didn't want me. Maybe out of state. *Yeah, and how long will I last on the run?* Backlog was national. I headed for the front doors, wondering if my third chance was still available.

"Coop! Shit, I mean, Eric." Karma's voice stopped me in my tracks and made everyone in the room stare at me.

Great. So much for the low profile.

I glanced back at her, my heart pounding in my chest at her beauty. I wanted her so much, but I had no idea where we stood. She'd told me she loved me and she'd visited the infirmary. Dollhouse said Karma loved me, but she'd never talked to me about what happened after I healed, and I wasn't looking at a lot of friends in the room.

"Hey." She gave me a warm smile though it faltered when I didn't return it. "Are you okay?"

My mouth flattened into a sarcastic line but I managed to stop the sharp words from escaping. "I'm fine. What's up?"

She frowned and tilted her head, her gaze scanning me with unnerving intensity. "You're angry. And scared, which just makes you more angry." She nodded sharply and took my good arm. "Come with me."

She pulled me out of the clubhouse toward her cabin. I didn't have anywhere else to be and I liked being with her despite my unease, so I followed along without complaint. She opened her cabin door and stood back.

"Go on in."

I met her gaze as I hesitated. "Why?"

She sighed. "Because I want you here. You're my Marshal, my sexy former lawman, and my mate. Didn't you believe me in the hospital?"

I nodded with a shrug. "Yeah, but that was days ago and I don't really know what's going on." I held up my hand when she opened her mouth to protest. "I know it's not logical, but it's how I feel and feelings aren't really logical, either. I'm out of my element here and I already fucked it up enough. I don't want to make things worse."

"Okay." She stepped across the threshold and turned to face me with her hand out. "Please, come in, Eric. I want you here in my life and in my bed...if you're a good guy." She gave me a sexy smirk that jumpstarted my heart and threatened to harden my cock. "I want you to be mine forever, or as close to it as we can get, and I promise to take care of you as your Madam for all that time." She wiggled her fingers. "Will you accept my invitation?"

You have a second chance, Eric. What will you choose to do?

Nightingale's words echoed in my head as I stared at Karma's hand, and I knew the answer before I could utter it aloud.

"I will." I stepped forward and grasped her hand, allowing her to tug me into the room. The smirk widened into a genuine smile and I realized she'd been uncertain how I'd respond.

She released me and closed the door before taking my bag from my hands and dropping it in the bedroom.

"Now, come sit down. I need to tell you what we have planned."

"Why does it matter?" I shrugged again. "I'm not in any condition to help." I lifted my splinted arm. "Not really up to anything physical."

"Don't worry. We can work around that." She smirked again and I suspected she meant something else. "But that's later. Right now, we're gonna take your car out to an abandoned area, put a body in it dressed in your clothes, and set it on fire. Everyone will think you're dead and you'll be safe."

I ignored the stab of pain at the thought of Rosé being burned. "They'll test for DNA, fingerprints, and dental records. They'll figure out it isn't me."

She shook her head. "Not the way the body will be burned. We're going to leave your badge and your service weapon on the seat, and make sure the tail of your shirt gets closed in the door so it survives the fire. Torch is that good at burning things."

I shook my head. "What about DNA, fingerprints, and dental records? I haven't forgotten to go to the dentist once. They'll know it's not me."

"We got that covered. Neo's changing the records to make sure the body we have will match when they run tests. It'll be damn near charred to nothing, but we'll leave just enough for them to match it to "you", meaning the body. Genius, right?"

"Maybe, but someone will recognize me if they see me walking around after. Like my boss or my old partner and it'll get out. I can change my name, get rid of my car, and color my hair, but my face is my face." I spread my hands. "Unless I totally disappear, someone's gonna know."

"Don't worry about the local Backlog guys, and Neo's fixing the records, including what you look like. Eric Marshal and Cooper DeVille will have different faces in the digital world."

I opened my mouth to ask how, but she shook her head. "Don't ask. You don't want to know. As for your partner and your boss, how important are they to you?"

Alarm zipped through me. "You're not going to kill them."

"No, no." She waved her hand, dismissing the idea. "But we do have ways of making them forget. It's not harmful or invasive, but it is permanent. They literally won't recognize you or your name or have any memory of their connection to you."

That sounded creepy as hell. How could they make someone completely forget? Did they use drugs or hypnotism?

"What are you going to do?"

"I'm not going to do anything, but Loki knows a guy." She shrugged and refused to elaborate.

"I shook my head. "There's one guy I don't want messed with. But the rest of the Denver Marshals' office is fine. Gary Battlebourne is a good man and he might be a good contact on the inside in the future."

"Don't Marshals have partners? What about them?"

I grimaced. I still didn't know if Anna was in with Backlog or clean. "Yeah, her too."

"Her?" Karma's voice sharpened. "I didn't know your partner was a woman." She eyed me narrowly. "Did you ever sleep with her?"

"No, Karma. Stop. Contrary to what Hollywood and TV likes to say, men and women can work together without having sex." I scowled and looked away. As much as I'd liked working with Anna, I'd never been sexually attracted to her. "Would you have asked me the same question if my partner was a man?"

She shook her head. "No, because I know you're attracted to women."

"Still, give me a little credit to see my partner as a person rather than a pretty decoration."

"So she's pretty?"

I groaned and rubbed my face with my hand. "I never considered. She was my coworker, not someone I lusted after. Besides, I don't know if she's part of Backlog and I can't take the chance." I sighed. "I'm really doing this. I'm really disappearing."

She crouched in front of me and rested her hands on my thighs. "I know it's an unfair change, a huge unfair change. But you'll be getting a life back, free from Backlog, and you'll have me, your Madam."

She stopped as she met my gaze, waiting for me to say something. When I didn't, she bit her bottom lip.

"I'm still your Madam, right?"

Dollhouse's words about Karma believing she'd caused this drastic change in my life came back. Part of me wanted to punish her a little for telling me to leave and ripping out my heart. But that was the childish toddler in me and I told it to go fuck itself and locked it in its room.

"Yes, Ma'am, if you'll allow me to serve you. No secrets."

"No secrets." She nodded and pushed between my legs, resting her breasts on my groin.

Oh yeah, my cock liked that, but I reined it in and held out my working hand. "Hi, my name's Eric Marshal and I'm a private investigator."

"It's very nice to meet you, Eric." She took my hand and squeezed gently. "I'm Karma, and yes, I mean that literally. I'm the physical manifestation of the energy of consequences and I'm the Enforcer for the Concrete Angels Motorcycle Club."

"You're beautiful, Karma, and I want to stay with you." I meant the words. So much of life had thrown me out various windows with me frantically trying not to fall. I just wanted a safe place to land with people who'd have my back. Battlebourne had, but even he'd been limited by the threat of Backlog.

"Forever?"

I nodded, very well aware that forever could last a blink. "For how long forever lasts."

She rose up and wrapped her arms around me, pulling my lips to hers. Her kiss hinted at more than a simple promise, but it still felt like coming home. *Maybe I've finally found the safe place to land.*

CHAPTER TWENTY-TWO

Cooper

It took us a few more days to organize everything so it would play out the way we wanted Backlog to think. I kept asking Karma what she was going to do about Ainsworth. He knew my face and would know the records had been changed. She just gave me an enigmatic smile and said it would be fine. A little voice in the back of my head reminded me I might not want to know what that meant.

By then, my arm and chest no longer felt like they would fall off and break at any given moment, and I could breathe again. It made walking a helluva lot easier. Karma or Loki must have said something because the rest of the Concrete Angels stepped up to help get me ready for my dramatic ending. Well, most of them. Scott and Numbers remained aloof, and Dollhouse worked at calming Scott down about it.

Still, it was a lot like Spy Boot Camp. People would show up out of the blue and start a conversation with Eric, who I was supposed to be, and I'd have to respond like a normal guy. Like it was me and not a made-up identity. I screwed up a few times and they'd call me on it like the Russian KGB instructors trying to beat me into shape. I definitely learned fast.

But I was still Marshal Cooper DeVille for my final performance and I had to make it look good. Neo had changed all my records, including my face, fingerprints, dental records, and even my DNA profile. I had no idea where they gotten the body that would be my death substitute, but I didn't really want to know. Torch had tried to ease my mind by telling me the guy would essentially get a Viking funeral, but it didn't really help.

I pulled open the doors of the Fort Collins police station and strode inside, bold as brass in my US Marshal's coat. No one noticed me until I met the desk clerk. But I gave the woman a professional smile and showed her my badge.

"Marshal Cooper DeVille to see Commissioner Ainsworth."

The clerk clicked a few things on the computer. "I don't have you on the schedule, Marshal DeVille."

"No, he just called me about an hour ago and said to drop by whenever."

The clerk frowned but nodded. "I'll call him and tell him you're here."

"Thanks."

We didn't actually have an appointment but I figured my name would get me in the door. He'd probably want to know why the hell I was visiting after disappearing from the hospital almost a week before.

I glanced around the station. No one else paid me much mind. I wondered if Backlog hadn't infiltrated the precinct as much or if they were just good actors. *We'll find out soon enough.*

"Marshal DeVille? The Commissioner will see you now."

Yeah, I just bet he will. "Thanks." I followed her to the office near the back and stepped inside, leaving the door open behind me.

"Marshal DeVille. So good to see you. What can I do for you?" Ainsworth's greeting was pleasant enough but his eyes glittered like a rattlesnake's.

"Actually, it's what I can do for you, Commissioner Ainsworth. I wanted to thank you for the beating you gave me with the help of your friend Officer Kinsley. I needed to give you a heads-up so you and Backlog can make sure to line up your lawyers and judges on the take." I'd raised my voice so it carried out of his office and into the station. As I'd hoped, the conversations outside had stopped or slowed, and people were staring in our direction.

Ainsworth's expression hardened and he lost his smile. "Those are serious allegations."

"They're not allegations. I'm still living despite the punctured lung, broken ribs, and the concussion you gave me. Check the hospital records. You'll see I was there."

"That could've been anyone who beat you."

I nodded. "Could've, sure, except you were there threatening me and my girlfriend if I didn't lay off investigating Backlog, the shadow organization that's been infiltrating law enforcement agencies across the country for the last decade."

He bit back a snarl and headed for the door to close it. I turned to keep him in my view, though I suspected he didn't hit people. His people hit people. Despite his best efforts, everyone in the station was focused on us and I bit back a smile. It was all going according to plan.

"We warned you, DeVille. If you kept coming after us we'd kill your slut girlfriend."

"Let me stop you right there. One, she's not a slut in the way you mean the word – I doubt she'd give you a look more than to avoid you on the street. Two, you should know better than to threaten a member of law enforcement. We don't take it lightly or with much amusement. And three, I owe you this."

I took three steps to him and clocked him hard with my

fist, right across the jaw. He went down with an indignant grunt and fell against his old-fashioned coatrack. I'd hit him hard, so hard my hand ached, but I didn't wait around for him to get up. I was out the door and across the room before he managed to scramble to his feet. I heard him roar about catching me just as I sailed through the front doors.

It's a damn good thing I'm gonna be dead soon. I'd assaulted a police commissioner. I would've been reprimanded and more than likely fired, even if Backlog hadn't had a grip on the Marshals.

I slid into the seat of my bright Pompeian Red Caddy and waited just long enough to give my pursuers a good look at her taillights before heading out of town. I needed to be far enough ahead to set the trap, but close enough for them to follow me.

Rosé's engine rumbled and purred as she sped through the streets, heading for the freeway. Most people were still at work so getting out of town before the flashing lights made for a pretty easy drive. They caught up to me right around the time I hit the highway up into the mountains and I opened her up.

Gotta say one thing for good old Detroit steel. They made engines that didn't quit. I roared up into the mountains, my back window full of lovely patriotic lights when my phone rang.

"Hello?"

"How's it going?" Karma's voice flowed over me and settled some of my nervousness.

"Good. I've pissed off the entire Fort Collins police department and Commissioner Ainsworth. They're now chasing me. How are you?"

She laughed and my heart rate increased with the spike of joy and adrenaline. "We're ready for them. How much of a lead do you have on them?"

I glanced at the rearview mirror. "Only about thirty seconds."

"Widen that please."

"How would you like me to do that?" I leaned into a sharp turn, slowing a little.

"Around the next curve is a road to the hiking trails. We're waiting for you at the trailhead. That's where Torch'll switch out with you and take care of the rest. Just leave your badge, wallet, phone, shirt and coat there."

I shook my head. "Yeah, I got it. Comin' around the turn now."

I dropped the phone and focused on keeping the old girl on the asphalt. I'd widened the gap between me and the cop cars and they hadn't sent up a chopper yet, so I still had the advantage. I saw the trailhead sign to the right and yanked the wheel. Rosé fishtailed but made the turn and the trees swallowed us. I kept glancing back at the road behind and caught the cop cars continuing on their original path as the road wound through the rocky hills.

I blew out a relieved breath and continued to the trailhead where Torch, Karma, Attila and Viper waited for me. Karma watched me drive in but the others kept their gazes on the road behind me, watching for unwanted company. I kept my focus on the plan even if it ended with a dead guy in the driver's seat and Rosé on fire. I gritted my teeth and pulled into a parking spot for easy egress.

Oh glory, we're really doing this.

I knew the reasons it had to be done and I agreed with them but the potential loss gnawed at my gut and made me want to weep like a man losing his wife and family. I was losing my family. I shot a look at the Concrete Angels waiting for me to get out. No one smiled as they converged on the car. I wasn't sure I'd gained anything.

"How was the drive, laddie?" Attila gave me a mild smile as I stepped out of the car and headed for the trunk.

"Oh, you know, uneventful." I couldn't keep the dry sarcasm out of my voice.

He snorted as I opened the trunk. The body there lay in

a twisted mess and I'd banged him up a bit taking those corners as I did. I felt kinda bad until I remembered he was dead and no one would see the damage once he burned to a crisp.

I stepped back out of the way and shrugged out of my overshirt and coat as the men lifted the body out of the back. Viper took the clothes and threw them on the body, working the sleeves onto the arms like dressing a doll. She was surprisingly efficient and I wondered how many other bodies she'd dressed for things like this.

They set the body in the passenger seat and Torch hurried around to the driver's side. He winked as he settled inside and I tossed him the keys.

"I'd tell you to take care of my baby but that seems to be at cross-purpose to our goal. So, good luck."

"Luck's got nothin' to do with it." Torch winked as he closed the door. He rolled down the window. "Damn, this body stinks. I'll be glad to set it alight." He glanced up at the sky to the south. "You better get under cover. There's a chopper coming."

I frowned and glanced at the sky, but Karma grabbed my arm and pulled me toward the building holding the bathrooms as Torch backed Rosé out of her spot. We'd just stepped into the women's restroom when a helicopter crested the trees to the south. Torch floored it and Rosé sped out of the trailhead parking lot, headed back to the main road.

The Bell helicopter with Denver PD markings pivoted in the sky to follow as the tail end of my car headed out of sight. I let my breath out in a long sigh, the ache of loss already grabbing my heart. No family, no friends, no job, and no cool car. I'd really given up everything.

I have my life. Kinda.

I shot a look at the three other people around me and wondered what lay ahead. I had a name, a social security number, and a black Toyota sedan I'd have to sell.

And I have Karma. I'd figure out the job part later.

"Okay, chopper's out of range." Viper stepped out of the bathroom and headed for the bikes parked in the trees behind the building. "Let's see what they see."

She opened the flap on her nearest saddlebag and drew out a remote control. She flipped a few switches and a soft high-pitched buzzing drew my attention to a little drone parked in a spot of sunshine beneath the trees. Viper revved the little machine up and it zipped into the air like an angry hummingbird, sailing off after the cops. We all huddled around her screen to watch the show.

The action on the screen played out like a movie, with the cops and helicopter chasing the fugitive through the winding mountain roads. Viper kept the drone low enough not to get in the chopper's way but still high enough to keep all the action in view.

I had to admit Torch handled Rosé with confidence until he got closer to the end of his run. The car fishtailed a couple of time as if he'd started to panic as he ran out of road. Up ahead, the land ended in a fairly deep gouge from a stream cutting through the hillside. The canyon wasn't narrow enough to jump and the steep sides made driving anything down them impossible. Trees and jagged chunks of rock protruded like odd teeth beyond the edge of the ravine.

As he sped to toward the canyon at full speed, I caught sight of something diving from the driver's side just before the car shot over the edge. I whimpered in dismay as the tail lights dropped from view and Attila's hand dropped onto my shoulder, squeezing sympathetically.

The drone moved closer enough to see the car explode into flames as the gas tank went up. I'd filled it up before I went to piss off Ainsworth so there'd been plenty of fuel to allow us to make our getaway. It created a flaming vessel worthy of a Viking funeral as Torch had said.

The cops skidded to a stop before they followed Rosé

into the canyon. The helicopter flew into the open space and circled around to get a better view. I'd bet my life savings that Ainsworth sat in the front, scanning the wreckage for signs of life.

Not gonna find it, asshole.

I hoped Torch got away as Karma touched my arm and motioned me toward her bike.

"You okay?"

I shrugged. "Yeah, I'm fine."

"I'm really sorry about your car." She grasped my hand in sympathy. "I know she meant a lot to you."

I nodded. "And I know why she had to go."

"But it still sucks. Let me take you home and make you feel better." She straddled her bike and held out a helmet to me. "Put this on so no cameras pick you up."

I put it on my head and buckled it as I settled on behind her. Viper retrieved the drone and packed it up in her saddlebags. Attila swung his leg over his bike, his kilt swinging behind him. I wondered if he froze his balls off when he rode around in the winter, but the thought was left behind as we rumbled out of the trailhead and pointed our wheels back toward the compound and for me, the unknown.

****

Karma

I felt Coop/Eric's silence behind me as we headed into the forest to pick up Torch. Of course, he wore a helmet that disguised his face so I couldn't hear him, but his withdrawal settled deeper than that. I wanted to tell him it would be all right, but I sensed he wouldn't believe me at the moment. And honestly, the plans I had in mind still needed a little more time to develop.

Torch met us at another picnic spot three miles from

where he'd sent the car off the cliff. I didn't doubt his ability to survive jumping out of the moving car, but I still breathed a sigh of relief when I saw him waiting for us, leaning against the fence with his ankles crossed. Smoke trailed from his nostrils and his eyes glowed with internal flames but he wore a relaxed smile.

"Lookin' good, hot stuff." Viper laughed as he winked. "Come on, I'll give you a ride home."

"Actually, I have an errand to run in town. Would you mind droppin' me there?"

I raised my eyebrows but Viper nodded. "Sure. That'll give me a chance to stop at Michael's favorite bakery and get him something sweet. He's been extra irritable since he came back from taking the brothel victims to the shelter."

Eric lifted the face mask on the helmet. "Everyone get out okay?"

Viper shrugged. "Yeah, but I think it shook him just how evil people can be to each other and he's having a tough time regaining his perspective. A treat might mellow his sharp edges."

"Okay. We'll see you back at the compound then." Michael wasn't the only one with sharp edges. Eric had grown stiffer and stiffer the longer we waited to get going.

Attila and Viper revved up their bikes and headed out, but before I could follow suit, Eric thumped my arm. "Ma'am, what's gonna be done to Ainsworth? He's a direct link between the Fort Collins' PD and Backlog, and nothing happened to him today."

I shook my head. "Nothing's happened that you know of. But karma doesn't always come to people where their victims can see or in the way they expect. Just trust that the consequences of his actions are already in the works and will become clear shortly. And even better, they won't lead back to you."

He studied my face, searching for answers with his chocolate brown eyes, but that's all I would tell him. He didn't need to know that Ainsworth's rash actions in beating Coop up and Coop's subsequent reveal of Backlog's presence at the Fort Collins police station had required Backlog to take action to remove Ainsworth, permanently. Turned out it wasn't the first time Backlog had to clean up one of Ainsworth's mistakes, but it would be the last.

"But he will get what's coming to him?"

I sighed. "Are you really that bloodthirsty?"

Eric shook his head. "No, not for what he did to me. What he might do to you. Plus he knows what I look like. I can't be Eric Marshal if someone who knows what Cooper DeVille looks like. Or I'll have to leave Colorado for good."

The idea made my stomach cramp, but I reminded myself that retribution had already been set in motion and Ainsworth wouldn't live through it.

"Your secret is safe within the Concrete Angels. Michael and Luke are making sure. By the time we get back to the compound, only the inner circle, Attila, Viper, Torch and I will remember you were anyone other than Eric Marshal."

"Wait. How are you gonna do that?"

"Do you really want to know? Or are you content to know it can be done in world that contains a physical body for karma?" I'd asked the question flippantly, but it was far more serious than that. Could he understand the magic Loki had brought to bear to give me the life I had? *And apparently the mate who's sitting behind me?*

He stared at me a long time, thinking over my words. "Are you telling me that when we ride back into the Concrete Angels' compound, everyone will have forgotten I was US Marshal Cooper DeVille?"

I shook my head. "Not forgotten. As far as they're concerned, US Marshal Cooper DeVille never existed. They won't recognize you. I'll introduce you as Eric

Marshal, a private detective, and that's how they'll know you."

He raised his eyebrows. "Even Scott and Oriana?"

I grimaced and shrugged. Messing with their memories had sucked, but was necessary.

"What about Gopher?"

"Oh, particularly him. Do you think that jackass could keep a secret? His mouth would run faster than Speedy Gonzalez."

Too my relief, Eric laughed, his eyes crinkling at the corners in that oh-so-sexy way.

He nodded. "Yeah, I can totally see that."

"So let's go home where it's safe and I can explain everything I've been planning while you rested up. I promise, I have a lot to tell you."

He tilted his head, his eyes growing curious. "Yeah, a lot to tell me?"

"Yeah, and a few things to ask of you." That's where I grew nervous. I wanted to make our relationship permanent. I wanted to be sure I could take care of him and fulfill his needs every time. But I'd need his permission and the last few days had been tricky at best.

"Okay. Take me home, then."

I didn't have the words to describe the pleasure of his declaring the Concrete Angels' compound as home, but I gave him my most brilliant smile before I kick-started my bike. I hoped everything would be ready for when we came back, but if not, I'm sure I could improvise. And Eric was definitely worth a little improvisation.

CHAPTER TWENTY-THREE

Eric

Karma had said everyone would think of me as Eric Marshal, but I had my doubts. I shouldn't have worried or even questioned. I mean, if she really was the physical manifestation of the energy of consequences, then it stood to reason she was right about everyone getting a mindwipe straight out of a sci-fi flick. But remembering how things had gone when everyone found out I was a US Marshal stuck with me.

We rode in through the gates and Karma parked her bike in the barn workshop. I kept the helmet on until we stopped and dismounted. I took a deep breath and pulled it off, expecting people to give us the hairy eyeball about my presence. Karma had explained to people why she'd brought me back from the hospital—I'd been injured by the guys who'd stolen their money and I had no one else. But now? After we'd kicked their asses? Yeah, I didn't expect much of a reception.

A couple of the scooters meandered by, eyeing Karma with appreciation and me with curiosity. *Like they don't know me.* I frowned as I set the brain bucket on Karma's bike and she secured it before taking my hand.

"Let's go talk to Loki and let him know how it turned out." She pulled me toward the clubhouse, but I tugged back.

"Are you sure you don't want to do that alone? I'm not part of the inner circle of the Concrete Angels, and I'm a former US Marshal." I rubbed the back of my neck as I shot a look around at the other members in the yard. "I can accept that you want me with you, but I also know no one wants a stranger in the know."

She squeezed my hand. "But Loki likes to meet all the newcomers to take their measure, and he'll want to meet you as his new private investigator for the club. I have a feeling this Backlog thing is going to be a long-term endeavor that's gonna take a lot of investigation and research. Loki will want an expert on it. Today was just the first engagement."

"Private investigator for the club?" I allowed her to tug me through the clubhouse doors.

"Yeah. You'll need a job and we need to keep an eye on what Backlog's up to. Win-win."

I tilted my head. "And does that mean I'll be staying or living here?"

"Would you like to?" She gave me her best enigmatic smile.

Would I? Spending my time working on ways to take Backlog down while still getting to serve my Madam and pleasure her until she screamed with ecstasy? *Let me think...*

"Yes, Ma'am."

Her smile grew wider. "Let's introduce you to Loki, then."

We passed by Dollhouse sitting with Scott and Oriana, and I waited for the protests at my returning to their home. But while Scott scowled, it wasn't with the furious animosity I'd seen when I'd left that morning, and Oriana merely watched me with wary curiosity. Dollhouse nodded, but I suspected it was to Karma rather than to me.

Seriously? They don't seem to know me. At all.

We found Loki in his office with Neo and Michael while Viper and Attila finished telling them their part of my death deception. Neo didn't bother looking up from his tablet but Michael nodded to Karma before his gaze landed on me. He'd grown more serious since he'd rescued the sex slave victims, but I didn't feel any animosity.

Thank glory. I still wasn't sure who he was, but I definitely didn't want to be on his bad side.

"Ye shoulda seen those wee bastards swarming around the wreckage like ants." Attila shook his head with a wry grin. "We couldn't stay to see that Ainsworth fella get all bent outta shape, but the helicopter kept circlin' the wreckage."

"Ah, Karma, glad you got out okay. You, too, Mr. Marshal." Loki shot a look at me and winked. "Sounds like everything worked like a charm."

"Yeah, I guess it did." I nodded as I glanced around the room at the others. "Thanks for all your help."

"Och, 'twas a pleasure. I love watchin' cops run around chasin' their tails." Attila gave me a nod. "Not bad driving either. They thought they had ye until ye gave 'em the slip up there in the toolies."

I raised my eyebrows. "How do you know that?"

"I was listenin' to the police bands. That's why they brought out the helicopter."

I laughed and Loki grinned. "All's well that ends well, *ja*? So, we help you fake your death, give you a new identity, and in exchange, you become our pet dick, *ja*?"

I didn't like the way he'd phrased it, but it was a reasonable deal considering all they'd done for me. And despite their nefarious reputation, I liked the Concrete Angels. *And I definitely don't have room to talk about operating outside the law.*

I nodded. "And if I refuse?"

Karma's eyes widened and the others around me stiffened. Loki didn't move and his smile didn't change, but his eyes became harder.

"Then we return you to your life." He shrugged but I got the impression he meant my life as Cooper DeVille, U.S. Marshal. "And you'll have to watch your back for both Backlog and the Concrete Angels, *ja*? The choice is yours."

I nodded again. "Yeah, that's what I figured. I just wanted to see what I'd be missing, and it turns out, not much. I'm happy to stay and help you find out more about Backlog, and be Karma's mate."

The tension drained out of the room as if everyone had breathed a sigh of relief. Viper shot a look at Karma and winked before she turned her head back to Loki. *What's that about?* Attila grumbled something about contrary Americans and Michael's lips curled into a half-smile. Only Neo kept his stoic expression.

"*Det er bra*. Welcome to the Concrete Angels, Mr. Marshal. Over the next few days, we'll set up your office here in the clubhouse and you can continue your investigation, *ja*?" Loki grinned but the humor had a calculating edge to it. "Neo will put together your email and phone, Numbers will set up your expense accounts, and Viper will help you with surveillance equipment. But this can be done over the next few days, too."

"Thanks." *I think*. It was everything I wanted, right? Well, almost everything. I didn't have a cool car anymore, but I thought I might be able to find a good chassis in a junk yard somewhere and start building again. "I look forward to having a new base of operations."

Loki nodded. "You might also need to look into personal issues of the clubmembers as part of your inclusion here. Everyone has something worth looking at, *ja*?"

I snorted. "Yeah, most likely. Sounds fair. Should we

get this in writing, just so there's no misunderstanding or wiggle room?"

His grin widened. "*Ja*, that's a good idea. Neo?"

Uh-oh. Neo tapped a couple of things on his tablet and the printer in the corner of the room spit out a couple of pages. He gathered them up and handed them to me. I looked over the contract, reading it carefully just in case his name gave evidence of who he truly was. *Do I really want to make a deal with Loki, Norse God of Mischief?* When put like that, I'd have rather eaten an entire rattlesnake carcass coated in gangrene, but the contract read clearly and the terms were acceptable.

"Looks good. Got a pen to sign with?"

Loki laughed and chills ran down my spine. "*Ja*, this one."

He held up what looked like an old-fashioned quill pen, but it had a small, sharp blade on the grip. He scraped his finger across it until it bled, feeding the pen with blood to use as ink. *Holy glory.* He signed his name with a flourish then handed the pen to Michael. He dropped the pen into a small bowl of water, swirling it through the liquid until it turned pink and the pen was clean. He dried it and handed it to me.

"You want me to sign with blood?"

"*Ja*, this is how we do things here." He nodded to the pen. "It makes the contract completely binding to everyone involved."

I raised an eyebrow. "Even you?"

He smirked. "Especially me."

I narrowed my eyes at him but followed his example by pricking my finger. The blood oozed down to the tip of the pen and I signed my new legal name. I could try to weasel out of the contract by insisting I was Cooper DeVille, but I wasn't planning to go back to that name. Besides, I wasn't in the habit of breaking contracts, particularly with people like Loki. Something told me the havoc he'd wreak would be astronomical.

The air rippled as I finished signing my name and the hair on the back of my neck stood up. *What the hell was that?* I shot a look at the others in the room, but no one else seemed to have seen it. Loki grinned.

"It is done. Tomorrow we'll have an office for you to start your work, but today we celebrate your escape from the police." Loki rose and gestured toward the door. "We'll send Gopher for the beer."

Attila groaned. "Och, not Gopher. Knowing the clueless lad, he'll bring back a lawyer this time."

Everyone one laughed, but I agreed with Attila and wouldn't put it past Gopher to do just that in his quest for alcohol.

"Are you okay with this?" Karma squeezed my hand as she tugged me back toward the front doors.

I shrugged. "Yeah, I think so. It's kinda new right now and it hasn't sunk in yet."

"Not to overwhelm you, but I have something for you."

I raised my eyebrows. "What is it?"

"Come with me to find out." She gave me a secret smile and dragged me to her cabin. "Ready?"

"Close enough."

She followed me inside and closed the door behind her. "Go sit on the loveseat. I'll bring them to you."

"Them?"

She winked. "Just sit." She pointed and I plopped my ass onto the loveseat. "Good guy."

Her approval warmed my heart as she disappeared into her bedroom. What could she have for me? I took a deep breath and my ribs twinged, reminding me I'd had some fairly traumatic injuries recently. I'd have to figure out where I'd be staying or find myself an apartment nearby. With the documentation the Concrete Angels had provided, housing wouldn't be a problem.

"Close your eyes, Eric." Karma used her Madam voice and my eyes closed on their own.

I heard her come back into the room carrying something. She sat down beside me and rearranged whatever she had on her lap. "Okay, open."

I opened my eyes and found her holding a large box wrapped in brightly colored paper.

"What's this?"

"Just open it." She grinned as she handed me the large box.

Stripping away the paper didn't help reveal what it was so I pulled the lid off the box. Inside rested a black leather jacket with the club's patch on the back, the gargoyle with a maniacal grin on a motorcycle with flaming wheels. The banner at the top read "CLUB P.I." and the rocker at the bottom read "PROPERTY OF KARMA." I stared at the jacket and my throat closed. Tears didn't quite hit my eyes, but it was close. I raised my gaze to Karma.

"Are you sure, Ma'am? After everything?"

The smile she gave me warmed me better than a leather jacket. "Yeah, I'm sure."

I ran my fingers over the supple leather. "Thank you. I'll wear it with pride."

"Good. Then I can give you this." She handed me a much smaller box wrapped in the same bright paper.

I opened it to find a set of keys on a keyring with a Marshal's star hanging from it with the words "Deputy Dick" inscribed. I laughed as I held them up. "What are they to?"

"This cabin and the gate, so you can come and go as you need to." For one moment she looked hopeful and insecure as if she wasn't sure how I'd take having keys to her place. "That is, if you're okay staying here with your Madam."

I set the box with the jacket on the floor and dropped the keys on it as I rolled to my knees in front of her, taking her hands. I met her gaze and put my whole heart into my eyes and voice.

"I'd be honored and very pleased to stay here and serve you to the best of my ability, Ma'am. I'm much happier with you than without you." I meant every word. She was the only woman for me, even if she wasn't completely human.

She swallowed hard and her smile wobbled a little as she cleared her throat. "Good. Then I can give you this."

The last box was long and narrow, and had a fair amount of weight to it. I sat back on my heels as I unwrapped it then lifted the lid. Inside, nestled in black satin, rested a thick, silver herringbone chain. At one end it had an open loop and at the other, a small, elegant brushed gold padlock lay unlocked with a small key. The words "For Karma" had been engraved into the back side of the padlock.

This time, I couldn't stop the tears from flooding my eyes. "Is that what I think it is?"

"That depends. What do you think it is?"

I cleared my throat to keep my voice level, but it wobbled anyway. "It looks like a collar, the kind a Madam will put on her devoted submissive." I raised my gaze as the tears spilled over. "Are you collaring me, Ma'am?"

She nodded, her smile hopeful. "That's exactly what it is, sweet man. If you're okay with it, I'd like you to be my mate, my sub, my handsome Marshal from now until forever. What do you say?" She lifted the chain out of the box and held it up. "No one has to know what this means, beyond you and I, but it's my equivalent of a wedding ring. Would you accept my collar, Eric? Would you be my committed submissive?"

I barked a laugh as the tears ran down my face. "Yes, Ma'am. Oh glory, yes, Ma'am."

Karma reached out and fastened the chain around my neck, closing the padlock with a tiny click. Again, the air swirled like it had when I signed Loki's contract, and it felt just as binding. The chain settled onto my shoulders and chest, the lock resting between my collar bones and most of my worries fled from my awareness. Whatever happened after, I'd have my Madam at my back, and I'd serve her forever.

"Thank you for this, Ma'am. I lost the last piece of jewelry you gave me." I grimaced to hold back the disappointment. "I don't know what happened to it, but when I woke up in the hospital, it was gone."

"Are you talking about the cock jewelry?"

"Yes, Ma'am. I'm afraid they destroyed it when they took me in for surgery." It still pierced my heart at the loss.

"Were you wearing it during your beating?"

I blinked and nodded. "Of course, Ma'am. I would never remove it unless you gave me permission."

She gaped at me. "Even after I asked you to leave me alone? You still kept it on?"

"Yes, Ma'am. It was a way to stay close to you after I left." I glanced away and bit my lip. "I needed to feel it there in hopes I hadn't lost you forever."

"Oh, Eric." She gave me a watery smile. "I wasn't thinking very clearly. Can you forgive my stupidity?"

My own smile was pretty damn watery too. "Of course, Ma'am."

"Good." She reached out to smooth the necklace against my shoulders. "This is beautiful on you." Karma closed one fist over the key. "And I'll keep this safe for you." She sniffled a little and gave me a warm smile as her phone buzzed with a text. She picked it up and smiled wider.

"What is it?"

"I have one more thing to give you." She pushed me back and stood, lifting me to my feet.

"More? Why are you giving me so much, Ma'am?" I'd never needed much and it seemed an abundance after the way things had fallen apart a week before.

Karma stopped, her expression unusually solemn. "I'd give you the world if I could, Eric. I love you to the moon and back. You're my everything."

Her statement struck me dumb and I allowed her to tug me back out to the yard where we found Torch waiting on us. He leaned against a peacock green and cream 1956 Chevy Corvette soft top, a cocky grin curling his lips.

"Wow. That's a helluva car, Torch." I was rather envious.

"Do you like it?" Karma bit her lip, her expression hopeful.

"The car? Yeah, it's sexy and sleek."

"Good. Then it's yours." Torch tossed me the keys and I caught them out of reflex.

"What?"

"It's yours. I figured since you had to sacrifice your Caddy to save your life, we should make sure you had a nice ride to replace it." He pushed off the car and waved at it. "A buddy of mine had this baby lyin' around his junkyard and I was workin' on it for fun. I fixed it up and had another friend paint her. He finished cleaning her up today. She's all yours now."

"Aw, Torch, man, I don't know what to say." It was true. Thanks seemed completely inadequate.

"You're welcome, Marshal." He grabbed me and gave me a back-pounding hug. "Good to have you as part of the Concrete Angels. Don't fuck it up, okay?"

"Yeah, gonna do my best not to."

"Good. Enjoy your car." He tilted his head a moment to take in the new necklace around my throat. "That's fuckin' sexy right there. And it looks good on you. Congrats." He winked as he sauntered away and I rubbed the back of my neck as my emotions overwhelmed me again.

"You okay?" Karma stepped up, trailing her fingers

over the chain around my neck. I shivered at her touch and nodded.

"Yes, Ma'am. I'm better than okay. I'm home."

It had been a long time coming, but I'd finally found what I was meant to do. I'd continue to investigate and hound Backlog, and I'd serve my Madam to the best of my ability. And I'd drive my cool car. *I guess I finally got some good Karma.* Good karma and a good future. I was all for it.

EPILOGUE

Michael

I'd seen a lot of shit over the millennia, stuff that
would curl anyone's toes in horror. Humans had the
amazing capacity to hurt each other in ways even my older
brother Luke hadn't devised. But they also had an
overwhelming capacity for love and compassion that
outstripped the ugliness every day and twice on Sundays.
I'd seen both in one day and I reeled from the tug-of-war
between the two extremes.

When we raided the sickening brothel filled with sex
slaves, I'd damn near hurled my breakfast onto my shoes.
The women and children of both genders we found wore
expressions of defeat and despair, their bodies the only
thing keeping them alive. I was certain most of them
would've chosen to die if they could have.

Some had been drugged, other beaten, and still others
had been bound by fear of retribution from the guards
keeping them in. All of them had made so much profound
sorrow rise up in my chest I feared I'd stop breathing. It
was all I could to do to load them into the van and clear the
tears from my eyes enough to drive.

Nightingale performed triage in the back despite the

cramped quarters and her face told me more than I wanted to know. She and I had often worked together to protect the people around us from the rigors of human existence, but it was the first time I'd questioned why I stayed when such evil existed in human hearts. As an Archangel, my job was usually pretty easy. I gave counsel, I helped people see a different, less violent path, and when all else failed, I committed violence to make sure the evil deeds didn't get out of hand. But the sight of these people so hurt by others made me want to do harm in ways that wouldn't bring redemption or healing to anyone.

Sweet glory, we're gonna take down those Backlog mudfuckers and give them a helluva retribution. I clenched my jaw and pulled into the parking lot of the Hopeful Heart Shelter. Oriana had found it to be the best shelter in Fort Collins for victims of sexual assault and I couldn't think of a better place for the people I'd help rescue.

It took all my grace as an angel to convince some of the women and kids to come out of the van. To them I represented the biggest, baddest, most frightening man they could imagine with my dark hair, scruff, and arm tattoos. They didn't know the tattoos represented challenges I'd overcome, like the one they faced. But I tried to smile at them with all the compassion in my heart as I fought tears. None of these people deserved the damage done to them.

Nightingale led them inside and stopped to talk to the director of the shelter, a tall, slender woman with weathered skin on her face. She looked as if she'd lived as hard as her charges had, but her core of steel had allowed her to help others. She didn't hesitate to take in the victims and find places for them.

"Haley, could you come help me with the kids, please?" The director waved at another woman across the room.

"Sure, Evelyn."

I froze.

The woman named Haley had a soft smile for the children that made my heart ache and her rich brown eyes crinkled at the corners with her warmth. She'd pulled her dark hair into a ponytail and the luxurious waves brushed her shoulders as she turned her head to listen to one of the youngsters.

Sweet glory of all, she's the One.

I'd been with the humans for millennia, watching and learning from them all the time. I envied their ability to love so completely and fiercely that they'd give their all for their loved ones. It was both inspiring and baffling. I'd always protected the people around me, stood up for them, and defended them, but I'd never experienced the love they displayed, even for the littlest things like kittens or a garden.

Hell, I wondered if I was even capable of feeling that kind of love. Watching my friend Scott fall for Oriana had made me wonder if love was only a human emotion, something denied those of the Elder Races. Oh, sure, I'd felt love—the pleasure, kindness, joy, and compassion held for people who needed protection, whether human or not. But never the gut-wrenching, bone-deep love that made people sacrifice everything for someone else.

But Karma had fallen for Cooper-cum-Eric with the same desire and fervor I'd seen in human couples, and he'd returned the feelings. I'd never been jealous of anyone before, but the green monster had flared in my chest when I looked at them.

I stared at Haley and I couldn't take my eyes off her. She listened to the kids with patience and focus, never touching or intruding on their space. Her whole body radiated calm, patient, kindness, and I wanted to stand with her to boost her signal.

Yeah, she doesn't need you. She didn't. The kids were drawn to her strength and followed her as she led them toward the dorms of the shelter. I could stop watching her and my heart pounded with the need to speak to her before she got away.

But at the last moment before she left the room, Haley looked up and met my gaze. Time stopped and I fell into her eyes, seeing the heart inside. I'd been chosen to protect the people of our world and to help them in any way I could. But Haley had been born a protector, too, with a core of steel and a heart of fire, and she'd fight for those she loved.

I want to be one of those loved ones.

Then she looked away when one of the kids tugged on her sleeve and the moment was gone. I blinked, released from her spell, and time resumed its relentless forward motion. Except instead of the usual calm, boring progression, my heart pounded and excitement flooded my system.

"Hey, Michael, are you okay?" Nightingale touched my shoulder, her eyebrows up.

"Yeah, I'm good."

Better than good. I had research to do. I needed to find out more about Haley-who-worked-at-the-shelter because I'd gotten a glimpse of my mate and I wasn't about to let the opportunity escape.

THE END

PLAY LIST OF SONGS
FROM THE STRIP SHOW

"Bad Romance" by Lady Gaga - The Kilted Nutsack

"Hot Hot Hot" by Buster Poindexter - Firehose

"You Can Leave Your Hat On" by Joe Cocker - The Schlong Ride

"Wild Wild West" by Escape Club - Deputy Dick

"Come and Get Your Love" by Redbone - Pocket Rocket

"Infinity" by Guru Josh Project - Kiddie Pool Shark

"Concrete Angel" by Gareth Emery - Hank Hardon

"All of You" by Betty Who - Harry Longballs

"Get Me High" by Kelde - Wally Ballbanger

"When Can I See You Again" by Owl City – All

MY FOREVER COCKY BIKER ENCOUNTER
CONCRETE ANGELS MC, BOOK 1
SNEEK PEEK

Leather, Lies, and Larceny…Forensic Accounting was never so sexy!

Oriana Hunter

I don't trust many people. Most especially, the bikers from the Concrete Angels Motorcycle Club. When I'm abducted by my "best friend" to come work for them as a forensic accountant, I pretty much have zero choice. They're not the typical biker club. And some of their members make my hair stand on end. Hey, I got them to sign a contract, and it comes with dental. All I have to do is find out who's embezzling from them and I can go home. It would go a lot faster if I didn't have a sexy cocky biker hanging around. I have far too many personal demons, and then I start seeing angels. Literally. The question is which folks are more scary, those wearing the Concrete Angels' cuts or the FBI jackets?

Scott Free

Oriana Hunter is the most beautiful and dangerous woman I've ever seen walk through the gates of the Concrete Angels' compound. She's badass, through and through. I don't believe in mates-for-life, but Oriana makes me want to give it a try. But she doesn't trust anyone, me especially, and I can recognize the signs of someone dealing with PTSD from my time in the Army. Turns out, she's a former FBI agent and has major trust issues. Not that I blame her. With Loki at the helm and his habit of making people squirm, I wouldn't trust us either. I know she'll figure out our money leak, and quickly. Which means I'm popping the clutch and going in full throttle to prove I'm not what she thinks. And that she's safer with me.

COURTING THE DRAGON WIDOW
CLOUDBURST COLORADO, BOOK 6
SNEEK PEEK

Everyone has demons, but Lissandra's date might have it worse than most...

Lissandra Charforest is finally stepping back into the dating game after three decades of widowhood. Accepting a blind date, she travels to a small town in upstate New York to meet an eligible dragon bachelor. Too bad the guy seems determined to stand her up.

Denarrion Goldencoat wouldn't have agreed to a blind date with the Widow from Colorado if his father hadn't insisted. Happy being the perennial bachelor, he has no desire to settle down on one woman, much less one with kids already. Until he falls into the reservoir with her.

But everything's not as it seems. Beneath the quaint façade of Redfield, darkness and decay lurks to ensnare the unwary. When Lissandra discovers she's been lured to Redfield to kill a demon under the pretense of a courtship, she almost walks away. But the truth jeopardizes the life of her True Bonded mate, leaving her with one choice: Destroy the demon or die trying.

OTHER BOOKS BY SIOBHAN MUIR

Queen Bitch of the Callowwood Pack
Her Devoted Vampire
Second Chance Succubus
Wildfire's Heart
Darwin's Evolution

Bad Boys of Beta Squad Series
Bronco's Rough Ride
The Navy's Ghost
Rimshot's Hard Target
Bam-Bam's Inked Hart
Deli's Take Out

Cloudburst Colorado Series
A Hell Hound's Fire
The Beltane Witch
Christmas I.C.E. Magic
Cloudburst Ice Magic
Cloudburst Coffee & Spa
Courting the Dragon Widow

Concrete Angels MC Series
My Forever Cocky Biker Encounter
Dude with a Cool Car

Rifts Series
Take the Reins
A Centaur's Solstice Wish
In Death's Shadow

The Ivory Road Serial
A Walk in the Sand
Outback Dreams

Triple Star Ranch Series
Rope a Falling Star
Star Light, Star Bright

Warbler Peninsula Series
Order of the Dragon
The Valkyrie's Sword
Burning Yuletide

Coming Soon
Angel Ink (Concrete Angels MC #3)
Star Spangled Banner (Triple Star Ranch #3)
Stars & Stripes (Triple Star Ranch #4)

ABOUT THE AUTHOR

Siobhan Muir lives in Cheyenne, Wyoming, with her husband, two daughters, and a vegetarian cat she swears is a shape-shifter, though he's never shifted when she can see him. When not writing, she can be found looking down a microscope at fossil fox teeth, pursuing her other love, paleontology. An avid reader of science fiction/fantasy, her husband gave her a paranormal romance for Christmas one year, and she was hooked for good.

In previous lives, Siobhan has been an actor at the Colorado Renaissance Festival, a field geologist in the Aleutian Islands, and restored inter-planetary imagery at the USGS. She's hiked to the top of Mount St. Helens and to the bottom of Meteor Crater.

Siobhan writes kick-ass adventure with hot sex for men and women to enjoy. She believes in happily ever after, redemption, and communication, all of which you will find in her paranormal romance stories.

Connect with Siobhan online at:
http://siobhanmuir.com
http://www.facebook.com/siobhan.muir.35
http://twitter.com/SiobhanMuir
http://siobhanmuir.com/siobhans-blog
http://pinterest.com/siobhanmuir.35

www.ingramcontent.com/pod-product-compliance
Lightning Source LLC
Chambersburg PA
CBHW031004260626
47169CB00002B/692